Long JOURNEY HOME

Shirley Harrison

Long JOURNEY HOME

sepia™

LONG JOURNEY HOME

A Sepia Novel

ISBN-13: 978-1-58314-809-9
ISBN-10:   1-58314-809-4

www.kimanipress.com

Printed in U.S.A.

This Book Is Dedicated
To My Mother

And
To my Loving Sisters,
Deborah (deceased), Brenda, Carol Jean,
Harriet, Sharon, Diana, Jean, Claudette,
Lolita, MarvAnn, and Carol (aka Skip)

Each contributed to the journey in her own special way
Proving that when it comes to shared experiences and
defining sisterhood
There are no half steps...
Just sisters for life

CHAPTER 1

"Uncle Byron is dead."

The four words leaped from the phone and shattered Grace Morrissey's composure. She leaned forward in the office chair, as though she hadn't quite heard it right, and managed to whisper a response.

"When?"

"A few hours ago this morning." Melissa Johnson, the baby in their family of six sisters, and called Missy by everyone, made the announcement.

Caught in an eddy of grief, the file Grace had been engrossed in a moment earlier was dropped to join similar ones scattered across her government-gray metal desk. She turned away from the clutter, aware that Missy was mercifully silent.

In the span of that moment Grace's thoughts tumbled in controlled sorrow, barreling over a collage of memories of the uncle she loved dearly. It was funny how death had a way of pushing its own agenda to the front of the line. Grace blinked hard and corralled her thoughts.

"I just talked with him the other day," she said wistfully. "He liked this time of the year. He said the leaves were already changing to red and gold down there."

"Down there" was little Oxford, Georgia. Grace wondered about that conversation and the small talk they'd made. Had he known it would be their last? She hadn't—wouldn't have even considered it. She should have shared more, listened carefully. The heat built around her eyes and she fought off the tears.

"Mama said to call you first. You're the oldest. I tried to get you earlier this morning at home, but you had already left."

Missy's voice was light and blameless as she laid the groundwork for fault aimed elsewhere for the delayed news, redirection being a natural occurrence among twenty-somethings, Grace concluded.

Grace had no words, profound or otherwise, to offer her sister. And while she wanted to be alone to mourn her loss, Missy's call had a twofold purpose. The nobler one had just been served in the notification; which set into motion the other: preparations for the family gathering.

"Is Mama all right?" Grace asked. She worriedly drew her fingers across her head and smoothed the French braid she'd hurriedly plaited that morning.

"And what about Reba?" she continued.

Rebecca Beneby, their fourth sister in birth order, was a shy and sensitive woman who could be unduly affected by death and illness. Despite that, she had also recently joined the ranks of single mothers with the birth of her son, now four months old.

"Yeah, yeah. We're all fine."

"I guess we knew it would happen soon, didn't we?" Grace spoke as if the question was directed to Uncle Byron.

She had sensed, in the end, that maybe he'd even preferred death to the incessant pain and medication. Still, with a degree of naïveté, Grace had hoped for a miracle-like reprieve from the inevitable. It hadn't come.

She sat back in her chair in the tiny work cubicle and sucked in a large gulp of the too warm recycled office air.

"So," Grace said into the phone. "Tell me when it happened."

"Grandma Rhoda was with him," Melissa began. "She said he was all right last night, but by morning he had just…gone. It was all real quiet-like." She sucked in her breath in finality. "'Course, to me, if you gotta go, hell, I think that's the best way."

With her heart hurting from grief, Grace considered Missy's words as bordering on callous; but that was Missy—frank and to the point. Yet, at Uncle Byron's end, with his only ally being a morphine drip hanging over his bed, maybe her sister had it right.

"Uncle Byron was like a daddy to us," Grace chided. "Give some respect for how much he cared. At least he showed an interest."

"Now, don't be gettin' ticked with me 'cause I'm not screamin' and cryin' all over the place." Missy's voice turned huffy. "But don't get me wrong, either. I loved Uncle Byron 'cause he's family and I could laugh and talk with him anytime I needed to. But he kept coming around all the time 'cause of you and Mama. Anyway, you just said it's not like we didn't know he was gon' die."

"Missy…" Grace was used to her sister's bluntness, but she didn't intend to excuse it today.

"Okay, okay." Missy managed to turn her petulance into an apology through the phone. "I'll keep my thoughts to myself."

Not likely. "Where's Mama now? I know she's relieved that he died in his sleep." Grace could only hope his end had really been that peaceful. It was what they all deserved after his living had become a choice between lucid pain and medicated oblivion.

"She's over at the house with Aunt Evie. And you *know* Evie, the drama queen, is putting on a show with enough tears for everybody." Her voice turned hard. "I guess she'll have to give up trying to get him back now."

Grace didn't miss the triumph in Missy's gossip. With Uncle Byron dead, some in the family would dredge up the stories about his freewheeling ex-wife Evie. Grace saw it as more disrespect at his passing.

"You know what's gettin' ready to happen," Missy added. "Uncle Byron was tighter than a drum about his personal life. Everybody down here wants to get into his business 'cause nobody ever could while he was alive."

"You don't have to sound so excited about the prospect."

"Girl, I don't even want to hear that. I wonder if Aunt Evie gets to keep his house and his big ol' car she been riding 'round in since he got sick?" Missy grunted. "Give it up. You probably wondering, too."

Grace closed her eyes for a moment, ashamed that five minutes of grief had been invaded by, of all things, talk of what Uncle Byron did or didn't have. With no children and an ex-wife with a strip-joint past, his exceptional life had always been easy fodder for dissection.

"I'm not going there," Grace said, lowering her voice.

"Why you whispering?" Missy quipped. "Uncle can't hear you and, personally, I don't think he ever cared a damn about what anybody else thought, anyway…well, except for maybe you and Mama."

"Still, it don't seem right discussing that kind of stuff today, and it's nobody else's business anyway."

"Least of all Aunt Evie and her two brothers from hell."

At the mention of the brothers, Grace's eyes narrowed as unease crept into her voice. "Just stay clear of them."

CHAPTER 2

Aunt Evie's brothers were nothing but trouble; and when none was present, they managed to create it. And that was the way it had been since Uncle had divorced Evie.

"Aunt Evie makes sure they don't come around Grandma Rhoda's house starting trouble," Missy said. "But since Uncle got sick, I can tell they been telling Aunt Evie what she ought to do to favor herself."

Grace sighed, though she did agree about the brothers being hell's spawns. "Missy—"

"Besides that, she and Aunt Cora already trying to take over everything in between all that crying they doin', and he's not even cold yet. Everybody knows Uncle Byron was closest to Mama. They were two peas in a pod, so wouldn't you think they'd just back off and let Mama and Grandma Rhoda do all the arranging?"

Grace opened her mouth to respond, but Missy was on a roll.

"Grandma Rhoda even said so. 'Course, Grandma also thinks he shoulda had her some grandkids. But you know Evie wasn't 'bout to let no stretch marks mess up her stomach. You think that's why he divorced her, 'cause she didn't want kids? If that's the case, I'm guessing he don't want her to be the one to decide how he'll be put away, either. That's why you need to be here with Mama—"

Grace's attention drifted, her sorrow irreparably invaded by the certainty that Uncle Byron wouldn't get to enjoy peace—even in death, or at least not today, in this place, and with her.

Why did all hell break loose so easily during weddings and funerals for her family? Fortitude was a requirement for either, and anticipation of the latter had already started her stomach to churn.

It hadn't been enough that Uncle Byron and Evie's wedding had been a carnival; his funeral was now destined to resemble a zoo. But not if she and mama had anything to do with it. She rested her head against the back of her chair.

"So, when are you coming?" Missy asked, expertly re-entering Grace's consciousness. "Mama thinks you're coming tonight. You know how Aunt Cora can be when she wants information. She'll ask Mama about every one of us, so mama's got to say something back to her."

Home. Grace frowned amid her strewn and littered thoughts. "I—I don't know yet." She managed to mumble something about arranging time from the office and talking things over with the kids.

"You're bringing Dee and Jamie, right?" Melissa asked.

Feeling unduly pressured, Grace's tone turned sharper than she'd intended. "Missy, I'm not sure what I'll do."

"You don't know? But you're coming home, right?"

"I don't know if my car can make the trip," Grace

said, trying to explain away her anxiety. "And airfare is pretty expensive for three people on such short notice, even if I can get a special rate. I've got to figure out things."

"Aw, Grace, you have to bring the kids. Everybody wants to see them. Work something out with Bobby. He can help out—that's what the daddy's supposed to do—so long as he keeps his sorry ass up there."

Grace expelled another tired sigh as the conversation flipped once again with Missy's sarcasm. "Everybody's a sorry ass with you these days."

"Excuse me for pushing your buttons. I guess baby daddies is the wrong subject."

"C'mon, Missy. The least you can do is cut the crap one day for Uncle Byron's sake. He is why you called, right?"

"Okay, I'm re-ally sorry." Missy's voice mocked her regret. "Aw, Grace, I didn't mean anything. I know how much he means to you."

"To us," Grace corrected.

The humor spilled from Missy's voice. "Hey, we talkin' 'bout Uncle Byron or Bobby?"

Grace ignored her gibe and rubbed her temple. A headache had now made a formidable entrance.

"You *will* come as soon as you can, won't you?" Before an answer was given, Missy began to wheedle. "It'll take days for y'all to plan everything, and everyone still has to get into town. You gotta come early 'cause I don't know if I can take that loudmouthed Gloria and her clan without you here."

Goodness, here we go again. Grace pressed her fingers against her temple. Gloria, the second oldest, and Missy were the original oil and water and, though Gloria was married and living in Miami, distance hadn't changed much.

"When is she getting in?"

"I talked with her earlier this morning. And would you believe her fat ass is driving here tomorrow? To comfort Mama, no doubt." Missy's short snort echoed through the phone. "Everybody knows the only reason she's bringing her tail up here so fast is so she can start suckin' up. You know Gloria, and she always wants something, and when Mama gets wind of whatever it is—"

Grace didn't want to hear. "Missy, you don't know—"

"—Mama will give her money or whatever Gloria says she wants."

"Will you listen to yourself? Stop it." Grace breathed in deeply. "I don't know why I want to come home just to keep grown women out of each other's hair."

"Well, she's the one who'll show up taking over everything with all those kids and a no-good husband," Missy argued. "It'll be a wonder if she don't show up pregnant...a-gain."

Grace's fingers moved to press against her eyes. "You fuss every time Gloria comes to the house, and then you're the first one inviting her home again."

"Yeah...so she'll pay me back what she owes me. But I swear, Grace, if that bastard husband of hers hits on me again, I'm telling her about it this time."

"Goodness." Grace sighed, changing the subject from

Gloria and that whole set of touchy issues. "What about space at the house? Isn't Reba and the baby there?"

"She'd planned on staying a month, but she's leaving tonight since Gloria will be here tomorrow."

"Why?"

"The way I heard it from Reba, Gloria told her she needs to find another place to stay."

"No, she didn't."

Missy let out a harsh chuckle. "Get this—Gloria told her that the family coming from out of town should be the ones using space at the house."

"What?"

"And don't you say nothing to Mama, 'cause she don't know about it." Missy snorted her contempt. "Can you believe that hard-ass Gloria had the nerve to call Reba selfish for moving her and the baby back into Mama's house in the first place?"

"I swear, I don't know what gets into her," Grace said, and sighed. She didn't like to admit it, but Gloria did have a dangerous mean streak that she managed to share regularly with her sisters. Grace couldn't understand the cruelty; even sadder was how Reba never stood up for herself and allowed this recent abuse to be heaped upon her.

"Somebody needs to talk with Reba," Grace continued. "Find out where she and the baby are going tonight, and let me know."

Their mother's modest house with its two small bathrooms and three bedrooms had been sufficient for them all back in the day. Now the place seemed barely large enough to hold her mother, two sisters and a baby, not to mention the numerous temporary residents who passed through the revolving doors all too often.

"Poor Reba and her screwed-up life," Missy said. "Her baby's daddy must be pretty damn disappointing if she won't even tell us, her family, who he is."

"What does that say about us?"

Missy sniffed at the point. "I swear I'm not having kids if a man is part of the deal."

Grace ignored her sister. She made some variation on that vow every time she was between boyfriends.

"Maybe I can stay with Grandma Rhoda." Stressed by the prospects before her, Grace spoke her thoughts out loud. "But if I bring the kids, I may have to just get a hotel room 'cause everybody's going to be scrambling around for a free bed." She couldn't see her way to pay airfare, so how she planned on paying for a hotel room was a whole other question.

"I want you at the house," Missy whined. "Let all the other poor-ass relatives go to a hotel."

The weariness in Grace's spirit had moved lower—to her belly—and now manifested into nausea, a malady she was familiar with, and that seemed to strike with an inevitable visit back to home. Her stomach fluttered as she stood in the work cubicle, as though to proudly proclaim she was one of those *poor-ass* relatives her sister so indiscriminately scorned.

"Anyway," Missy continued, "Mama's not gonna ever

hear the end of it from Aunt Cora if she can't even put up her own children for a visit. So, we'll just have to fit everybody here in the house, for Mama's sake."

"Missy, I've got to go."

"When do you think you might get here?"

"I'll call tonight," Grace began weakly. "After...after I talk with the kids."

"Promise?"

"Yeah. Promise."

"All right, then." There was a slight pause before Missy added, "I love you, Gracie."

Sisters. Childhood nicknames were always handy when an immediate connection was necessary—or to inflict a stab of guilt, a tool their mama had honed well in the house.

"I love you, too, Missy."

The connection worked. Grace gently replaced the receiver on the phone, overcome by an insistent and familial need to see her sisters, comfort her mama and realign herself with the people who'd helped shape her life—for better or worse.

Yet, in that same instance, she recognized that the cost for reaffirmation was likely to be as debilitating as it was exhilarating.

It would all be much more than she wanted to handle over a few days' time, let alone the week's stay her family would demand of her. Still, she felt compelled to go, the pain be damned.

Grace leaned against the gray cubicle wall and closed

her eyes, now warm and damp from a few escaped tears. Sweet Uncle Byron.

His death, the numerous unknowns that awaited her back home—they were more than she cared to digest right now. She was mentally and physically drained.

And what of the dreams that had returned to haunt her sleep? Grace opened her eyes and straightened from the wall. What about them? Were they a byproduct of her tired body and exhausted mind, too?

She'd almost forgotten the enigmatic nightmares that could hold her in such thrall that she couldn't discern sleeping illusions from waking reality.

This morning's nightmare had been a perfect example...

CHAPTER 3

Last night had ended for Grace like most of her evenings. It had been late—way past midnight—when she'd finally climbed the stairs of her modest Maryland home.

Hushed quiet had filled the Prince Georges County house and accompanied her to bed like an old friend. She'd welcomed it, loving the late-night stillness. In fact, Grace sometimes found herself intentionally delaying the sleep that would bring on a new day and its companion problems.

That was because her weekdays began at 6:00 a.m. and held her in a relentless grasp until she made the inevitable trek to bed some eighteen hours later. It was no more than Grace was willing to bear. A full-time job along with tailoring piecework—courtesy of the local dry cleaner—meant extra money to hold things together. It was as simple as that.

God makes the back to bear the burden. Her mother's prophetic words, uttered throughout Grace's childhood, had become her mantra for strength.

When she finally pushed through her bedroom door and stepped unerringly into the dark to switch on the small bedside lamp, she was already anticipating the sweet rest her body craved and knew was within reach.

She had settled lightly onto the bed's edge, shrugged from her robe and then turned off the light.

Stifling a yawn, Grace had slid under the covers and closed her eyes. A smile formed as she savored the luxury experienced from total relaxation of tired bone and muscle.

Grace had also murmured a simple prayer. *Please, no dreams tonight.*

She had thought the extreme night terrors that haunted her when she'd first left home to get married had dissipated for good after her divorce years ago. However, in recent months, and with alarming regularity, Grace's sleep was frequently stormed by dreams so vivid that their ferocious tap into her subconscious emotions would jar her awake.

Sloughing off the day's troubles, Grace sighed and easily drifted into sleep.

A familiar prod soon came to her leg—again and again, as if to test to what degree her sleeping state had reached.

Grace let out a grunt tinged with loathing.

Go away. The thought escaped the clutches of her mist-shrouded sleep.

A grazing touch slowly moved up her leg, stopping at her waist. Grace flinched. When it lingered there, she grimaced and automatically curled her body defensively, drawing her knees up and into herself.

The nudges to her waist had become persistent, demanding her attention.

Grace slowly surfaced from her misty stupor as the insouciant flickers of unwanted familiarity grew more and more intimate.

She grunted her disapproval at the jarring interceptions coaxing her awake. Unwilling to raise heavy eyelids captivated by sleep, Grace pulled away, clutching the covers to her chest and shrugging off the disturbance.

"Wake up."

She surfaced into consciousness and fought off the command. "No. Leave me alone," she mumbled.

"What's wrong? Wake up."

Grace felt a hard grip shake her shoulder.

"It's late. I need a ride to school, Mama. Mama…"

The whiny, singsong voice pierced through the foggy cloud that shrouded Grace; she became acutely aware of her surroundings with startling swiftness.

Grace threw back the covers in one motion and sat straight up in another.

"Dee, I told you not to wake me that way." She had snapped the words in embarrassment.

"What way? All I did was shake you," had been her teenage daughter's shrill retort.

"Not when I'm asleep. I told you that," Grace replied sharply, rubbing her eyes. But when she raised them and witnessed Dee's upset stare, she was instantly contrite.

"I'm…I'm sorry, baby. I guess I'm tired, that's all." She sighed. "Looks like I overslept, too. I'll be ready in a bit."

Grace watched her daughter turn and saunter from the room, mumbling discontent, and more than likely with a pout in place.

"Make sure your brother's up and ready." She spoke to a straight back that cleared the doorway, shaking her head at another lost chance to connect with her increasingly distant daughter.

Grace quickly stood from the bed and made her way to the adjoining bathroom.

As an image of puffy bed hair and tired brown eyes gazed back at her from the mirror above the sink, Grace's thoughts flitted back—to before her daughter appeared.

She had dreamed again. It had started out much like the others, too: Sunday afternoon at her grandmother's house, relaxing on the back porch, eating desserts, playing hide-and-seek with her sisters and cousins, and waiting for Grandma Rhoda in the sewing room for another lesson.

But sometimes Grandma never appeared, and that's when the lighthearted, sunny daydream morphed into a nightmare of dark memories, launched this time, Grace was sure, by her daughter's innocent touch.

A wave of shame swept over Grace at how she'd reacted. She was even more humiliated over the fact that it had been witnessed.

Bewildered, she stared down the reflection mocking her in the bathroom mirror. *Lord, why do I still act that way?*

Now, hours later, standing in her cubicle, Grace still didn't have an answer. A shiver sliced through her at the memory and she shook her head to clear it. She hugged her arms to thwart another chill, but it was clear the earlier nausea was preparing to rear its ugly head. She clenched her mouth in readiness.

Uncle Byron was dead. Nothing would change that. His was the easier duty now. While he need only make the final appearance at his funeral, Grace, on the other hand, was obliged to live through it. She only hoped it wouldn't be the predictable zoo she envisioned.

The acid bile from her stomach pitched and sloshed in waves, splashing its way high into her throat. Grace moved through her cubicle door and into the carpeted office space as each heave reached higher than the last.

Forcefully tamping back the results of her frazzled nerves, Grace darted through the hall to the restroom located just beyond the office door.

What is wrong with me?

CHAPTER 4

For the next hour—in between fruitless attempts to reach her mother—the upcoming journey back home weighed heavy in Grace's head. Keeping in mind she'd be absent from the office for at least a few days, she reorganized her work calendar, though the miserable news Missy had delivered was firmly encased in her thoughts.

So when her phone rang at her desk, the caller was an unexpected surprise.

"Mama?"

"Grace. You doing all right, honey?" Corinne Wilson never failed to use an endearment whenever she could with her daughters.

"It's you I was worried about," Grace replied, releasing a sigh. "I've been trying for a while to get you on the phone."

"Didn't Missy call you about Byron early this morning like I told her to?"

"Yeah, Mama, she did. But I wanted to talk with you."

Grace recognized the petulance that had crawled into her voice. It was a custom she'd noticed with all her sisters when they wanted their mother's undivided attention—an understandable trait among six girls.

"You knew I was gonna call you, dear, but I was with your grandmamma all morning."

Grace thought she sounded tired. It was to be expected, though, what with all she had to contend with on a daily basis, and now her brother's death. Still, it was unusual, given her seemingly boundless strength at handling most anything.

"Are you holding up okay?" Grace asked.

A deep sigh preceded Corinne's reply. "Yesterday was pretty bad for Byron, and he told me he was ready...if it was his time." Her words were unsteady, her voice feather-light, as though strained through a sieve.

A pause floated between the women.

It was unfair and equally unlikely that cancer would attack and bring Uncle Byron down so quickly. He had bucked the norm for black males, making it his business to visit his doctor on a regular basis, in good health and bad. Unjust or not, the prostate cancer had finally won out after only a year's siege of his body.

"Grace?"

"I'm here, Mama."

"It's finished, you know. This is all God's will and His way of seeing a thing through."

Although not particularly religious, Corinne could effectively invoke the claim when it was necessary to make her point.

"Yes, I know that." Grace squeezed her eyes shut, fearing she'd break down. "But, I miss him already."

Corinne didn't immediately respond, but cleared her

throat. "I know one thing, I'm gonna end up joining him myself if these sisters of yours don't get their acts together." Her voice was strong again. "Sometimes I feel like washing my hands of all of 'em."

The subject had been purposely misdirected from Uncle Byron to some form of drama-in-the-making that Missy must have forgotten to share. Although Grace wanted—no, needed—to talk with her mother about her uncle and the burgeoning tear to her heart, she allowed the moment to pass.

The older woman continued gruffly. "Now, I want you down here with the rest of us as soon as you can. With all that's got to be done, I need you here. Are you coming tomorrow?"

Grace considered her mother smart, with lots of common sense. So she never understood how her mother could condemn her own household's melee, yet invite Grace to join her there in the very next breath.

"Missy said Gloria would be in tomorrow. Have you heard from Belinda?" Belinda, Grace's next to youngest sibling, had been married less than a year and would be traveling from Birmingham.

"I think Belinda and Glenn plan to drive down, depending on what day we have the funeral."

"I don't know if I'll be able to get there too early, either," Grace said gently.

"You have to get on down. You know we need to plan a funeral, honey. We got to do things just the way Byron said he wanted them done."

Grace listened in on her mother's plans for Uncle Byron's special home-going service, abandoning any attempt to further explain her own situation.

With marked chagrin, she pressed her fingers against her eyes and welcomed the pressure. Their conversation had shifted from shared grief to role-playing, wherein they denied the family problems that made up the river of reticence that flowed through Grace's veins at the simple prospect of going home.

Grace ended the conversation with the promise that she would work on a final obituary for the funeral director; and, no, she wouldn't leave any family members out. Or at least, she'd try. At the last family funeral, that small act of conciseness had become a bone of contention for many since their employers wouldn't give them the day off unless they proved, through a written obituary, that they were kin to the deceased.

Grace said goodbye and hung up her phone—strangely cold, always conflicted—and marveled over the way so many of her conversations with Mama ended: as though they left something unfinished, unsaid.

Still, troubling concerns invaded her head. Why was it necessary that she engage in the funeral preparations when she was hundreds of miles away from home and the rest of the family? Gloria was the next oldest and obviously had the time—she thrived on attention. Let her take on the responsibility. And for chrissakes, what about Missy and Reba? They were right there in the house.

Grace already knew the answer, and it wasn't based in

any deep reasoning, either. In her matriarchal family, with its deep Southern roots, to be the eldest daughter was to forever be the *bearer of burdens*. It was a silent gift passed on without benefit of rejection.

"Home" was Martin Luther King Jr.'s South, where Grace had grown up juxtaposed to sixties' enlightenment and innate ignorance, conspicuous wealth alongside hopeless poverty. Her mama believed that only in the South could you manage to snatch hope from despair. And she'd been right. After all, Grace had survived childhood there like all the family women. They were all intact, more or less.

Grace sighed as her prior irritation dissipated. She glanced at her watch and acknowledged her workday as pretty much shot. It was close to lunch and there was a lot to handle and work out if she planned to leave soon, so why not get the worse of it over with right now? She frowned, knowing that meant a talk with her manager, Miles Samuel.

Recognizing this as the true starting point of her journey, Grace rose from her chair and girded her resolve.

Because just as there was no getting around the dread that waited for her back home, the same could be said of this visit to Miles.

CHAPTER 5

Within fifteen minutes Grace had made her way to the administrative wing on the twentieth floor and laid a courteous rap to her manager's cracked door—his idea of an open-door policy.

The door widened to a noticeably cooler waft of air. The view overlooking the city was pretty magnificent through the wide floor-to-ceiling windows. And if one harbored a penchant for jealousy, something Miles would understand and appreciate, a visit to his office might easily stir the emotion. He had nothing Grace coveted.

Miles looked up from his desk and quickly gave Grace one of his patented head-to-toe once-over glances coupled with a broad Management 101 smile. Clean-shaven and manicured—no doubt pedicured, as well—he was the embodiment of a success story. And he knew it.

"Grace," Miles said, and slowly stood from his chair. "Come on in."

Faced with slick manners exuding like wavelets from his business suit, Grace's stomach began its familiar churn. Miles was the only black managing attorney in the Justice Department's Maryland Field Office. Constantly on the prowl—though he could now stalk his women legally since his divorce became final—his was a position he made sure no one forgot. He was embodied with his own self-importance.

Grace, on the other hand, was a paralegal in an office with no shortage of minorities in lower to mid-level dead-end positions. So, it was quite natural that she, along with others, embraced Miles's professional debut there—that is until it was clear early on that he wanted her to ride with him through the ranks; and he didn't mean in the seat alongside him.

The man's climb within the organization had been swift and remarkable, particularly when coupled with the common belief that minorities were generally expected—at least on paper—to supersede their white counterpart's ability. Miles didn't even meet that general expectation, which only managed to deepen the enigma on his rising excellence.

"What can I do for you?" Miles actively pointed out a chair as he came around the desk with a self-assured swagger.

Grace lingered at the door, declining the proffered seat.

"I just received some news from back home." She paused, not quite willing to fully share private information with a man she held in such low regard, but aware that their positions required that she at least reveal the basics. "A member of my family has died, and I'm going to need some time off."

Though his ready smile properly disappeared, it was rapidly replaced with a thoughtful slant that feigned the job of sincere concern. "I'm sorry to hear about that." He gestured her further into the office.

"Come on in, sit down, and let's talk." Joining her at the door, he firmly closed it behind her, effectively denying her escape.

Conceding she was trapped for at least the length of a short conversational exchange, Grace sank her weight into the chair nearest the door. As Miles moved back to his desk, she plunged in to get it over.

"I may have to take off as early as tomorrow, but I'll be away a week."

"You need to take annual leave...for a week?"

She arched a brow at Miles as he folded into his chair. "It is my leave, and I have to travel to Atlanta." She didn't bother to explain her actual destination was a bit farther south in Oxford.

"Can I ask you something?"

Through his eyes, Grace could see the dusty tumblers in his brain slowly click into place and prayed he wouldn't ask her to explain in any more detail.

"Of course," she responded.

"Who died?" At Grace's frown, he added, "I mean, was it expected? You don't act like an accident or something like that happened to...say, your mother."

Grace feared her eyes would pop out she was so irritated with this man, but he noticed it, too.

"You know what I mean," he continued. "You're pretty composed for hearing somebody died."

The man had presumptuous gall—either that or he'd

been born in a barn. Regardless, the details were none of his business.

"It was my uncle," she replied evenly.

When it was obvious that Grace wouldn't be offering anything more, Miles shifted in his chair.

"And you say you need to be out a week, huh?" He shook his head with skepticism. "Really, Grace, our un-expected leave policy is to be interpreted liberally only when it comes to immediate family."

"As far as I'm concerned, my uncle is immediate family." She pressed her lips together in finality.

"I don't know." His voice took on a patronizing tone behind steepled fingers. "We've got that big case coming up for trial next month. Your attorneys need you."

To research, shepardize results and assemble all the casework, Grace silently finished the sentence with her own version.

"Mildred will pick up the slack," she said out loud of the other paralegal. "I've done the same for her in emer-gencies. Anyway, my work is already on disk." He's enjoying this, Grace decided as she watched him study her.

Miles reached among the executive playthings that dotted his gleaming desk surface and selected one of many slender designer pencils from a gold-embossed cup, all the while keeping a trained gaze on Grace.

"We'll see." He tapped the eraser head of the pencil against the desk. "We'll see. Oh, I meant to remind your attorneys about this earlier—you know your annual review is coming up."

"I hadn't thought about it, but yes, it is." She frowned. "Is there a problem?"

"That's for you to decide. I'll send an e-mail out to your work group members and solicit their input." He leaned back in his oversized leather chair and toyed with the pencil. "You don't think they'll complain that you don't pull your fair share, that you're not a team player?"

"No, Miles, they won't." She straightened in the chair until her back was ramrod-stiff. "You're not bringing up my evaluation because I asked for time off—?"

"No, no," he interrupted in Management 101 speed. "That's just an oversight on my part to be corrected."

"Then, accept my apology that my uncle didn't die at a more convenient time for the office."

"Grace, Grace..." He offered a toothy white smile. "Don't be so touchy." Leaning forward, he peered at her. "This extra business you're pursuing...what is it, tailoring, sewing, something like that?"

She gave a curt nod. He knew exactly what it was. In fact, she had been required to seek his approval for the outside business activity last year.

Shifting in her chair, Grace recrossed her legs and felt them suffer his appraisal. "And your point?" she asked.

The grin disappeared as he sat back. "Just observing, that's all, that you've taken a lot of time off since you started it. Make sure you don't confuse your roles in and out of the office."

"I don't." His loathsome mistrust and twisting of facts was no surprise, but she bristled that he questioned her integrity when she gave so much of herself to her office duties. "In fact, I'm quite clear on it. My time away from the office handling my other business has always been on personal leave."

The delicate pencil snapped in two and broke the prickly silence.

"So, when is this funeral?" Miles casually placed the pencil pieces to the side and reached for another.

"The plans aren't finalized."

"In that case, maybe asking for a week's unplanned leave is premature." He rested his forearms on the desk. "Let's look at something less than that for now, say the two days at the end of this week," he said, his tone condescending as he drew her gaze. "In the meantime, why don't you talk with your group about that court case? If it turns out that it's in pretty good shape, we can discuss more days if you need them."

Grace could feel the flush of anger pour into her face, and jerked up from the chair. "Fine, Miles."

"Good. We're clear on this?"

"Of course. You see things your way, and I'll do the same."

Turning for the door, she took in a deep breath, calmly tamping back her dislike of the man. Grace intended to talk with her group, all right. She'd inform them that she planned to be away for at least a week, the consequences with Miles be damned.

Without a backward glance, Grace strode through his door and pulled it closed behind her before she took a moment to exhale. Shaking her head, she moved away. To hell with Miles.

He still carried resentment from their bungled date years ago when he first arrived. Actually, it had been more his octopus limbs and uninvited tongue invading her mouth that had changed the tone of their evening. Of course, he hadn't attained the level of manager at the time; he'd just been a charming black attorney in the office who paid her some much-needed attention and eventually talked her into going out on a date.

Grace's mouth tightened at the memory. Miles had taken her dancing, of all places.

CHAPTER 6

"Unh, unh, unh." Miles grunted pleasantly. "With legs as fine as yours, Grace, you should be out dancing. I know just the place for some fun."

Miles' spirited words were like a shot of adrenaline to Grace's single-parent mind-set. And like that, her moratorium on dating was broken.

"Okay. I'll go," she said.

They'd gone to a local salsa club, and though Grace wasn't adept at the Latin moves, a surprisingly adroit Miles showed her the ropes. Before Grace knew it, her butt twirled and her limbs twisted as smartly as the other women on the floor.

The evening had started out easy and relaxing, and Grace had indulged her excitement at going out with a man by wearing a soft, swingy skirt with her normally bound hair loose on her shoulders. She had forgotten the fun in pleasing a man who so obviously liked what he saw.

"Damn, girl, but you are looking delicious tonight," he whispered at her ear as they undulated in near touches amid a floor of dancers.

"I've never done this before," she replied, laughing. The

Latin music had encouraged Grace's carefree mood. It wasn't often that she had the chance to give in to blithe pleasure; after all, she was a divorcee raising impressionable children.

"I'm loving all of this," she admitted.

"The pleasure is mine." He slid his hand from the small of her back to a spot that was lower—much lower. In fact, his hand came to rest comfortably against Grace's butt cheek.

"All mine," he finished. "I can make it yours, too." He pressed her against his rocking crotch.

Initially, Grace was taken aback, but considered the move more mischievous than serious, and pulled back at the same time she slapped away his hand. But as the evening wore on and Miles persisted at every opportunity to take liberties, Grace called him on it in no uncertain terms.

"Miles, stop." Beneath the table, she removed his hand from her thigh. "I thought we came to dance, and have a good time. This is just one date and you're acting like I'm sleeping with you."

He grinned and sipped at his drink. "The evening's not over yet."

"Sure it is," Grace said sternly, sliding from the booth. "Please, take me home."

And that was the end of her uncomfortable evening. Or so Grace thought. When Miles parked in front of her house, he turned to her in the car, and what Grace thought would be a heartfelt apology for his behavior became a forced, openmouthed kiss and grope. She struggled for the door before she quickly sought her front latch, only to have Miles hike after her.

Standing at the front door, searching her purse for keys, Grace was the one surprised by what he had to say.

"Listen," Miles started, "I admit, maybe I had a drink too many, but I thought you wanted to have a good time tonight, too. I mean, we've laughed and joked over coffee at work, so I thought you were...you know, feelin' me."

Grace's words were clipped. "Being groped all night by someone I trusted is not my idea of a good time, Miles."

He nodded, though his eyes were scornful. "Yeah, you're coming through loud and clear. We can look, but we can't touch the merchandise."

Surprised by his insult, Grace silently whirled from him and fumbled with her key until it slid into the lock.

He stepped back to the edge of the porch as if to leave, but didn't. "Listen, about what happened earlier. So, maybe I didn't read you right. But, that's all it was. We have to go back to the office and, maybe work together. I think we ought to chalk up tonight as nothing more than an evening between consenting adults that just didn't go well. Can we, ah, agree on that?"

Grace didn't look around. "Go to hell, Miles." She pushed open her door, stepped inside and then slammed it before he could say anything else.

The embarrassing bad memory on the heels of their hu-miliating meeting was yet another shock to Grace's already overloaded emotional circuitry. She blinked it away as she now strode down the hall from Miles's office.

In retrospect, his parting words that night long ago had been a classic Miles moment. He'd made sure to cover his own integrity-lacking ass before he'd left her.

Grace never mentioned his slimy actions to anyone else, despite the common knowledge that he'd dated others in the office; and she wondered how many other women had heard his speech. After all, he had a career to protect; and look at where he'd landed—in a position where he could make her life hell anytime he wanted.

It was too late to claim foul. That was the trouble with secrets—they lay dormant inside, and before you know it, you've learned to live with them, something Grace had experience with.

Anger sluiced through her body again and reactivated the bile in her stomach to a bubbly roil.

Grace reached into her pocket and extracted an antacid, quickly popping the chalky mint disk into her mouth to calm her belly.

The impulse to vomit again had died away by the time Grace made it to the timekeeper's station to sign for a week's annual leave.

CHAPTER 7

Ring...ring...

"Okay, okay. I'm coming." Grace muttered with general discontent as she entered her tidy kitchen and then, with a shift of her hip, pushed the back door shut.

Amid the phone's incessant din, she set the bags of groceries onto the table. In the same motion, she grabbed up the wall extension and answered in a none-too-friendly tone.

"Hello?"

"What're you doing home?"

Recognizing her ex-husband's voice did nothing to eliminate Grace's melancholy mood.

"I live here, Bobby. What do you think?"

"Aw, Grace, you know what I mean," he said in a sober tone. "You don't usually get home until later. I was expecting the kids to pick up."

After seven years of divorce, Bobby Morrissey still tried to know everything that went on in her household.

"I left the office early." She dropped her keys next to the bags and began to unpack them. "A lot's happened today."

"Yeah, I know. I heard Uncle Byron died this morning. Why didn't you tell me?"

"Does it matter now?" Grace replied quietly. "You obviously found out." *No doubt from that nosy sister of yours.*

"Jeannie called me," he answered, referring to his sister back in their hometown, "asking about the kids coming to the funeral. She said to tell you Big Mama's looking forward to seeing them and having them stay with her if you don't have space at your mama's."

Bobby spoke in unenthused tones, as Grace methodically folded one of the brown grocery bags along its creases, resentment rising at the added pressure his sister and mother forced on her.

She hadn't even told the children, let alone decided on how to get them all down there. Yet, everybody was already making plans for them. *It's what you get for marrying a high school sweetheart. Even divorce can't cut the damn hometown ties.*

"I told Jeannie I'd let her know something later on," Bobby finished with a sigh.

"So, why are you calling Dee and Jamie?" Grace challenged as she shoved the folded bag under the sink. "I know you didn't plan on telling them about Uncle Byron before I did." Cautious silence flooded the line as her suspicions were raised. "Bobby…"

"Well, it's already close to the trip I promised them on their next school break, so I was just checking to see if they really wanted to go down to the funeral, too."

"No, you didn't," Grace blurted, her voice rising with her anger. "Their uncle is dead and all you're concerned about is trying to figure a way out of paying for two trips?"

"Now, Grace—" he started.

"And you were making them choose between respecting their uncle and Six Flags Amusement Park?"

"You got it all wrong."

"I'll make the decision on whether or not they go to the funeral, Bobby. And yes, if they do attend, you *will* have to help with the air fare."

"You f-flyin'?" he sputtered. "Why you gotta fly? Why can't you drive?"

"I'm not driving twelve hours by myself, and especially not in a ten-year-old car that needs a lot more work than a tune-up."

"Then…then I'll drive you—we can all go in my car."

"Now that's just great," Grace said, sighing. "Your old family and your brand-new wife, all cozy together for a day's drive to a funeral. Bobby, are you crazy?"

But Bobby quickly launched into an explanation about money being tight, and that Marilee wouldn't mind the drive.

Of course, she wouldn't, Grace thought indignantly, and tossed the last grocery bag under the sink. The young thing—no more than ten years Jamie's senior—would probably take it in stride, reminiscent of her senior class road trip.

"Well, it's just an idea," Bobby said.

Grace glanced at her watch and frowned. Dee and Jamie were seriously overdue from school. They should have been home at least an hour ago.

"I have to go," she said. "We'll talk about this later." At that moment, the sound of loud, laughing teenagers came from outside. Grace turned to the window. The kids were home.

"Oh, ah, Grace. Before you go, what's this I hear 'bout you seeing somebody? You dating again?"

Caught off guard by the unexpected question, a slow flush crawled up her face as she stammered a reply.

"W-who told you that?" *It had to be the kids*. Having answered her own question, she wanted the subject dropped. "It doesn't matter. It's none of your business anyway."

"Well, I hear you go out to meet him someplace else." Silence. "So, who is he that you can't even bring him home to see your kids?"

Grace heard the front door locks turn. And while she wanted nothing more than to set Bobby straight and remind him that he was married and had no say about her life, she decided to stay civil in front of the kids.

"You know what? I've had bad news from home and one problem after another at the office, and the day's not even over yet. So back off." She lowered her voice. "But you'd best remember that whoever I date and when I let him meet the kids is *my* business."

"All right, all right. But you know I can always get Norris down at the station to run a check on him. All you got to do is say the word."

Grace rubbed her forehead. It would be funny if he weren't serious. "No, Bobby, and you keep that crazy friend of yours out of this, too." She could hear young voices at the front door filtering into the kitchen. "The kids are home—I gotta go."

She didn't wait for his response and quickly replaced the wall receiver before she headed into the living room.

Just as she cleared the wide, arched doorway, two teenagers strolled through the front door, arm in arm. Each lugged a bulging gym bag. When they looked up and saw Grace, they froze in their tracks, the carefree grins dropped.

While Grace acknowledged her wide-eyed, sweat-suited daughter with a quick glare, it was the lanky, jeans-clad boy sporting mini dreads that garnered her undivided attention.

Dee sputtered her surprise. "Mom?" She took a step forward. "What are you doing home?"

"Lucky me." Grace crossed her arms and readied for the verbal battle even as her mind briefly slipped into the past. What a wonderful moment it had been when her baby girl was born. And then, incredibly, when the bundle of joy reached her teens, she turned into this alien.

Grace's eyes remained on the friend. "And, who are you?" Though her question was obviously directed at the surprised boy, he seemed to have lost his tongue.

"His name is Julian and he's new on the swim team. We're studying this afternoon, Mom. That's all."

Grace hated when her daughter whined. It reminded her of Missy's bad habit. Grace walked past them to the front door, and opened it with a flourish.

"You know the rules, young lady. No friends in the house after school. Julian, it was nice meeting you, and if

Dee ever gets off punishment, you might get to visit again."

"Y-yes, ma'am," he stammered, and hastily retreated with his bag through the opening being offered.

Grace closed the door behind him, deciding his impromptu visit was probably all Dee's idea. Poor boy.

Dee had left the room. Grace found her in the kitchen pouring a glass of orange juice. She was beautiful, her almost-fifteen-year-old child-woman. With her fair complexion, flawless skin, and average height and build, she was so much like Grace. But she also managed to practice feminine wiles far beyond her age. And that was very much unlike her mother.

Lord, Grace prayed silently, just help me to get her through her teens without getting pregnant, and then into college before I lose her attention completely.

Dee turned from the sink with her glass and, as she sipped, cagily eyed her mother over the rim.

"Where's your brother?"

"You mean, my babysitter," she huffed.

"How can I trust you when you pull a stunt like this?"

"It wasn't a stunt, Mom, I promise. We planned to study. Jamie knew, and he said it was okay." Her brows knitted together. "I could have called and asked you about it if you'd let us have a cell phone like everybody else."

Grace sighed at this old family argument. "Don't start with that phone business, Dee. Where's Jamie?"

"He'll be here in a minute, and he'll tell you the same thing."

"What? That you let a boy in the house?"

Her daughter's voice traveled an octave higher. "You think I'm gonna do the deed with my brother in the house?" She swung her head and her shoulder-length braids fanned out in a black swirl. "Gross."

Grace moved beside her daughter and stroked the long braids she favored for the swim team. It was just like her misguided Dee to redirect blame for her own lack of judgment.

"You know there's a price to pay when you break house rules. Anyway, the *deed,* as you call it, isn't always planned. We've talked before and you know what to avoid." She rested her hands on Dee's shoulders. "You don't put yourself in situations where kissing and petting can get out of control."

"As if you'd know anything about that."

The barely discernible words muttered against the glass hadn't meant to be heard, but Grace didn't let that fact override her response to her headstrong daughter.

"What did you say?"

"Nothing," she quickly retorted in a facile lie.

Grace sighed at her immature daughter's insight. It stung to remember that it had been years since Grace had engaged in worthwhile passion, but that didn't mean she didn't know of it. She took a deep breath for the problem at hand.

"There's no point sulking. Get up to your room and start on your homework. We'll talk about the punishment later."

"Aw, Mama, I didn't do anything," Dee whined.

"And when your brother gets here," Grace continued, "I'll speak with both of you." She would tell them together about Uncle Byron.

"Then, I have to call Julian since he was gonna pick me up for school in the morning."

Grace frowned as she listened to her manipulative daughter, and shook her head. "No. And if he's smart, I'm sure he got the message not to show up. Anyway, I plan to give you and Jamie a ride."

"How can I even show my face at school now?" Visibly upset, Dee tilted her oval face at her mother. "First, you embarrass me in front of Julian and now you won't let me call him. He's gonna tell everybody what happened if I don't explain."

"Stop with the drama," Grace demanded evenly. "Maybe you'll consider the consequences next time."

Dee set the empty glass in the sink. "You just don't understand."

She left the kitchen in a huff, her gym bag dragging behind her. At the same time, the front door locks turned again. Grace stepped back into the hall as Jamie came through the door.

Only fifteen months his sister's senior, Jamie was on the path to be tall, like his daddy, but more angular. He seemed a perfect natural for basketball; yet, his first love was swimming—a good thing since Grace could trust he'd see what his teammate sister was up to at least part of the school year.

"Mom," he greeted her, "you're home early. I didn't see

the car out front, so I hope that don't mean it's in the shop again." He dropped his books and gym bag on the floor near the sofa and continued past her into the kitchen where he made a beeline for the refrigerator.

That explained Dee's surprise, Grace thought as she turned to join him. "I pulled around to the back because I had groceries. Why didn't you and your sister ride the activity bus home together?" Grace watched as he peeked from around the refrigerator door, his eyes cautiously gauging the room's mood.

"What's up?" he asked. "Did Dee do something?"

"She showed up just before you with some dread-headed boy."

"Yeah, I know him." Seemingly unconcerned, he buried his head in the refrigerator once again. "He did a favor and gave Dee a ride home. The activity bus broke down and we had to wait for the second bus—but it never came. So, Julian and some other guys at school with cars gave a lot of us a lift home." He darted another glance from around the refrigerator. "Dee got in Julian's car, but it filled up before I could get in. But, hey, he's pretty cool, Mom, so don't stress."

Cool, don't stress? Sure, while you and your boy-crazy sister crowd into some teenager's car? Grace shuddered inside as she imagined all that could go wrong.

"Okay, this was an emergency," she obliged. "But next time, use a phone and let me know what's going on."

"I tried. I borrowed somebody's cell phone and called your office. They said you'd already left."

"I—I see." A wave of guilt flowed over Grace. She hadn't been available when the kids needed her. Maybe she should try again to fit a cell phone in their already strained budget.

With his hands and arms filled with juice and sandwich fixings, Jamie kicked the refrigerator door closed. As he set his bounty on the table, he turned to Grace and asked, "So, if it's not the car, why are you home early?"

Grace hesitated. She should call Dee down and tell them now.

"Mom?" Jamie was staring at her with a frown. "What's wrong?"

"Your uncle Byron died this morning."

He looked at her, a mixture of disbelief and earnest concern in his young eyes. "Aw, man, that's messed up. You were real close to him, too."

The phone's jarring ring interrupted the moment, signaling the start of an evening ritual that would spirit her children away. At least for now, Jamie resisted answering. His avid face held steadfast to Grace's as they heard Dee yell from upstairs that she'd get it.

"What about you, Mom? You straight with things? You all right?"

Only now did it dawn on Grace that, in all the flux of activity that had occurred in the wake of Uncle Byron's death, this was the first time anyone had inquired of her state, of her own well-being at hearing this news. Being asked a simple question like, *Are you all right?* was a luxury to savor. She pulled Jamie into a hug, the top of her head just reaching his throat.

"Thank you for asking," she said, her eyes squeezed tight. "And, yes, I'll be fine."

CHAPTER 8

The next few hours offered no respite for Grace and passed quickly. And though the phone interruptions continued at a regular pace, a truce was negotiated with a pouting Dee as she helped prepare their spaghetti dinner.

Later, around the dinner table, they all joined in with quiet talk of Uncle Byron, with Dee's surprising admission that she liked talking with him because he made her laugh. But when the question of attending the funeral together came up, it was met with some resistance from the kids, who pressed their own agendas when Grace said they had to go.

"Mom," Dee whined loudly. "Why do we have to go?" She plowed her fork thoughtfully through the remnants of spaghetti and meat sauce that dotted her plate. "I don't want to miss the big swim meet this weekend."

It was code that she preferred to hook up with this Julian kid as soon as possible.

"Oh...and when did you get so dedicated?" Jamie joked as he piled another helping of salad onto his plate. "Coach should hear this."

"Shut up," Dee snapped, her eyes flashing and not a hint of whine. "Like, you really want to go down there to the country and see a bunch of people you hardly even know."

Grace wiped her fingers on her napkin. "That's a good reason to go—to meet the bunch of people that's family. I *have* to be there, and you know I'm not leaving you here by yourself. Anyway, I want you to pay last respects to your Uncle."

"I know what—" Dee sat straighter, a bright smile on her young face. "I can stay with Monica while you're gone."

This girl didn't hear a word I just said. Mother and son knew that if any other teenager's obsession with the opposite sex eclipsed Dee's, it was her friend, Monica.

Grace tried to keep the cringe from her face. Jamie, though, let out a great, whooping laugh, blowing salad from his mouth across the table.

"That is so-ooo gross." Dee made a face at her brother and defiantly crossed her arms.

Sighing, Grace watched the kids go at each other with their usual verbal zeal of one-upmanship. Dee was bold to a fault and afraid of nothing; Jamie was much more thoughtful and even-tempered.

Finishing her dinner, she ruminated on how she had been as a teenager. As the oldest child, she'd had to forego childhood to be the supportive and empathetic daughter to her mother's growing family that always required something of her. She didn't want her children loaded up with responsibilities that were not their call. But hadn't she already started doing that to Jamie, making him accountable for his headstrong sister at school?

Unnerved, she shook off the shadowy thought. *Of course not.* She closed off the reflection and returned her attention to the table.

"All right, both of you cut it out. And no, you can't stay with Monica. If we go back home, we'll do it as a family."

"So, how are we getting there?" Dee slumped in her chair, her brows raised. "We're not gonna drive Bertha, are we?" It was her nickname for the family's aging Volvo.

"I'm still figuring that out. We may have to fly."

"Hey, now that's all right," Jamie offered, and looked up from the attention he was giving his food.

"And why you so pumped about going?" Dee continued to beat that dead horse with her brother. "Don't you want to compete at the meet so you can work on your times for the championship finals?"

"Yeah, but I don't mind being out of town *this* week." He grinned. "I've got an English lit unit test Friday."

Dee's fork clanged to her plate. "Mom, that's not fair," she whined.

Grace glowered at her disingenuous son. He may be supportive but he was, after all, still a teenager. "You didn't tell me about that."

"See, we can't go now," Dee offered lightly, striking at this new opportunity. "We can stay with Daddy and Marilee."

The stepmother's name brought to Grace's mind yet another man-obsessed female, and she ignored her daughter.

"I'll talk with your teacher tomorrow, Jamie. I'm sure she can figure out something, maybe give you a take-home test to work on."

Jamie's smug demeanor had turned stricken while Dee's laugh crackled the air.

"That's not fair," he argued.

"Everybody wants to see y'all again, especially your grandma and aunties."

"Mom, how many husbands did Grandma Corinne have?" Dee asked.

"She had three," Grace answered, and looked up. "Why?"

"Is it true they kept on dying?" she asked, then looked across at her brother. "Jamie said she's like a black widow Grandma."

"Jamie," Grace said chidingly, and cut a look at him. "They died by accidents and sickness, and it wasn't your grandma's fault."

"I didn't say it like that, Mom." Jamie glared at his sister.

"Yes, you did," Dee argued.

Grace pressed her fingers against her eyelids as the doorbell rang.

No sooner had she looked up than both of the kids jumped from their chairs, shouting in unison, "I'll get it."

She watched them race from the table and into the living room.

Propping her elbows on the table's edge, Grace rested her head against her palms. Mentally drained, there was just too much to do before she could leave town for as long as a week.

As a tailor affiliated with the local dry cleaner where most of her business emanated, her customers had to be contacted, the school had to be notified—the list seemed endless. And she absolutely couldn't forget to handle the utility bills tomorrow. The grace period for payment would be over within a week and she didn't want to return home with no power or phone service.

She kneaded her brow and mentally checked off her list.

"Mom?"

Grace pricked her ears at Dee's shout from the front door, suddenly aware that neither of the kids had raced back to the kitchen. Rising tiredly from her chair, she left the kitchen.

"Yes?" Grace called as she traveled a few more steps and entered the living room. Both Jamie and Dee had crowded the front entry. Mildly alarmed, Grace quickened her steps. "Who's at the door?"

The kids fanned out to either side of the opening.

"Who...?"

Grace saw the tall, commanding frame she recognized as Theo Fontaine's step into the house from the porch, and stopped in her tracks.

"Grace." His resonant voice smiled her name as he moved across the threshold, into her living room, and into her life.

A bona fide stream of panic, much like the cacophony of a symphony warm-up, scraped its way through her senses.

What was he doing showing up here?

CHAPTER 9

Grace never expected to see Theo Fontaine in her home without first having prepared her children for the event. So his sudden appearance both stole her breath and released a mother's guilt at being found out.

If anything, though, Grace had become adept at handling the unexpected, and in a moment, she had recovered her aplomb.

She strained through the first-time introduction between Theo and the kids, and at the same time juggled the loud voices from her head that hammered at her logic.

While one voice explained there was no reason for Dee and Jamie to be leery, another confirmed Theo as a friend, not a lover—yet. But the third came full circle and acknowledged her guilty pleasure in a friend who made her heart beat faster, her mind lose focus and her thoughts linger on the sweet possibilities. All of this swirled in Grace's head at breakneck speed before she even asked Theo to join her in the den.

Dee and Jamie's interest in her guest was as keen as a razor's edge, and they preceded her and Theo into the den, quickly plopping down comfortably across the sofa.

As Grace unconsciously smoothed stray strands of hair with one hand, her cursory dismissal of the kids with the other failed to uproot them with any speed. She raised her voice and spoke sharply.

"Jamie, Dee, did you hear me? Finish your dinner and then get on your homework."

Though her short, energetic burst of authority got everyone's attention, in the kid's eyes, she knew it managed to thrust Theo in the untenable position of being responsible for their dismissal. They filed out of the room, eyes slanted at Theo in accusing silence.

So much for a smooth first meeting.

Grace watched the kids amble off, then turned from the doorway to join the tall, dark-suited man she'd begun to fall for on their first date. It was a fact she had not admitted to another soul, and had difficulty coming to terms with herself.

She had first noticed Theo as a repeat client for her tailoring work. It had been all business between them, but she had come to look forward to his appearances.

Their deciding encounter had been straight out of a romance novel, though. Grace, in a crouch, had been measuring his inseam in a workroom at the back of Monroe's Dry Cleaning—one of the businesses that contracted tailoring work to her—when she'd stumbled headlong against him and they'd both ended up in a tangled heap on the cement floor. Theo had been so gracious at her embarrassment that, when asked to join him later for dessert and coffee, she'd agreed.

From the beginning, Grace had been reluctantly drawn to what she attributed to his masculine strength, not to mention his confidence, of which he was in no short supply on that first date. And despite Grace's misgivings, the date had gone very well...

An exchange of basic, personal information between cheesecake and java had given them both an opportunity to digest what each considered essential. The rest of the time, Grace realized, had been easygoing small talk that was, surprisingly, easy. And over too soon.

Grace glanced at her watch. "Theo, it's late, and I'm afraid I have to get home." His full name was Theodore Fontaine Jr., and he warned her he wouldn't answer to anything other than Theo.

"So..." He reached for her hand across the table and lightly lifted her fingers. "Can I see you again?" he asked.

An unbidden smile had already flowed from Grace's heart to her face; but before she responded, Theo continued.

"I hope you say yes," he said, smiling. "I've just about run out of clothes to be altered. Pretty soon, I'll have to buy more for you to fit."

"You've..." Grace laughed. "You've been stalking me?"

He joined her with a deep chuckle. "Since that second fitting. You had that cool, ice-beauty thing going on, so I kept coming back to figure you out, break your reserve, and ask you out."

"And?" she prompted.

"Well, that tumble of yours was serendipitous."

"Serendipitous?" she asked, laughing again.

"Okay, so I read a lot."

"That's a good thing."

He grinned. "That I read or that you fell?"

"Both."

"It definitely broke the ice."

"The fall...definitely." Grace looked down at his long fingers curled under hers. She hadn't laughed this freely with a man in a long time. "Yes, Theo. I'd like to see you again."

When he squeezed her hand, she added, "But you understand I'm a single woman raising two teenagers, and I'd prefer to get to know you—away from them—before I introduce you into their lives."

Theo agreed, respecting her decision. And so began their meetings, each of which had left her longing for the next...

Now, standing face-to-face with Theo, Grace knew she was long past the girlish notion of romance, what with being divorced and closing in on forty, and simply waited for Theo's initial "romantic" effect on her to wear off—though it hadn't yet. She decided he probably harbored no such schoolboy notions about her, either. He'd been widowed for at least a decade, and was in his mid-forties with two grown children. Still, Grace enjoyed how he made her the center of his universe when they were together—even now.

She stared bravely into Theo's cautious eyes, with her chin raised. The past few months of quiet, public meetings, frequent innocent touches, goodbye kisses now and again that were growing more desperate, and then off in separate cars to separate lives, had been nice—and safe. Their times together had been like island retreats from the caprices of fate that could visit without warning.

Theo risked everything with this deliberate appearance; showing little respect for the promise he'd made when they'd first embarked on this dating journey.

"Grace…" Theo raised his hands in quiet exasperation. "I didn't mean to disrupt your evening with your family." He glanced in the direction the teens had gone.

"You've got yourself a couple of good-looking kids. I imagine you're proud of them."

She watched his long fingers splay as they raked across his head, touching a graying temple in the process. He was exhibiting a measure of vulnerability that had not been apparent to her before. It was a simple revelation that was endearing, and Grace almost smiled, but instead she bit her lip.

"I am proud, but this isn't how we agreed you'd meet them."

"I know." He caught her eyes with his. "And I'd like to explain."

Theo had broached her set borders on…what, a whim? And now he wasn't sure how she'd react to the invasion; but then, neither was Grace. How this turned out could test the direction of their relationship. Surprisingly, Grace wasn't ready to give up those island retreats he represented. Not just yet.

She pressed on. "We agreed that I would decide when you'd meet my family, but you just—" She shook her head with uncertainty and then moved past him. "Just show up without so much as a warning." Out of habit, Grace began to arrange some of the untidiness that came with a family.

Theo slowly moved with her. "I was worried about you, so I took the chance and came over."

"What's that supposed to mean?" Before finishing the sentence, enlightenment widened her eyes and she whirled to him. "Theo, I forgot. We were supposed to meet—"

"Tonight because I'm going out of town tomorrow," he finished, and stopped in front of her. "I called your office this afternoon, like I always do before we meet, but you'd left early. So, when you didn't show up at our usual place and you didn't call, that wasn't like you. I wanted to make sure nothing was wrong."

He showed up out of concern. The idea of such a thing almost made Grace giddy. She realized her anger at his appearance was dissipating, and she no longer trusted herself in such proximity to him. Grace turned away before she bent to clear school papers from the coffee table.

"You know, you took a big chance." She flicked him a fierce look from over her shoulder. "What if I'd lied to you about my circumstances and my big, hulking husband answered the door?"

A resonant chuckle rose up from him, the tension between them seemingly broken. "I would have tried to sell him insurance, or something like that, and hope for nothing more than a slammed door."

Theo's deep voice quickly sobered. "But, I never even considered that you'd been anything but honest with me from the start, Grace." He moved a step closer. "We've talked about a lot over the last months, and you wouldn't have lied."

Uncomfortable, Grace moved to the couch to plump the cushions. "Okay, it's my fault. I should've called and let you know something came up."

"Maybe things worked out for the best, after all, and stop with this damn cleaning." Theo gently pulled her away from the sofa and, turning her to him, tenderly rested his hands on her shoulders with a smile.

"You weren't going to keep me away from your family forever, were you?"

Is that what she'd been doing? Grace blinked through reason as she felt his hand, a big hand that suggested tender, intimate abilities, stroke her neck before tilting her face to his. And then he was kissing her.

It was a warm, urgent, "Damn, I miss you" kiss, in her house, with her kids in the next room, and who might even be watching. In this moment, Grace didn't care, and threw caution away.

With a low moan, she grudgingly broke away from Theo's sweet mouth and hands. No, she wasn't trying to keep him away from her family forever; she was just being extra cautious for her children's sakes; that's all.

"Theo, I just wanted a little more time."

Grace wanted to draw him into her confidence and share what happened today—including her doubts about returning home for the funeral; but experience told her that to do so would invite an inevitable regret. Her problems were of little interest to anyone else, least of all a would-be suitor. Avoiding disappointment had always been a good practice.

"So, that *was* your plan, to keep me away?"

Theo's words hit home, and she looked up at him. "You think I'm overreacting to you showing up?"

He smiled at her. It was a deep, honest smile that brought crinkles to the corners of his eyes.

"Maybe a little." He took up her hand in his and pulled her along with him to the sofa where they sat. "I've learned enough about you over the past weeks to know you're cautious and prefer things at a slower pace."

"Oh" was all Grace said. He was right. Already, Theo knew way too much about her, even her hopes and dreams.

"Don't you think it's time for me to see you at home and meet the people important to you? I love your smile, Grace. It's a little crooked, and dimples on the right side. And, you know, you've been hard pressed to give me one since I got here."

It was Grace's turn to smile, and she touched his arm in a silent apology. In hindsight, maybe she had blown Theo's visit out of proportion.

He gently stroked her hand. "I was beginning to feel like this shameful secret you wanted to keep hidden."

"I'm a little on edge tonight, I guess," Grace began. "A lot happened today, and I can't seem to find the time to deal with the consequences, let alone accept them."

"You have time now. Tell me what happened."

She dropped her head back against the couch and tried to gauge how much of her troubles she should share—how much he really wanted to hear—before, like most people, he reached his saturation level and became patronizing.

Grace turned her head to draw his gaze. "Do you remember my uncle I told you about, with prostate cancer?" When he nodded, she continued in a whisper, "Well, he died this morning."

Theo jerked around to face her. "Grace, I'm sorry to hear that," he spoke quietly. "You thought a lot of him."

The memories Grace had managed to keep at bay for most of the day coalesced to form a hard lump in her throat. She nodded, unable to speak the words as her eyes burned to shed unspent tears.

"Hey, you're more upset than you're letting on." Theo's words projected sincerity. "If you want to talk about him, I'd like to hear it." He leaned back and pulled her head to his shoulder.

Grace swallowed hard. "My uncle Byron, he was a good man. At least he tried to be, and that's better than most. But he wasn't understood all the time." At Theo's nod and quiet interest, Grace decided to tell him more.

"He knew about you." She glanced up for his reaction.

Theo's slowly growing smile was a gentle line. "You mean, you didn't keep me a secret from everyone?"

Her head shook in reply as her own weak smile formed.

"We talked some almost every day when his condition worsened. He thought my seeing you was a good thing."

"I see."

Grace looked up at Theo pointedly for a moment. "I don't think so. He figured that if I went so far as to let someone into my life again, they must be having a positive effect on my fear."

"Fear?"

"He said I was infected with what he called a fear of living." Grace smiled again at the memory, but it didn't reach her sad eyes. "Uncle Byron liked to say that I worked harder than anyone he knew at keeping things the same. Sometimes, I'd get mad when he said it. But in the end, I always forgave him."

"Because in your heart you knew he was right?"

"Maybe." She closed her eyes against his shoulder. "He also called me a dreamer. Well, I'd tell him, dreams don't cost a thing, but try making them real, especially when you're raising two teenagers alone."

Grace realized she was dangerously bordering on pity. She abruptly opened her eyes and sat up, and effectively stemmed the bittersweet reminiscing.

"Your uncle was a man who spoke his mind. I think I would've liked him a lot," Theo said.

"He was the father I never had."

Theo nodded sagely. "Your father died when you were young."

They all died and left us. Grace closed her mind to the haphazard thought, running her hands down her face with a sigh. "The truth of the matter is, I didn't spend nearly enough time with Uncle Byron. We never do with our loved ones, do we?"

"In retrospect, probably not," Theo agreed.

"We're busy being adults and parents ourselves. And when we realize time has passed, well, it's too late." She turned to Theo, her voice wavering. "I'm going to miss him."

"Come here." With gentle coercion, Theo tucked Grace into the crook of his arm and they both settled back against the sofa in a hug that was more comforting than anything else. "Give yourself a moment to relax."

It was the first time today Grace had lowered her guard long enough to immerse herself in memories. She'd been afraid that unrelenting grief would overtake her and breach her dam of control. She relished Theo's supportive shoulder behind her, his arm around her.

If she closed her eyes right now, she could imagine Uncle Byron's affectionate embrace, the smell of old-fashioned Aqua Velva aftershave, and the scratchy stubble from his not-too-close shaves.

What was it about a man's embrace that brought to mind thoughts of deep security and comfort? Grace struggled against the pressure from tears.

"I have to go back home for the funeral."

Theo brushed fine strands of hair from her face. "That's good. It's where you should be—with the rest of your family."

Startled, Grace realized she had spoken the sobering

thought out loud. She left Theo's arms, pushing off the sofa to walk over to the curtained window.

"Funny," she said. "My boss doesn't think so, and my ex-husband doesn't believe the kids need to go. On the other hand, everyone back home thinks all of us should've picked up and left tonight."

She pushed back the curtain and noted the black stillness that had settled into the neighborhood. Rather than being repelled by the quiet darkness, she was drawn to it, a kind of kinship of moods.

Theo joined her at the window. "Did things work out with your boss?"

"As good as they'll get. But he's the least of my problems."

"What about your ex?"

"Nothing unusual about where he stands or what I have to go through for any extraordinary expenses. You see, if there's money involved, and in this case we're talking possible airplane tickets for the kids, he freaks first and asks questions later." She offered a closed glance to Theo. "I've learned not to count on him in emergencies."

"This may not come out right, Grace, but if you need help with the tickets, I'll be glad—"

Her raised hand stopped him. "Please, I appreciate the offer, but I didn't tell you this for help. It's not your problem, so don't tempt me with your solution. I'll get through this the way I usually do." She attempted a smile to placate his concern. "If necessary, I'll borrow from Peter to pay Paul." She turned back to the window.

"I see that proud streak of yours is all fired up."

"I'll be just fine. I'll have something figured out by tomorrow."

He dropped his hands onto her slight but tightly held shoulders, and treated them to a light, lilting massage. "The upside to all this is that you'll be with family."

Grace grunted in disdain. "Why do people always say that? Family isn't always the answer, you know." She kept her face averted, lest he see the shameful truth in her eyes. "Sometimes they're part of the problem."

Only a slight shift in the rhythm of Theo's fingers indicated he had picked up on her annoyance.

"You've got—what? Five other sisters," he asked, although he knew the answer. "Will you see them all?"

"I imagine so. I've already heard from most of them."

"I have just the one brother I told you about. Hell, between the two of us, we'd be lucky to find ten relatives who even care enough to show up for a family gathering." He lay a light kiss upon her neck. "You should count yourself lucky to have a large and interested family."

"If there is an upside to having so many sisters, then it must be, if you don't get along with one at any given moment, there's always another personality waiting in the wings."

Theo chuckled at her analysis. "Well, I agree with your family. You should go on down and be with them, no matter what anyone says. Go see your mama and sisters, grieve for your uncle, and in the process, get some peace of mind for yourself."

Grace snorted at his enthusiasm, but he plowed on.

"Isn't that what makes going home good for the soul—seeing all those faces and places from your childhood, drawing on the memories?"

"No," Grace blurted. Theo's hands froze, but Grace seemed unable to stem the frustration that now poured from her. "It's not always good, you know."

"Grace..." He spun her from the window and looked into her eyes, bright from a sheen of unshed tears. "What's wrong?"

She stared back at him, trying to find the right words that wouldn't condemn her in his eyes, yet anxious to let them free.

"It's just that I..." She whispered the words. "I don't want to go home."

CHAPTER 10

"I don't understand," Theo said, puzzled. "You love your uncle."

Grace shuddered a deep sigh, sloughing off her candid admission with a wave of her hand. "Ignore me. I'm a little stressed from everything that's gone on today, that's all." She glanced his way and smiled. "I'll get over it. I always do."

The phone's shrill ring broke through their silence. Both of the kids could be heard shouting from upstairs, "I got it."

Grace stepped toward a lamp table and snatched up a couple of tissues from a box and dabbed at her eyes. It was too late to claim vanity. She hadn't looked into a mirror in hours; and as tired as she was, she and her straggly French braid must look a sight. She heard Theo's deep voice flow out from somewhere behind her.

"I'm still worried about you."

Grace turned and forced a smile onto her face. "I'm okay, I promise." He *was* worried. She could see the lines etched along his forehead, the concern reflected in his eyes.

From the doorway, she saw that Dee was slowly entering the den.

"What is it, honey?"

"Aunt Reba's on the phone."

Dee's inquisitive stare took in all there was to see. And more.

"One of my sisters," Grace explained to Theo. "Get her number," she said to Dee, "and tell her I'll call back in a bit. And then, I want you and your brother to come say good night to Mr. Fontaine."

When Dee left, Theo took Grace's hands in his. "So, it's come to this. You're throwing me out?"

"I have to. There's so much I have to handle before I leave, and I don't even know my travel plans yet."

"Believe me, I know how it is with traveling. Promise me, though, that you'll call if you need my help with anything." He squeezed her hands between his. "No, just call me, period, any time of day." He sighed. "I forgot, you don't have a cell phone."

She smiled at his attempts to be supportive. "They still install phones in houses, you know."

"After what you said about it being hard on you, I could come down to the funeral."

This time Grace vehemently shook her head. "Theo, that's not necessary. You have a meeting in New York for the next three days."

"I also manage the region. I can work something out."

She took a deep breath, uneasy that Theo might actually act on his suggestion. "I'll be fine, and I promise I'll find a way to call you while I'm there."

They heard footfalls approach the den. Grace pulled

her hands from Theo's grasp just as the children entered the room. Jamie remained near the doorway, slouched against the wall with his arms crossed.

"You wanted us?" His voice was sullen.

"Yes," Grace said, raising a brow at her usually considerate son's behavior. "Theo is about to leave. He only stopped by before we left town and…" She wasn't quite sure how to broach the subject.

"Are you two dating?" Dee had stopped in the middle of the room and now looked from her mother to Theo.

"Sure, they are," Jamie answered from the door. "Why else would he be coming over here?"

"We're not *dating* dating." It was a clumsy clarification, but Grace plodded on. "We're good friends and since…" She hesitated, and looked around to Theo for help.

"And since I'll be coming around more often, she wanted me to meet you two." Theo heaved a sigh as he moved toward the kids, smiling broadly into their glares. "And by the way…" His voice lowered conspiratorially. "If you ever need passes to get backstage to meet one of the groups performing over at the Rialto Strand, just let me know." He winked. "My brother is the manager."

It was the perfect icebreaker. Jamie straightened from the doorway and Dee's eyes sparked considerably as both teens showed a more respectful interest in Theo.

"O-oh…" Dee squealed in delight. "Wait'll I tell Monica at school." Her smile stayed bright as she shook Theo's outstretched hand goodbye.

"Yeah, that's all right," Jamie said, a wary grin slowly filling his face as he, too, walked over to shake Theo's hand. He gave his mother a fleeting glance before he added, "It was, ah, nice meeting you."

"Same here," Dee piped up.

"Okay, you can get back to your homework," Grace announced, and watched the two retreat through the door until they were out of sight.

Alone again, Theo took Grace's hand in his as they slowly walked to the front door.

"You didn't tell me you have a way with kids," she said.

Theo smiled. "I still have skills. It's the one thing that worked on my own two when they were teenagers—bribes."

He held the door, and Grace stepped out onto the porch ahead of him. She took a deep breath to steady her nerves, but it was mostly her heart that needed securing.

The darkness had taken over the twilight, and the slight chill in the autumn night was just what she needed. She heard the door close behind Theo, and knew it was the simplest defense for them against curious eyes.

He came up behind her, his hands sloping along her arms before he brushed her temple with a kiss.

"I like this, Grace, standing here on a beautiful night with a beautiful woman. I like coming to your house and calling on you." This time, he placed a lingering kiss to her cheek. "I want to keep on coming over."

Grace swallowed hard at the intimacy he'd sparked, marveling at the sizzle to her senses—like an egg on a hot frying pan—that his touch evoked.

She wanted it, the heightened intimacy; yet on some level, she was uncomfortable. If only Theo had given her a little more time.

More time? You don't think seven years without a man around is long enough? And how much longer do you think someone like Theo will wait? Soon, he'll grow tired, and he won't have any trouble finding someone who'll appreciate him.

Grace shook off the admonishment.

"I've got to decide on some things tonight." She didn't want to leave the comfort of his arms as she anticipated the kiss to come. "You must have a lot to do, too."

"Hey, don't change the subject," he teased, and spun her around so they faced each other. "You never said if it was okay to come here again." Theo didn't wait for her answer, but pulled her closer.

Grace's eyes fluttered shut and her breath held in her throat as she pressed against him and experienced an electric-like shudder. It was quickly followed by the indescribable intimacy of lips brushing against hers before they clung in a sensuous dance. Grace's insides yearned for the crackle of more heat, more pressure...more of it all. Too soon, she slipped from the silken kiss as though from a dream.

Theo lifted her chin with his finger. "Tell me what's on your mind."

Grace didn't say it, but she was reminded of their very first kiss weeks ago and how she would've been devastated had it been their last. Theo had seen her to her car that afternoon, and there, in the poorly lit parking garage, he had kissed her. It had been unexpected, but that had made it all the more pleasurable, his touch, strength, and she, lightly pinned against the car by his weight. Smiling, she remembered…

"You know I've wanted to kiss you since we first met for that fitting."

Grace tried to catch her breath as the last quiver of sexual energy dissipated.

"In that case," she said, "I hope it was worth the wait."

"Oh, it was," Theo assured her with a wide, white grin. "Something told me not to rush you, though—that if I did, I might lose you." He drew her gaze to his. "You aren't disappointed, are you?"

Her eyes flashed at him. "No, not at all."

"I didn't think so," he chuckled…

Grace smiled as the memory faded and found herself looking into Theo's intent stare. "I'm thinking you were right to stop by this evening."

"Are you now?" he said, his delight obvious that the evening would end on a high note, and he bent to pull her into another kiss.

As they broke apart, Theo whispered against her neck, "I'd better go." It was clear he didn't want to. "You already told me you have a lot to do."

"I promise to call you."

He squeezed her arm. "I'm sorry for your loss, Grace, but I want you to take care of yourself, too."

She watched him step down from the porch, and as he walked across the yard to his car parked on the street, she remembered his question.

"Theo," she whispered loudly at him. When he stopped and looked back, she smiled. "The answer to your question? Yes, you can come to the house again."

She could see his triumphant smile in the dim light and his hand raised in acknowledgment before he continued on to his car.

The road sign was clear. Caution. How things would progress with Theo Fontaine was a worry for another day, Grace decided. She had answered her own question about dormant passion, though. After seven years, she still had some. It remained to be seen what she would do with it.

Right now, she had enough problems to keep her more than occupied for the next few hours, let alone the days ahead.

She stepped back into the house and locked the door behind her. Standing there, Grace shook off her fatigue as she enumerated the things to be handled before she could call it a day.

"Jamie, Dee," she called as she headed for the back room she used for her seamstress jobs.

"Whoever has kitchen duty tonight, get started on it. And both of you, finish your homework. No phone calls until I see it."

She could hear their groans and smiled that they recognized the familiar routine. "I'll be in my sewing room with the phone."

And so it went until Grace's day quietly concluded near midnight. She wanted to sleep; yet at that hour, she still sat with her sewing, methodically repairing other people's clothes.

None of her own bags were packed, nor did she know the details for their tickets. She decided that, at this late hour, she'd carry those worries over to tomorrow with all the others.

She deftly maneuvered the sewing needle through the fabric, though weariness had begun to dull her senses. Soon, Grace's head nodded in unbidden sleep.

She felt herself dozing off, and then jerked awake, and looked down at the needle that lay slack in her hand. Grace could no longer hold off the inevitable. She knew she'd have to give in to the day. Throwing aside the sewing piece, she left for her own bedroom upstairs.

The quiet house contradicted the turmoil that swirled inside Grace. After looking in on her sleeping children, she moved down the hall to her bedroom and quietly closed the door before she walked to her bed. It was time to release her memories.

And she remembered it all.

Don't be so full of fear, Grace. That was what Uncle Byron would say to her when she talked with him about the things in her heart. Sitting on the corner of her bed, with her head resting against the tall post, Grace quietly wept.

She wept for the emptiness her gentle uncle's loss had

brought. She wept for her job that drained her of joy, the uncertainty of her new relationship, and the anxiety that most surely would remain her handmaiden for the next week as she reunited with her family.

But most of all, Grace wept for her lack of courage to change any of those things.

Soon, the tears were spent and Grace dried her face. Tomorrow, she would have to be strong.

CHAPTER 11

Corinne Wilson made deliberate, unhurried steps as she crossed the wood floor into the living room. She hadn't slept well last night, and didn't see the need for putting off the day's start once the light touched her window. Byron was gone now, and she suspected she'd be having lots of restless nights ahead.

Only if one peered closely at Corinne's gait could you make out the slight limp that remained from her accident over twenty years ago, and which precipitated so much change in her life.

A proud woman whose handsome face still carried traces of her classic beauty, Corinne seldom used the burnished oak cane Byron had given her from one of his trips to only God knows where. It stood in its usual place near the front door.

The promising Oxford autumn had turned balmy, and though it was barely seven in the morning, the fully occupied house was overly warm, but quiet and peaceful. Corinne liked this early morning calm before the day brought on the usual storm of commotion at her house. In and out, that was how her doors worked for anybody and everybody that wanted to use them.

Moving through the dim, curtain-shrouded living room toward her kitchen, she was careful not to wake her two granddaughters who fidgeted as they lay sprawled in sleep on makeshift beds fashioned from the two sofas.

Byron's death had been a shock. She might as well have had her right arm wrenched from her body. Oh, she'd known he might not survive, even with all that chemotherapy. He'd been terribly sick for the last few months. It was just that she couldn't remember a time in her life when she had been without him or his support. Born less than a year apart, they had gone through so much together.

Byron had grown up in a house full of girls; and when Corinne's babies turned out to be one girl after another, for each one, Byron would let loose with another of those wide grins of his, and present a toy truck as a gift.

Corinne smiled at that memory. She had been the only one of his sisters who could play just as rough as he did and, for that matter, get in as much devilment. And by God, did they get into a lot of trouble in their little country town. Yeah, she and Byron had known each other well. Each had been the other's solace.

Every time Corinne lost one of her husbands—and Lord knows she'd had a few—Byron had been there, urging her to go on and hold things together for the girls. First, Grace and Gloria's daddy, Richard, died. Then it was Rufus, Daisy and Reba's daddy; and finally Fletcher, Belinda and Missy's daddy.

Frowning, Corinne bit her lip as the panoramic pieces

of her life flashed in front of her. Byron had been there every time to hold her hand, wipe her tears. He even told her what to do. Who would be there for her at the end of the day now?

Of all her girls, Byron had been a steady fixture in Grace's life. And from Grace's voice yesterday, she was affected more than she was letting on.

The reasons weren't that complicated. Corinne figured it was because Grace had connected to Byron when her real daddy died. He'd been like a father and she'd been looking up to him alone ever since, even though Corinne had married two more times to give her children a daddy.

Over the kitchen sink, Corinne could see the morning light pierce the delicate eyelet curtains. Reaching up to push the cotton material apart, she winced from the sharp pain before her arm dropped uselessly to her side, bringing to bear the memory of her arthritic shoulder and leg.

Despite the joint pain that seemed to plague her aging body, Corinne began to hum a favorite hymn, willing the pain and sadness away—at least for a time.

It made her smile to know that the girls would be at the house tonight—all of them, God willing. That would be an unusual treat, indeed. She was going to prepare a special dinner regardless of how bad her arthritis flared.

She ticked off a plausible menu and opened the refrigerator door. Because everybody would be home, she made a special effort to stock it with her daughters' favorite foods, and over Missy's loud objections. Corinne's home cooking was something the girls and their husbands looked forward to; and with so many things to be done today, she might as well get started.

"Mama, Gloria's not down here yet?"

Missy had tramped into the kitchen with eyes flashing. A three-year-old rode her hip, his big brown eyes teeming with tears.

"She's upstairs with Rambo. They're still sleeping, if you didn't already wake 'em up with your yelling." Reaching over to take her grandson from Missy, she frowned as she asked, "Aw, what's wrong with you, Tavis?"

After handing over the child, Missy crossed her arms defiantly. "He's hungry and he wants his mama. Why? I don't know. You know she stuck him in my bed sometime last night? Now, she's upstairs lounging with her husband behind locked doors while we get the kitchen and baby-sitting duty."

"Don't cry, sugar." Corinne fussed over the whimpering child before she turned to her daughter. "I'll fix us all some breakfast, Missy. You don't have to do it. They're visiting us...let them rest."

"No, Mama. I told her a while ago she needed to get down here. We are not a hotel, and you know as well as I do that every time she comes, she brings her whole family, but she don't do a thing to help out. If we can put her up and supply the groceries, too, the least she can do is cook for her own family."

Corinne dried Tavis's tears while her daughter ranted. She watched from the corner of her eye as Missy sashayed to the doorway and stuck her head out into the living room. She drew a breath to stop Missy, but it was too late.

"Gloria," Missy bellowed loudly, "your children are hungry. You and Rambo need to get your shiftless asses down here and feed 'em."

It took only two beats for a response.

"I said I was coming, Missy," Gloria shouted in kind from somewhere upstairs before the door slammed for good measure.

"See, Mama?" Missy wore a self-satisfied smile as she turned from the door.

"Well, you didn't have to do all that screaming."

"Sure I did. That's how you get that lazy woman out of bed."

Corinne sighed deeply and sank onto a chair as she quieted her grandbaby. The earlier calm had been nice, she thought, but her day was just beginning. Get used to it.

She wondered again when Grace might get in.

CHAPTER 12

"Dammit," Missy muttered before she vehemently launched her fist at the car horn. *Beep. Beep.*

The tinny bleats filled the air as Grace braced for the inevitable braking. Sitting in the front seat of Missy's compact Sonata, she was used to the juts and swerves that usually accompanied her sister's erratic driving.

"Did you see that?" Missy asked, turning to Grace with brows furrowed in provocation. "You see how that bastard just cut in front of me?"

"For Christ's sake," chided Grace. "Watch the road, and your mouth, too." She made a surreptitious nod toward the back seat before Dee's giggle rose up from there.

"Aw, chill, Gracie. We'll be home before you know it." Her attention returned to the road and she gunned the little car forward.

We should be so lucky. Grace sighed and held on.

For as long as Missy had owned a license, she'd been a hellion on wheels. Coupled with a temper that gave short shrift to any driver that got in her way, it was a miracle she still *had* a license.

Grace suspected that for all her sister's in-your-face

derision, she kept things inside more often than she let on. There were more than ten years difference in their ages, and though Grace had not been home for most of Missy's turbulent high school years, she had tried to help her mother survive them. They shared the worry that it could be only a matter of time before Missy's lead foot and quick mouth did her in for good.

The little car hurtled along the Interstate, having already zipped past Atlanta's city limits and the heaviest airport traffic, as it headed to the little country town of Oxford, a place Grace had happily escaped.

She glanced over at Missy's glowing profile and smiled. Her fragile features were a stark contrast to decidedly chocolate skin and thick, curly hair that brushed her shoulders. As if she could read her thoughts, Missy returned Grace's glance.

"It's not funny, you know," Missy said, mirroring her sister's smile. "Wait until you get peed on by a three-year-old."

Grace didn't have a clue to what Missy was talking about. But it didn't matter that you understood—only that you listen, because Missy continued to talk. Grace looked out the car window at the rapidly approaching dusk and reflected on the past twenty-four hours.

The plane ride had been uneventful, though preparation for it had been anything but that. Exhausted now, Grace wanted only to sleep for a while before delving into Uncle's funeral preparations tomorrow.

The money for airfare had set her back big-time—she

had managed to get an emergency limit increase on her Visa *again*. However, if Bobby came through later on with his share of expenses, like he promised, Grace figured she just might make it through to next month…provided another crisis didn't rear its ugly head.

"Grace? You're not listening."

Grace jerked her head around to Missy with a guilty smile.

"Yes, I am. Go on," she urged as sincerely as she could before her train of thought jumped the track again. It was a no-brainer that Missy was either talking about somebody, or what they did, or where they did it, and she could do it nonstop.

Grace looked over her shoulder into the back seat where Jamie was still zoned out with earphones snugly entrenched in his ears and his eyes closed. It was what he had done most of the plane trip.

Dee, on the other hand, had put aside the *Essence* magazine to perch on the edge of her seat behind Missy, with arms folded at her aunt's neck. Dee idolized Missy, and now hung on to her youngest aunt's every word, giggling as they brazenly sped through the thinning late-afternoon traffic.

"Would you look at her up there, talking on that damn cell phone?" Missy huffed as she bore down on the slow driver just ahead. She slammed her horn before she darted into an adjacent lane and then passed the seemingly unwary driver.

Grace held her breath as the car jerked and surged forward under Missy's tutelage. Maybe she should have squeezed in the expense of a rental car because, after a week of this, her nerves would be shot.

She sent another testy glance to Missy. The reality was that Grace was back home and nothing had changed. Missy was still so young and foolish, and Grace worried about the day her little sister would chew off more than she could handle. She knew road rage could get out of hand—

"I'm so glad you finally got here," Missy gushed enthusiastically from behind the wheel. She grinned the wide, toothy trademark smile that tied them all together as siblings.

"Grandma said she was cooking something special for everybody," Dee piped in.

"You know Mama. She's been cleanin' and cookin' all day, and she acts like none of y'all ever lived in that house before."

"Yeah, sounds like Mama, all right," Grace agreed with a relaxed grin. "So everybody's here?" she asked, hiding her unease over Missy's driving.

"Didn't you hear me? I already said Gloria and Rambo and their whole crew got in yesterday." She swerved to pass another car. "The newlyweds got here about noon today," she added with a bit of sarcasm.

That would be their sister Belinda and her husband of less than a year, Glenn Townsend.

"They probably still over at Grandma Rhoda's," Missy added.

Grace frowned. "I thought Reba and the baby were staying with Grandma."

"They are," Missy agreed. "Belinda is just visiting over

there, that's all." She floored the accelerator. "Last I heard, she planned on staying with some college friends of hers in Atlanta."

"Oh," Grace said quietly, bearing down equally on the imaginary brake beneath her foot.

Dee combed her fingers lightly through the ends of Missy's dark hair, a mass of tight curls that brushed her neck.

"Mama," Dee said. "I think I want to wear my hair like Auntie's."

"You do, huh?" Missy answered. "Well, yours is softer than my coarse hair. I'll show you how to fix it without perming your brains out."

Dee let out a satisfied giggle.

"What about swim season?" Grace reminded her daughter.

"I can do it after, then." Dee's voice rose in petulant defiance, before she purposely slanted her conversation for Missy. "It was Mom's idea for the braids, anyway. She said they were the best thing for being in the pool every day."

"Yeah, I agree," Missy said. "Did she tell you how our hair turned green one summer from the chlorine in the pool at the Y?"

Dee laughed out loud, declaring, "Mama, you never told us about that."

Grace rolled her eyes at Missy. "You remember that?"

"I can tell you all kinds of hair tales that went on in our house growing up."

"Mama only wears her hair like that—pulled back in a braid or a ponytail pinned up," Dee said.

"I know," Missy said, and grinning, turned to Grace. "I keep telling her she not gon' get a man that way."

Before Grace could once again warn her sister about her mouth, Dee piped up from the backseat, "She's got a boyfriend."

Grace rolled her eyes heavenward before she turned to her daughter.

"I told you, Theo's not a boyfriend. He's...just a good friend."

Missy clucked gleefully. "Girl, if he's a man, claim it, okay? So why didn't you tell me about him?"

"We just met him," Dee offered quickly, obviously feeling safe while in the glare of Grace's evil eye.

"Oh, this is good stuff I can't wait to share," Missy said, glancing to Grace. "You're my girl, Dee."

Confident that she had an ally, Dee once again played with her aunt's curls.

"I'm gonna miss you kids at the house." Missy darted her eyes around to Grace again. "I'm figurin' you already told Mama about where they'll be staying?"

Missy's pleas for Grace to stay at the house had finally won out—that and the fact that Grace could hardly afford an unexpected hotel bill.

So, with the decision made to squeeze into space at the house, it made a lot of sense to take up the offer from Bobby's mother to let the kids stay with her. However, Grace knew it would be her mother who'd feel slighted when she learned of the arrangement.

"No, I didn't say anything to her this morning." Grace's

eyes turned apologetic. "I didn't have time to do much planning, and I didn't have a choice. We'll be like sardines in the house as it is."

"We could've worked it out, you know."

"Yeah, Mama." Dee chimed in with a whine. "I want to stay with Auntie Missy and you."

Grace was sure she had been the afterthought.

"Can you imagine all of us under one roof again…it'll be just like old times," Missy joked.

"There were four sleeping in your room back then." Grace added weakly. "Who wants to revisit that?"

"I guess now the bed would be a little crowded, what with Rambo squeezing into it with you and Gloria." She snickered as she looked at Grace and lowered her voice. "'Course, he's not the one who'd complain."

"Missy." Grace snorted a reminder, nodding toward Dee. "Anyway the old times are gone, and they weren't that much fun. Let them be."

A glance passed between the sisters, all too perceptive, even in its brevity.

"Well, it might not have been fun for you. You always had to take care of us, but you have to admit we had fun when we could get away from Mama and all that damn housework she made us do." She steered the car into a lower lane for their exit up ahead. "Hell, I can remember when Reba even made us laugh."

Grace grinned at her sister's confused memory. "You never did any housework 'cause you were the baby. While you and Belinda were in grade school, the rest of us older kids did all the work."

"That's a lie," Missy chuckled. "You and Mama both worked our tails off around that house, and then by sundown, Uncle Byron would drop by and whisk you and Gloria away 'cause y'all were the oldest."

Dee giggled as she listened to the conversation. "Mama never talks about the days when she grew up."

"Honey, I don't think she wants to relive that drama."

"You got that right," Grace opined. "I suspect, though, that we won't have a choice this weekend."

"Uncle Byron's gone, but he got us all together again," Missy said.

"Yeah," Grace said. She was watching the exit come up. "He always managed to do that."

"Dee, I can tell you everything you want to know about your mama growing up, but you're gonna have to be my ears while you're over at your other granny's house. So, if you pick up any good gossip, you have to share it, okay?"

Dee laughed again. "Okay."

"Missy, don't tell her that." While her sister and Dee giggled in conspiracy, Grace settled against the seat for their exit ahead.

They took the Oxford exit and sped along the two-lane asphalt strip of road that led to their hometown and most of their relatives.

Grace didn't like the fact that Jamie and Dee would be staying separate from her, even though it was their paternal grandmother. She remembered her anxiety from that first summer years ago after the divorce when Bobby had brought them here for a visit. She hadn't wanted them to go, but he wouldn't take no for an answer. She'd managed to survive it, though, and the ones after that, and she guessed she'd survive it this time, too.

Theo. He had called early that morning before leaving for his business meeting. In spite of herself, Grace smiled. He wanted to say goodbye again, and against her better judgment, she shared with him the phone number to the house after refusing his offer to leave her a cell phone. The nice gesture both warmed and surprised her.

She hadn't mentioned Theo to the kids again. For their part, they had been silent about him since their meeting. It wasn't an angry kind of silence, but rather a silence of omission, as though they expected something from her. Grace decided not to overthink the issue and adopted a wait-and-see attitude.

She looked out the window as they passed scattered wood-framed houses and landmarks, like the strip malls on the main road, and other childhood images assailing her sights once again.

Thornton's general store had been abandoned for at least five years and still sat empty, boarded and forlorn on the corner across from the small redbrick building used as the federal post office, the large-lettered zip code acting like a beacon on the front.

On the other corner sat a small grocery store, with a built-up lean-to next to it that sheltered a table and chairs.

Two men sat there playing checkers. They looked up as Missy's car drove by. It was Royce and Nathan Parker, Aunt Evie's brothers.

"How's that for luck," Missy said as she sped by for her next turn. "To have those two be the first people you see back home?"

Grace thought it didn't say much for luck.

It was here that Missy turned off the asphalt and onto a gravel road. Just ahead was the cemetery, pristine and green with the varying shades and shapes of headstones, in exacting rows, and erect as standard bearers.

Grace's stomach gave a quiver for a moment, as it always did, when she traversed this pastoral scene.

Looking across to Missy, she saw her sister's gaze already locked on hers. No words passed between them, just simple understanding.

"You might as well know Mama's already been talkin' about all us coming over here to lay down new flowers."

"I'm not coming," Grace said.

"Me, neither," Missy added.

It was no surprise to Grace. Each visit was sandwiched with this request, and all of the sisters were united in their lack of enthusiasm at performing what their mother described as duty in the cemetery that held an appreciable amount of their family history.

And indeed it was about family. Inside the cemetery lay their daddies. All three of the Wilson girls' fathers had come to bad ends too soon to get to know their children, and had ended up in this quiet space. Come this Saturday,

Uncle Byron would also take his place in the same wooded acreage behind the old A.M.E. church.

Missy took the corner much faster than was necessary, leaving the cemetery visible only through a pale cloud of road pebbles and dust.

They were now only a few minutes from the house. Thank God, Grace thought, and eased up on her brake.

CHAPTER 13

"Mama, Rambo's in here trying to sneak out with your fried chicken."

"Nah, I'm not. She lyin' on me, Mama."

Rambo's laughing baritone soared above the chorus of female dissents as everyone talked at once.

The high-spirited voices floated from the kitchen and into the living room where Corinne sat alone, attended by her own thoughts—for a moment, at least. The overstuffed armchair near the big picture window gave her an unobstructed view of the yard and empty street, where she peered vigilantly.

"We need a fan. It's hot as hell back there." Belinda had left the kitchen, rapidly fanning herself as she crossed the hardwood floor to join her mother in the living room. "Mama, what you doing in here all by yourself? I don't know how much longer you can hold off feeding everybody."

Corinne shifted in the chair, favoring her left leg, and then raised her gaze to Belinda.

"Rambo better not be in there eatin' up everything before Grace gets here," she chastised.

"Gloria popped him one, but she's no better. She's already stuck a spoon in the mac and cheese."

"What you doin' in here, anyway? Did y'all finish making the salad and corn bread?"

Belinda nodded before she perched her hip on the arm of her mother's chair and allowed her perfectly French-manicured hand, twisted around the straw fan, to dangle in the air.

"Daisy and Gloria are handling things just fine. But, you know me. I had to get out of that kitchen." She fanned herself rapidly. "Mama, you need some central air in this house."

"Like I used to tell Byron, I don't want no central air."

Corinne's attention gravitated back to the window. She wasn't surprised that Belinda had skipped out when it came time to help, and guiltily took on some of the blame that her two youngest daughters were more selfish and spoiled than she'd have liked.

She only meant to protect Belinda and Missy from the deprivation their older siblings had experienced; and since she couldn't love them any greater, she'd thought that meant allowing them more privileges. It backfired miserably; and by far, Belinda and Missy had given her the worst trouble while growing up.

Dressed in starched blue jeans and a crisp, white button-down shirt, Belinda was always the fresh flower compared to her wilted sisters in the kitchen. But, that was her Belinda. She wrangled her best interest from every situation; and she'd found a man at college in Glenn, who seemed content with her spoiled ways.

Corinne had been relieved when Belinda married, and she even liked Glenn, but Belinda kept him to herself, for the most part, and it had been hard to get to know him.

"So, where's that son-in-law of mine?" Corinne asked.

"On the back porch playing cards with Rambo and Spud."

She turned to Belinda. "Spud's still here?" He was the teenager who lived a few doors down.

"Uh-huh. He's been talking about how he does odd jobs around the house for you." She arched a brow at her mother. "You don't owe him for cuttin' the grass, do you?"

"No," Corinne said, frowning. "Did he say that?"

"No, so he must be serious about an invite to dinner tonight."

"He can come." But Corinne suspected his interest lay more in Tamika, Gloria's oldest daughter, than anything else.

Belinda followed her mother's gaze outside the window. "What're you looking at, Mama?"

"Nothing. I'm just resting some before we eat, that's all."

"No, you're not," she challenged, then paused a moment. "You're sitting here waiting for Missy to get back from the airport with Grace."

Corinne turned from her window vigil and instinctively masked her concern over Grace's continued absence.

"She needs to get on down here so we can finish the plans for Byron's funeral."

"Aw, Mama, she's coming. Missy would've called if she didn't show up at the airport or if they'd had a problem. And looking out that window won't make them get here any faster."

Corinne didn't like her tone and started to say as much; instead, she tamped it down and reached around her daughter's round and ample hips to squeeze her trim waist. "It's good having all y'all home at one time again."

"Not quite all," Belinda replied. "Mama, when did Reba start staying at Grandma Rhoda's with the baby?"

Corinne's arm slipped down to the chair. "Don't start up about that."

Belinda let out a hollow chuckle. "I swear, the things that girl does sometimes don't make a bit of sense, and you know it."

Corinne pulled her head back and rolled her eyes at her daughter. "I ain't playing, Belinda. Don't be startin' things up with a funeral going on."

Belinda's grin grew wide. "Aw, Mama, you know I'm kidding about that mixed-up child."

"Well, it's not funny. Granted, Reba's got her troubles, but we all do."

"So, you still don't know who the daddy is, huh?" She grunted. "You don't think it's that dude with the accent we saw her with a while back, do you? Wasn't he kind of funny-looking? Lord help that baby if it is."

"Don't be talking 'bout my grandbaby like that. He's beautiful and I miss him being over here."

"Guess that's why she named him Denzel." Belinda snorted. "He better be beautiful."

Sighing, Corinne crossed her arms over her chest. "Reba's a thirty-year-old woman who minds her business. She don't want to say who his daddy is—" her eyes sought the window again "—and I'm through asking."

"When Grace gets here, she'll find out." It was spoken as a matter of fact.

"Grace is not gon' force that out of Reba, and you know it."

"She don't have to force." Belinda's mouth curved into a soft smile. "We just, sort of, end up telling her stuff anyway."

At that moment, in the waning daylight, a dark car drove into their view. It quickly darted around the other cars parked on the street before swerving onto the aged cement slab that hugged the edge of the side yard, stopping with a visible jolt.

"That's Missy," Belinda exclaimed, leaning forward to peer through the window. "And she's still driving like a bat out of hell."

Corinne straightened from her chair, a wide smile reaching her eyes as she exhaled a deep breath.

"Grace is here," she announced.

It was just as Grace remembered it.

The two-story frame structure pretty much resembled all the other small homes set off the packed gravel road. The skyline was broken with tall, uneven pines; and in these moments before sunset, the shadowy surroundings appeared almost spectral.

"You can put your bags in my room," Missy was saying as she turned off the ignition. "I put an off-limits sign on my bed."

The words floated over Grace as she remained rooted to her seat and stared out through the windshield.

Nothing had changed. Fading grass and scrubby evergreen shrubs still surrounded the wide two-step porch. Mama's corner flower garden—where her colorful azaleas took center stage every spring—was overgrown and had yet to be weeded for fall's onset.

The familiar setting brought on a host of memories—some bittersweet, some poignant.

"There's Grandmama."

Dee's excited words were quickly followed by the sound of opening car doors as she and her brother got out.

Missy said, "Come on, girl," and nudged Grace's shoulder before they, too, followed the children.

Corinne was already through the screen door and stopped just short of the porch's edge. Her light-skinned face glowed in the dusk as it split into a wide grin.

"Come on, now, and hug your grandma." Corinne bent forward, spreading her arms wide to welcome Dee and Jamie heading her way.

Grace smiled, warmed by how her children showed their love for a woman they saw only a few times a year. She then glanced at Missy while they slowly made their way around the car to cross over the grass.

"So Mama's not using her cane these days," she observed.

Missy's grunt was a sneer. "You know how she hates that thing. Her leg probably hurts like hell. But, every now and then, when she can't help but rely on it, she'll give in."

"She seems to be holding up pretty good right now, considering all that's going on." Grace watched her mother, leaving her meaning unsaid between them.

"You know it," Missy quipped, joining her gaze with Grace's. "Puttin' up with all kinds of crap heaped on her by family, and all the while trying to please the same assholes."

Grace knew Missy excluded the two of them from the aforementioned family assholes. Of course, Missy never included herself and her listener in whatever problem or observation she happened to be discussing. But, no matter her sister's faults, Missy was right about Mama. Corinne Wilson seemed rooted in a perpetual "please everybody" mode.

Happy squeals came from the front step as Dee melted into her grandmother's embrace, all signs of her previous teenage petulance gone. By now, the front porch was becoming crowded with cousins and more sisters from the house. Jamie hung back for a moment before he claimed his turn and smothered his grandmother in a bear hug with his tall frame.

Grace smiled as her eyes spanned the happy group on the porch. Family connections. Despite the roadblocks, it's what she'd tried to preserve intact for her children, and hoped they'd remember something akin to love and security whenever they thought of home and childhood—unlike her own memories.

"Damn, Grace. Now that you're here, I've got to figure out a way to get you to move back down for good."

She turned to her sister's voice just as Missy reached for her hand, squeezing it tight like she did long ago when it was Grace's turn to take her to play.

As they neared the porch, Grace looked up and met her mother's gaze, and the anxiety of returning to the bosom of her roots melted away. Despite their past, or maybe because of it, they had connected. Corinne grinned a wide smile that reached beyond her eyes.

"Come on, baby, and give your mama a hug."

Grace was home again.

CHAPTER 14

By the time Grace hugged her way through the crowded kin on the little porch, she had made the full plunge back into the family bosom. Their loud, spirited renewal crackled through the tall pines and broke up the neighborhood's evening silence.

At the same time, the celebration kept the dull ache of Uncle Byron's death—along with the deep dread that inevitably accompanied Grace's returns home—temporarily at bay.

The group moved from the porch to the living room where Grace's senses were quickly assailed by a wall of dry heat—the byproduct of an overworked kitchen on an already warm day—and the delectable aromas that swirled in it.

As she moved deeper into the room, delicious whiffs undulated around her like teasing fingers, and Grace guessed correctly that dinner was fried chicken, beef stew and rice, and the ubiquitous macaroni and cheese—just a few of the dishes that waited in the kitchen. Dessert would most likely be a signature four-layer, coconut-cream cake. Corinne's cooking skills were legendary in the family and had not deteriorated one bit over time.

Once the adults had filed back into the living room, conversation ensued again—noisy exchanges punctuated with earnest, infectious laughter. From years of habit, Grace darted a glance through the front screen door and located her children. Oblivious to her gaze, Dee and Jamie seemed comfortable and showed no awkwardness with the young cousins they rarely saw. Relieved that they were fitting in, she let out a quiet sigh.

Dee and Tamika stood together and laughed with the tall boy from the neighborhood. Warning bells rang in Grace's head since, according to Missy, Tamika was hot to trot when it came to boys; that meant the two cousins could be toxic together—something else for Grace to keep her eyes on.

Except for Gloria's three-year old, all of the kids had remained on the porch in the humid twilight, ostensibly to avoid the scrutiny of so many adults in the house. Feeling the heat creep inside her collar, Grace thought the occasional floating breeze was another good reason.

From her end seat on the overstuffed sofa in the homey front room, and despite the overheated air that carried a cornucopia of smells, Grace allowed herself to relax for the first time since she'd left her own house. Settling back, she soaked in the simplicity of the small, closed-in surroundings.

The house's plain familiarity—dressed up with her mother's personal sewing touches—was like a caress to her soul that worked to loosen the knots in her belly. This was home, no matter the problems, no matter the memories.

Grace felt before she looked up to see her mother's smile aimed at her, with an expression that seemed to say, *I'm glad you're here. I missed you.*

She smiled back. *I missed you too, Mama.*

Corinne sat at the head of the room on a straight-backed chair in front of the big Sony television. She bounced little Tavis as he sat astride her good leg.

Despite the smiles, Corinne's almost lineless face wore a patina of weariness. Yet her age and wisdom spoke volumes in brown eyes haloed with pale shadows, all surrounded by a crown of soft, salt-and-pepper hair, cut to the length of a finger, and which curled effortlessly on its own, like some passé Jheri-curl do. It occurred to Grace that her mother had looked the same for a long, long time.

Grace's gaze soon left her mother and circled to her sisters. These were moments she considered her favorites and when she felt closest to them all—like time in a bottle—when they all came together and talked at once to bring everyone up to speed on what was happening in their diverse lives. Truly, this was as good as it got under the disparate branches that made up their family tree.

Listening more than she conversed, Grace watched Missy, barefoot and in a social mode, flit back into the room from upstairs. She comfortably planted herself on the sofa between Grace and Daisy.

Missy's shapely brown legs, always an attention-grabber,

stretched out, sylphlike, from her hemmed cargo shorts, attracting optimal attention that wasn't lost on the others. Missy could also be an exhibitionist, but only on her own terms.

A deep chuckle from the other end of the sofa drew Grace's attention. It came from Daisy, her round, rose-hued face sporting its usual impeccable makeup.

"Now, that's what I'm talking 'bout," she bellowed, slipping into comfortable slang as she responded to a comment. "Everybody 'round here oughta do like Uncle Byron did and plan your own funeral."

"That way all you need is somebody to put it in action," Missy said.

"No, that way, you don't put folks through Reverend Mitchell's preaching for a whole damn hour." This was met with laughter. "Mama said he only got fifteen minutes to roll Uncle into heaven. After that, Uncle's on his own."

"That's all the time Byron wanted on the program," Corinne said, bouncing the baby.

"Or figured he *needed*," Daisy added, warming up to the chuckling her humorous words elicited. "Y'all know Uncle had a *Saint* complex, and I *have* seen him a time or two, back in the day, down at the clubs." She finished with a wink and a grin directed at Grace. "But it sure didn't look like he was saving nobody."

Grace, helpless when faced with her sister's irreverent joking, joined the laughing with a shake of her head.

Everybody liked Daisy, what with her endless mocking and seemingly carefree attitude about most things. Only

Daisy could turn a put-down into an endearingly human quality, and make it funny, too.

In fact, everything about Daisy Beneby spoke big as life. Already twice divorced at thirty-four with no children, she offered neither excuses nor explanations for suddenly reclaiming her maiden name. While growing up, though, that same unanticipated audacity had added as much spark as it did punishment to their lives.

Daisy resettled her slimmed-down bulk on the sofa after another hearty chuckle. A yo-yo dieter most of her adult life, not only was her weight no secret, but she often made a point of declaring her new dress size at their infrequent get-togethers.

For this visit, Daisy now fit into a sixteen, down from her all-time-high, size-eighteen girth of eight months ago during that ugly divorce from Lester Parker—the divorce that garnered Mama a big Sony television.

True, not much made its way under Daisy's skin. Grace, however, suspected her sister wasn't totally unscathed. Lord knows there had been more than enough trouble to go around while they grew up; she just didn't know which tribulation had found its way inside Daisy and kept from prying eyes.

"I need to check on the children," Corinne declared, and slowly bent forward with Tavis tight in her arms. "They probably hungry by now."

"Aw, Mama, leave 'em alone, let them stay out there," Belinda said from a spot tucked somewhere beneath Glenn's shoulder. "They're just fine."

Just the thing somebody with no kids would say, Grace thought drolly, and watched her mother reluctantly reclaim her chair.

"Okay, now that everybody's here—" Belinda straightened from the love seat and enthusiastically clapped her hands together "—I can tell you about the new house."

"Go on, girl. Do tell," Missy purred sarcastically.

Belinda poured out her news, the children already forgotten. But Grace hadn't forgotten that everybody wasn't here, notably Reba and little Denzel.

Few worries, if any, marred Belinda's stylish brow for long. In her sister's universe, *something* always managed to supplant her need to deal with problems. And if *something* didn't intervene, *someone* would. While growing up, that someone had been her mother, or Grace, or one of the other sisters, respectively. There had been a collective sigh of relief in the family that it was now Glenn's turn.

Incredibly, after almost a year, her diva sister and Glenn still occupied a space in newlywed haze. Grace watched them lean into each other, literally becoming one on the love seat, and marveled that they could see light through that abysmally dark fog called marriage. But with all the examples of marital disaster languishing in the room, she wouldn't be surprised if they decided to run like hell.

You sure you aren't jealous just because they're happy? Grace quickly dislodged the self-deprecating thought. On the contrary, she was glad to be rid of primary responsibility for another adult. Jealousy—now that was more

Gloria's modus operandi. Grace's eyes shifted toward her other sister who sat near the large window.

In shadowed profile, Gloria's face was as perfectly sculpted as a Nefertiti cameo. In reality, she was a perfect example of a beautiful disaster. Gloria had confiscated the old La-Z-Boy lounger that Uncle Byron favored on his visits here.

Had favored, Grace corrected, and for a short moment, allowed his tender memory to hiccup through her thoughts.

Though Grace and Gloria shared the same father in Richard Brooks, and outward traits branded them sisters, the similarities ended there. Gloria Gatlin was a study in misery. She sat with all the hauteur she could muster while her husband, Rambo, towered over her from behind the chair like a sentinel. Notwithstanding the pride in her form, her eyes were severe, cold even, as on occasion she stared more than glanced at the others in the room.

Gloria's discontent didn't necessarily flow from any one inequality she experienced; she seemed able to find fault and dislike in most things. It had made her mean-spirited, selfish and the target for paybacks.

Grace had never joined in with her other sisters' some-times jointly contrived reprisals. From a very young age, Mama and Uncle Byron had required that she be the sensible, responsible one. Of this she had no choice; it came with the territory as the oldest. So, she had always been about setting the example for the others. In time, Grace could see that Gloria was her own worst enemy—that was punishment enough.

She lowered her eyes to a burgeoning paunch that Gloria's hands tented, and wondered if it was what Missy had suspected. She raised her eyes to the culprit.

Rambo, his muscle quickly turning soft at forty, was as close to no-good as Grace would care to label a family member—even if it was an in-law. Constantly on the make for a big break and, according to Missy, a willing skirt, he was not Grace's favorite person. In fact, Rambo didn't make any of their lists in that category—Grace suspected not even his wife's. But he was Gloria's husband, and for as long as they were together, he'd be accepted, warts and all.

As Rambo talked with Glenn, he indolently stroked at his beard. Missy was of the opinion that his always-immaculately-trimmed beard and mustache below those round, darting eyes gave Rambo the look of a low-rent Lothario. Missy could lean to the dramatic on occasion; but in this instance, Grace agreed her baby sister was pretty accurate.

"I hear y'all went on and bought that house in Birmingham, after all," Rambo said. "I saw the pictures, so I know it had to set you back a bit."

Glenn grinned proudly from the love seat where he held Belinda. "When my baby wants something, my baby gets it," he said, and squeezed Belinda. "You know how that is."

"Not Rambo," Daisy quickly responded.

"What you talking about now, woman?" Rambo demanded.

"You know you don't know nothing about that." Her bright eyes danced with mischief as the others let out hoots. "He knows about babies, though, Glenn."

Gloria's smile was pinched as she turned in her chair, not amused by the laughs directed at Rambo. "What's that supposed to mean?"

"You ought to know." Missy spoke up in a challenge, warming to the fun. "Last count, you had three of 'em."

Amid the chuckling, Glenn said, "C'mon, now. Leave the man alone."

"Those two always run off at the mouth, man." Rambo's white grin was affable. "But that's okay, 'cause when my ship comes in, I don't want neither one of 'em knocking at my door asking for nothing."

"Humph," Daisy snorted derisively. "That ship you keep bringing up, bro', didn't it sink years ago?"

"You must be talking 'bout after that husband of yours got hold to it," Rambo crowed right back.

It was a sore spot between the two, and Daisy jumped nimbly to her feet with her hands akimbo. "Nee-gro, please. That was between you and that no-count ass I divorced. So I don't want to hear no—"

"Don't y'all get started with that old mess," Missy cut in. "You see Mama in here trying to enjoy everybody in town for the funeral."

Grace had listened and watched the jocular exchanges, and they were nothing unusual. She had grinned along with the fun and winced when a jab went too deep. Old business did have a way of cropping up, like that messed-up, too-good-to-be-true deal Rambo'd had going with Les Parker that signaled the sorry end of Daisy's second marriage.

But this was, after all, what her family did when they

gathered together. A playful nick was the order of the day, and everyone knew that past history was fair game, being careful to only make surface damage with cutting words. It would never do to draw too much blood—there was always the chance it could spray back on you.

"Grace?" Missy asked with a frown. "You not even listening."

Pulled from her reverie, Grace looked out at multiple sets of bemused eyes studying her.

"Yes, I am," she began, and then quickly followed with a sheepish, "Okay, I'm not. So, what did you say?"

"Honey, why don't you go lay down," Corinne suggested. "I bet you're tired from gettin' here."

"We all had to get here, Mama," Gloria said.

"Mama was talking about where everybody was gonna sleep. Including your kids," Missy emphasized, crossing her arms.

"I can't believe how all the children grew since I last saw them," Corinne declared. "I can put pallets down in here for the little ones, and the older children can sleep on the sofas."

"I think now is a good time to tell her your plans," Missy whispered out of the corner of her mouth. "Before she gets too carried away."

"What plans?" Corinne asked, ever alert, and turning to Grace. "Y'all not staying here, honey?"

Here comes the guilt. Giving Missy the evil eye, Grace turned to her mother and smiled. "I'm staying, Mama. I just thought that, with everyone here at the house, it was a good chance for the kids to see Bobby's mama and sleep over there."

"They can see her and still stay over here" was Corinne's quick response.

"Well, I'll just be damned, Grace," Daisy said, chuckling. "You gon' actually let the kids stay somewhere you can't keep your eyes on them?"

"I thought the same thing," Missy said.

"It'll snow in hell tonight," Gloria added.

Listening to them make fun of her, Grace didn't think she was nearly as bad as all that. She was careful, that's all. That didn't matter; she had hurt her mother with the decision.

"They'll only be with Big Mama at night. During the day, they'll be back over here with us." Grace could still see the hurt in her mother's face.

"Dee and Jamie don't get to see Mama in the summer unless they come with Bobby, and then they stay at his mama's house. And now," Gloria continued to preach, "you down here with them and she still don't see them."

Grace gave her sister, in rare form for drawing blood, a defensive frown. "That's not true."

"When they going over there, Grace?" Corinne asked.

"Tonight," she admitted, guilt-ridden. "She's meeting us at Grandma Rhoda's later on."

"I hear that's where Reba is with the baby," Daisy said. "I thought she was supposed to be here with you and Missy for a while, Mama."

Grace's glance automatically sought out Gloria, knowing she would never admit her part in Reba's leaving.

"She's at your grandmama's and they're fine." Corinne was clearly at a loss to explain much more.

"How come she's over there, anyway?" Belinda inquired innocently.

"I think she called and talked with Grace," Missy said, and swung a long leg beneath her before her eyes rested on Gloria, too. "I think."

Grace nodded. "She needed a temporary place to stay, and I told her to go to Grandma Rhoda's."

"Needed?" Belinda asked, and looked at her mother. "Mama, why she need—"

"I don't know why Reba up and left with the baby like that. She knows she coulda stayed here." The anger-tinged words tumbled from Corinne in rapid succession. "What I wanted was all my children and the grands here together."

"Mama," Daisy said, shaking her head. "You know that's not realistic. How many folks you think can fit in here for a night with three little bedrooms and two bathrooms?"

"We could've made it work," she argued quietly. "We have before."

Daisy laughed. "Back when Grace was fifteen, Mama."

"Enjoy this break while you got it, Mama," Gloria quickly pointed out. "You just had your hands full when Tamika came this summer, and Reba's been here since before Denzel was born."

Grace frowned and Missy sucked her teeth before rolling her eyes heavenward.

"I still don't get why she's not here," Belinda said.

Gloria's stern voice rose above the others. "Reba could've come over here for dinner tonight to see all of us."

"In what?" Missy asked, and directed a frown at Gloria.

"Just the same," Gloria continued. "Y'all know she got that bad attitude. She always sets herself apart 'cause she thinks she's better than us."

"Than you," Missy said simply.

"Huh?" Gloria looked around at her sister, puzzled.

"Gloria, I heard Reba's not staying here because of you." Daisy shook her head at her sister. "Did you tell her she needed to find her own place while all of us were in town?"

"You said what?" Corinne's brows gathered as she turned to Gloria.

"I didn't say it like that." Gloria's eyes grew wide as they sought out her mother, yet she spoke defensively to her sisters. "All I meant was—"

"Gloria, it doesn't matter now—the damage is done," Grace interrupted. "And leave her alone, Daisy." Grace looked at her mother before she spread her gaze to include her sisters and in-laws. "Please...let's not do this...Uncle Byron died, remember?"

"I don't know what Reba's been telling everybody," Gloria blustered on. "But I didn't tell her to leave the house—"

The dams broke and everybody talked at once.

"You know good and well you told Reba to go somewhere else," Missy intoned through bared teeth. "That's just like you to do it, too."

"I don't blame Reba for leaving if she's not wanted." Belinda's voice slipped out from the comfort of Glenn's arms. "I know I would."

"I thought she had her own apartment before the baby came? What happened to that?" Rambo inquired.

"I love all of my girls, and it hurt for her to leave like that." Corinne spoke in a wounded tone. "Reba knows I want her here. My house is open to every one of you."

They all talked at once, and nobody listened.

From a wealth of prior experience, though, Grace knew family unity always managed to get trumped by the inevitable spontaneous arguments sparked by multiple opinions that ruled the air.

Grace launched herself from the sofa and raised her voice above the din. "Why don't we get ready to eat?" she suggested, drawing the expected attention. "I'm hungry, and I'm sure the kids are, too."

She walked across the room to the front door. And with the noisy tantrums and recriminations from the adults temporarily staunched, Grace opened the screen door to the peaceful children and ordered them to come in and eat.

CHAPTER 15

"We're leaving for Grandma Rhoda's house in fifteen minutes," Missy announced from around the kitchen door.

Sitting at the dining room table, Grace glanced toward her mother who stood near the ancient maple buffet that was laden with two layer cakes and a pie under glass.

"We'll be ready," Grace replied, aware that Missy hadn't waited around for an answer.

Grace and Corinne had cleared the table after dinner while the others had moved into the kitchen to tidy up and put away the considerable amount of food. Now, Grace contemplated the slice of pie Corinne had determinedly placed on the table in front of her and realized that her appetite—the one thing she could always count on in the presence of her mother's cooking—continued to elude her.

"Look at you, Grace, dawdlin' over that potato pie, and it's your favorite. You sure you all right?"

Grace forked a morsel of the sweet, golden custard into her mouth, if only to appease her mother, but found no solace in the mixture of seasonings that smoothly flavored her mouth. In another time, this would have been heaven. But she was here and other things, like death and funerals, crowded her mind.

"See, Mama? I'm eating." She pulled out the chair beside her. "Now, I get to check on you."

"You don't need to be worryin' over me." Corinne moved around the table and slowly dropped her hips onto the cushioned chair beside Grace before she settled her hand on her left knee. "I'll be fine. Like I say, God makes the back to bear the burden."

"Sometimes I wonder, Mama," Grace said in a voice laced with concern. Her eyes followed Corinne's small, rough hand, no stranger to hard work or arthritic contractions, as it kneaded the painful joint.

Corinne straightened in the chair and met Grace's gaze head on. "I was so glad to see y'all drive up tonight. It took you long enough to get here."

Grace's sigh became a smile at her mother's less than believable show of strength and her redirection of the subject to one of her own choosing.

"I told you, Mama. I had to make…arrangements at work, get the kids checked out of school, that sort of thing. I also had to find the money to get us down here."

"What about Bobby? I know he would've helped you get the children here."

Mama's delusion over Bobby hadn't changed much, Grace thought. Corinne still deferred to a perceived goodness in the men who populated her universe that could sometimes border on naïveté.

"Bobby has his own problems, but let's not talk about that. I'm here." She pushed the pie away and then folded her arms on the table.

"Death don't usually give a notice, so we have to be ready," Corinne said.

"It was so fast, Uncle's dying. I talked with him practically every night, and we always ended on this hopeful note. I don't know, maybe I was just being hopeful."

Corinne nodded. "He did a lot of talkin' these past weeks, but mostly he talked to me about you."

"He did?" Grace looked up. "What did he say?"

"I know he wanted to see you one more time."

Grace swallowed the strong surge of guilt that rose in her throat. "I should've tried harder to get home."

Corinne shook her head. "No, I don't think it was like that. Byron understood that you lived way up there and that you'd just been here for his surgery a few months back. He was making his peace while he had time, that's all."

She reached over and gently nudged Grace. "And don't think I don't know you don't like coming down here."

Grace frowned and, for a moment, thought her mother had somehow discerned the increased unease that accompanied these returns home. However, that wasn't the case.

"I can see how upset you get when everybody acts a fool, especially Missy and Gloria. Still—" Corinne's voice softened and the high cheekbones widened to accommodate a smile "—all that don't keep me from missing you and Dee and Jamie."

"It's not like we live on the other side of the world, Mama."

"You might as well for what I see of you."

Grace swallowed her annoyance at the repeated guilt mantra, hating she had been led into it like a lamb to slaughter. "I've offered to send for you to visit."

"You know I'm not flyin' nowhere, and that bus ride is too long, what with my leg and shoulder."

This was how their conversation on her traveling always turned, so Grace dropped it.

"You should be using your cane more. Your leg's bothering you because I bet you spent all day on your feet in the kitchen."

Sighing tiredly, Corinne's hands raised up in simple supplication. "Grace, honey, what do you expect me to do? I had to cook for y'all." Her eyes reflected frustration at what Grace had not said, and she quickly shook her head defiantly.

"You're not here to deal with everything that's got to be done, so I don't want you tellin' me I don't have to cook or clean, 'cause I do. Even though other grown people stay here, this still my house."

Grace was immediately contrite. "I won't say it, then, Mama. It's just that…we're grown, and can take care of ourselves."

"There you go again about how I'm supposed to be resting now that y'all grown, just like Byron."

"We should've been the ones cooking dinner for you, not the other way around."

A smile cracked Corinne's previously serious countenance. "At least Gloria and Missy *can* cook, but then, you got to keep them from fightin' like cats and dogs. Daisy's more comfortable hanging out at clubs with those hellion friends of hers, and you know Belinda not gon' mess up her nails. As for you, you just got in, and Reba, well…"

Corinne's voice trailed off as her hand traveled back to her knee. She massaged it vigorously for a moment, but it was plainly evident that no amount of kneading would assuage her deep pain.

"Mama," Grace said gently, and covered her mother's hand with her own. "I know you're feeling bad about Reba. She'll be okay with Grandma Rhoda."

"Tell me the truth, Grace. You really think she left from over here because Gloria told her to?"

Grace nodded. "That's what she told me. But Grandma can use her help this week with so much going on over there, so it worked out fine."

"For a while—" Corinne looked up and a shimmer brightened her eyes "—I was thinking she'd left here on account of me."

"You? No, Mama. Why do you say that?"

"Aw, it's nothing," she said, and waved her hand in dismissal. "But I don't understand that Gloria. Sometimes she can say the meanest things."

"I think she's unhappy, Mama, and can't help herself. Also, she's probably stressed over Uncle Byron's death like everybody else. How're you handling him gone?"

Corinne leaned in and whispered loudly, "Lord, you think she's pregnant again? Missy says she is."

Grace let out a reproachful groan. "Missy says a lot of things. We'll all know soon enough, and it's something for Gloria and Rambo to work out, not you." She watched her mother's attention return to the aching knee. "You didn't answer me about Uncle Byron."

Corinne raised her eyes. "You know I can't even remember a time when he wasn't around." She raised her eyes. "To tell you the truth, I don't even know how I made it through these past days."

"You made it because you're strong," Grace said, not liking her mother's tone. She covered Corinne's hand with her own and gave it an affectionate squeeze. "And you'll keep on because that's what Uncle expects you and Grandma Rhoda to be."

"Byron didn't tell anybody that the cancer had spread."

Grace's head stiffened, surprised at this news. It explained why Uncle had abruptly stopped the cancer therapy and opted, instead, for admittance to a hospice where, a short time later, he died.

"Not even Evie knew," Corinne continued. She shifted her legs, toppling Grace's hands on hers. "In the end, all he wanted was to come home and wait out his time."

Grace sat back and took a deep breath, comprehending what she now saw as the full spectrum of Uncle

Byron's suffering. These past weeks had been worse than he'd let on. So much worse. And he'd wanted to see her.

She wanted to cry and drown her sorrow at losing her sounding board, her guiding star that saw in her a bright future. But, maybe it was even worse for her mother. While Grace knew what it was like to be alone, Corinne had never been without her brother's guidance.

"He wasn't afraid," Grace said. "And we shouldn't be, either."

"Byron was always right there for me through all my troubles." She paused before she rattled off the husband's names she'd outlived. "Richard, Rufus and then Fletcher. I buried them all. Who can forget that?" Her voice had become flat.

Certainly not your children, Mama. Grace shut her eyes as the fathers in her life marched across her mind's eye. She would have been hard-pressed, as would any of her sisters, to forget the tragedies, one after the other, that had marked them so intimately.

"You'd think by now we'd be used to it." Corinne's melancholy voice wavered a slight bit, heavy with obvious heartache.

Grace opened her eyes. "Used to what, Mama?"

"Death, baby. Used to death." She dropped her head against her chair. "I been numb ever since Byron died."

"That's normal—"

"You don't understand." She turned her head to Grace and struck her chest hard with her fist, the prior shine in her eyes squeezed into a tear that rolled onto her cheek.

"I couldn't feel nothing, Grace. Not a thing. That's why I needed you here, and quick."

Grace raised her brows in a quizzical arc.

"You see now, with you here, I feel like Byron's come back, too, and everything's gon' be all right."

Grace nodded, silently interpreting her mother's words and expectation that she would step into Uncle Byron's tall boots.

"I know he's watching over us like he always did," Corinne said.

Profound sadness engulfed Grace. "He was a good man," she whispered.

At her mother's nod, Grace added, "Daisy did say Uncle acted like our Saint. And we were his cause. He was serious about it, too."

"Almost like he was doing penance," Corinne whispered.

"That's a strange way of putting it," Grace observed. "He wanted us to be better than the circumstances we'd been dealt."

Corinne reached out and tucked a strand of hair back into Grace's braid.

"Look at you, still wearing your hair pulled back like you been doing forever. You not gon' change, either. That's why Byron used to stay on you about things."

Grace sloughed off her mother's tangential comment with one of her own. "So, what about that cane, Mama?" She stood from the table. "Where is it, anyway?"

"I know more about my own body than Dr. Matthews

ever will." Corinne grunted. "And I know when I have to use a cane. I told you not to worry—"

"But we do worry about—"

"Y'all still in here?" Gloria's voice boomed through the kitchen doorway before she marched over to the table, her small kitten heels clicking across the hardwood floor. "Mama, come on. We gettin' everybody in the cars to go over to Grandma Rhoda's right now."

"Gloria, we were talking—" Grace started, but then abruptly stopped as her sister took their mother by her arm and pulled her to her feet.

"Gloria—" Corinne, on the other hand, only mildly protested this seemingly innocent kidnap of her person.

"I don't know why you acting like this, honey," she said as she was directed away from the chair and then led across the floor.

"Humph," Gloria snorted, calling back over her shoulder, "Grace showed up last, so she shouldn't be hoggin' you from everybody else."

"I'm doing what?" Grace sputtered lamely at her sister's back. Before she could form the words to hurl back, she remembered to smoothly handle Gloria's barbed response the way she'd handled most of her sister's passive aggression growing up. She ignored it.

Corinne's head bobbed as she willingly trudged along-side Gloria. "I was coming. I know how long it takes y'all to get ready." She glanced back to her eldest. "Come on, Grace."

"I'm right behind you." Crossing her arms over her

chest, Grace stepped back to the table and regarded her mother and sister's retreating figures.

When they were through the kitchen door and out of sight, Grace sat down, took up the fork from the napkin and quietly ate the rest of her cool pie. There would be time enough to be divided into a car, and Lord help her if she had to sit next to Gloria.

CHAPTER 16

"Grandma," Grace said, and bent to hug the small, golden woman who stood in the narrow doorway. "Oh, it's so good to see you again."

She inhaled the bouquet that was her childhood and was immediately transported: vanilla, ginger and cinnamon swirled in her wake. A hint of gardenia rose from her hair.

"And you just never change, girl. You're my same pretty li'l Gracie," Grandma Rhoda announced with one of her trademark beaming smiles, standing back to take in her granddaughter.

Grace believed her grandmother was still the real beauty. Her smile was as wide and white as ever; it had always been enhanced by full lips—something they had all inherited from Mama's side of the family, a healthy swipe of lipstick, and quality dentures. She wore no other makeup to conceal the tiny lines at her eyes and her mouth, but her forehead remained as smooth as a new baby's behind.

"All right, now, where are those young'uns Corinne been braggin' about?"

Grace stood aside so Jamie and Dee could come forward, and then she proudly watched as they shared hugs with their great-grandmother, who then made a big fuss over them with her quick touches, brushes and motherly pats.

Quietly closing the front door behind them, Grace thought it was a good thing to have made this trip together. She crossed her arms and smiled, satisfied with the sacrifices made to bring it all about. Actually, she felt genuinely happy at this moment.

They had just arrived, Grace and the rest of the family, in two cars. After Rambo and Missy had parked their cars along the gravel road—the grass around the house had already been filled with other cars—they had poured from the cramped vehicles and filed into the house, with Grace bringing up the rear, Dee and Jamie in hand.

Corinne, her daughters, and their families greeted Grandma Rhoda in much the same way Grace had been welcomed before they disappeared into the house with the others who had gathered out of respect for Uncle Byron's death.

At four-eleven, Grandma Rhoda was a worthy matriarch in a tiny package. She had birthed seven children without benefit of a hospital, was about to bury her second, and still had, as everyone around her would attest, every lick of sense God had presented her with over eighty years ago.

She also still had every lick of hair God gave her. It was long—very long, and silvery gray, which she kept caught up in a tight chignon clamped to the back of her small head. No one could every remember Grandma with hair other than down her back, not even her children.

"Oh, my," Grandma Rhoda exclaimed, stepping back from Dee and Jamie. "Just look at how y'all done grown since I saw you last."

Jamie smiled and slouched against the wall while Dee preened for all she was worth, with both basking under the older woman's affectionate gaze.

"Grace," Grandma Rhoda said, whisking her head up to her granddaughter. "All I hear from everybody is that you got two fine children. Don't forget that's a blessing to be proud of."

Grace smiled. "Yes, ma'am. I know." She bent and pressed a kiss to Grandma Rhoda's cheek. "You holding up all right with the funeral plans and all?"

The older woman nodded. "I'm glad you helped with some of it before you even got down here. People been in and out visiting since Byron died and we can't seem to find time for the little things."

"I can tell you're getting visitors by the cars parked outside," Grace said.

Grandma Rhoda stretched her eyes. "Most of them were here earlier, but I sho'nuf thought I was gon' scream if Rev. Mitchell stayed here one more minute today. In fact, he just left not too long before y'all got here, and I suspect it's only 'cause the chicken's gone."

When Jamie and Dee snickered at her words, she leaned in toward them and whispered matter-of-factly, "He been here all day, just eatin' up that fried chicken."

Dee and Jamie laughed this time, and Grandma Rhoda waved her hand. "Lord knows we had enough of it from everybody, and I'm sure folks gon' bring more tomorrow."

Resting her hands against slight hips, she asked, "If y'all hungry, there's some more food sittin' out in the back parlor."

"But no more chicken, right?" Dee quipped with a grin.

Grandma Rhoda squinted her sharp eyes at Dee. "I can tell you a firecracker," she said, and waggled her finger at her great-granddaughter. "But don't let me have to pop you one like I had to do with that Tamika."

"What did Tamika do?" Jamie asked.

"Just know, if one of you do it, I'm gon' pop you, too." She moved between the grinning children. "Y'all come on in here with everybody else."

Raising her arms, she slipped one around Dee's waist and curved the other somewhere in the vicinity of Jamie's hips, and the three of them began an odd trudge down the hall at the tiny woman's pace.

Grace smiled and followed them. At the end of the tight hallway, a bright light glowed overhead and a stream of voices grew steadily louder.

"I'm gon' sit and talk with y'all some more 'cause I don't get to see you too often," Grandma Rhoda explained, "but I need to talk to your mama for a minute." She dismissed them with her words. "So go on in there and visit with your cousins, get you some desserts—"

"There you are." Like magic, Tamika's girlish tone had

soared up from the chattering voices before she appeared as an elongated shadow at the end of the hall. "I been lookin' for y'all," she exclaimed.

Y'all, of course, would be Dee and Jamie. Tamika then gushed into, "Oh, hey, Grandma Rhoda and Auntie Grace," as pure afterthought. It might have been the belated memory of Grandma Rhoda's pops. Grace still remembered them, too.

"C'mon here, and take care of your cousins," the older woman replied, stopping to turn to Dee and Jamie. "Y'all go on with Tamika."

As the kids disappeared into the other end of the hall with their cousin, Grandma Rhoda said, "That child knows everybody. She'll make sure Dee and Jamie meet everybody here."

"She came up for the summer." It was more a statement from Grace than a question.

"Gloria sent all three of her children up here on your mama, and you know Corinne don't get around near as well as she should on that leg."

Grace nodded. "I know."

"Come this way, Grace," the older woman said, and opened a door off the narrow hall, through which they entered a screened patio that was empty of guests.

"I don't think Corinne was able to keep up with Tamika this summer," Grandma Rhoda was saying as she walked briskly ahead of Grace. "That child just turned sixteen, but she act like she goin' on twenty-one. I don't know if Gloria sets limits for her back at home, but

Corinne said Tamika wanted to go up to Atlanta with 'Nard and them friends of his every weekend."

'Nard was Aunt Cora's youngest son, Bernard, who could also be affectionately described as a local up-and-coming criminal complete with a posse.

"Mama wouldn't let her go," Grace said. Missy had mentioned that their niece was used to partying down in Miami, but at sixteen? What was Gloria thinking?

"Corinne said she told her no, but these days that don't stop children from doing what they want to do. I told Corinne to send her butt right back home because she don't want her to get pregnant up here while she's watching her." She threw a glance to Grace over her shoulder. "Mind you, just watch your little Dee around that wild Tamika."

Grace swallowed hard as a skein of dread slipped down her back. How would she feel if the family thought of Dee as wild, boy-crazy and a party girl? Is this behavior what Gloria wrestled with? Was Tamika part of whatever her sister was struggling to handle internally? By Gloria's earlier actions, was she handling it at all?

They walked outside from the patio, Grace following her grandmother, and treaded along a breezeway that led to another door on an attached bricked room no larger than fifteen by twenty in size. They were headed for the sewing room.

"Come on in here," Grandma Rhoda said, opening the door, and going in.

Grace's grandmother's house was on the other side of Oxford, across the railroad tracks where, back in the day, that was the only side black folks lived. But even after equal opportunity foraged through Oxford, it still meant that no matter which side of the tracks you got to build your house on, you were still no more than ten minutes from anybody else's.

The cement block structure was a redbrick square ranch that had been added to about every five years for probably the last twenty-five years. And as such, it didn't so much resemble a house anymore as it did a rambling collection of connected squares centered in a manicured grassy field.

Grandma Rhoda was a superb and tireless seamstress who had dutifully passed her decades-old craft down to her daughters, most notably Corinne, and in some cases to an interested granddaughter, like Grace.

The sewing room was a profusion of color, texture and history. Beautiful quilts, coverlets and blankets languished in loose folds on shelves, most made by Grandma's own hands, others handed down to her from long-dead relatives, tatting for unfinished covers spilled from plastic bags propped against the walls, and an old-fashioned loom formed from light birch took up much of the room's center. Two sewing machines, one that looked like it came from the turn of the century, the other more recent, sat at the corners.

Many of the folded quilts had been shaped and sewn from a quilting form suspended from the ceiling. The quilts were then packed with real Georgia cotton. The wood suspensions had been right over there, she thought, looking around the room.

As the two women moved through the room, which could provide a shortcut to the back end of the house when necessary, the trek was not unduly slow. It was also not as fast as Grace would have wished it because in walking unhurriedly through the room, her mind began to ruminate on memories better touched with only a quick brush.

The colorful, textured blankets were opening memories that, for better or worse, were tucked away. Grace's eyes fluttered shut, though ever so briefly. It was in this room of sanctuary that Grace discovered the existence of good and evil, heaven and hell.

It had been her private retreat where her good-hearted grandmother taught and honed a lonely child's finesse and flair for the heavenly art of sewing. It had also been the place where she stumbled upon evil that was reminiscent of the devil in hell that Reverend Mitchell often referred to on first Sundays.

"Grace?"

Grace ascended from the eddies of her dark reverie, and bumped into a table holding piles of yarn.

"I been talkin' to you, and you ain't sayin' a word," Grandma Rhoda said, her hands pressed on her hips as she stood at the other end of the room.

Grace rubbed her eyes. "I'm sorry. There's a lot of memory in here."

"I know you always liked this room. That's why I kept it in here for you."

She had Grace's attention. "Kept what?"

Grandma Rhoda sucked her teeth and shook her head at Grace's continued ignorance. "Something for you, child."

"For me?"

"Your mama didn't tell you?"

"No." Grace felt light-headed. She needed fresh air out of this room. "Tell me what?"

"That Byron left something for you. It's a letter, and I hid it in here."

CHAPTER 17

Grandma Rhoda stepped up on the footstool in front of a tall bookcase that was crammed with linens and cardboard boxes marked as sewing supplies. Showing remarkable agility for her age, she stretched out, extending her arm between the multipatterned quilts folded tightly on an upper shelf.

"Let me get that for you," Grace said, and made her way around the colorful materials stacked on the floor.

"I can do it," Grandma Rhoda huffed. "It's right here."

"Why'd you put it way up there?" Grace's interest had peaked.

"To keep it out of Cora and Evie's way," her grandmother grunted. "You know how nosy they can be, wantin' to know everybody's business."

When Grandma Rhoda pulled her arm out from between the plumped covers, her fingers clung tightly to a white paper.

Grace moved closer, her eyes drawn to what she could see was an envelope. "When did Uncle Byron give you this?"

"Let's see, it was 'bout a week before he died," she answered, and stepped off the footstool with Grace's support at her arm. "He made this big fuss over me not giving it to nobody but you." She handed the envelope to Grace. "So, here 'tis, honey."

He made a big fuss? Grace turned the envelope over in her hand, but that was secondary to her roused curiosity. In all these last weeks when she and Uncle had talked, he had ample opportunities to tell her anything he wanted her to know.

They had spoken on a lot of subjects, including recovery, his funeral, her future and their past, but never once did he mention this envelope.

"It's probably nothing but more funeral plans," she surmised, and tapped the envelope against her hand.

"I don't know. Between me and your mama, and with you here now, I think we done finished all the details for the funeral." She smiled. "I guess you gon' have to open it up to figure out what it is, baby."

"I know," Grace said, and sighed tiredly. "But maybe not here with everybody around. Later on, when I go back to Mama's house."

"Suit yourself. You know he was so proud of how you, being the oldest, helped Corinne raise your sisters after every one of them husbands of hers was gone. Lord have mercy." She shook her head sadly. "That child of mine has had her share of troubles."

Grace nodded. "She got through them, though, with the family's and Uncle Byron's support."

"He always did what he could. But I think he counted

on you when he couldn't be around. I betcha that's why he wrote you that letter, to tell you thank you."

Grace wasn't comfortable with the praise, but that was probably what was in the envelope. Uncle Byron was the one who should be honored, though. In fact, she was sure he was responsible for them keeping the house after her first stepdaddy died.

"He missed you being 'round here, 'under foot' he called it, when you went off to school, though he never faulted you for leavin'." Grandma Rhoda chuckled at her thoughts. "Well, maybe he did when you left with Bobby."

Grace knew Uncle Byron's doubts about Bobby, but he never talked against Bobby to her. "I think Uncle and Missy are about the only ones who've ever come to Maryland to visit us."

"Your cousins—" Grandma Rhoda sucked her teeth. "They never really had the time for him—your sisters, neither."

"He could be pretty old-fashioned with those big old cigars, and he was set in his ways. Really old school." But Grace had loved him. She studied the envelope in her hand and deduced there was more than one sheet folded inside.

"—Except for Reba. Here lately, while Byron was sick, she came around a lot when he was here, she was even sittin' when your mama was with him over at the hospice, and comin' by herself sometime."

"Oh," Grace said, looking up, surprised by that bit of

news. "I didn't know—Reba never mentioned it." The door swung open with a creak.

"Here you are, girl."

Grace flicked her head toward the smoky voice coming from the doorway, and saw Aunt Evie's smiling face first, and then another peeking out just behind it—Aunt Cora's.

"What y'all doing back here?" Aunt Cora asked in a high-pitched voice, her eyes keenly surveying the room, as though the answer was right here to see, because nothing would dare try to get past her.

"Hey." Grace's smile was genuine for the women as she stepped toward the door.

"C'mon here, pretty girl, and give me a hug." Evie extended her arms wide.

Sliding the envelope into her pocket for later consideration, and away from her aunts' prying eyes, Grace allowed herself to be drawn into Uncle Byron's ex-wife's arms.

After a moment she stepped back from Evie, a fifty-year-old, still svelte former dancer—Evie swore up and down that she never stripped at the club where she'd worked in Atlanta decades before—in a becoming black dress.

Grace saw the circles that worried her red-rimmed eyes, and wondered again on the unflagging devotion Evie continued to slather on the man she had divorced.

"I want a hug, too."

Grace pivoted to Aunt Cora and hugged her, too. The Wilson genes were obvious in facial resemblance, but her aunt, who could be a formidable force, was tall and plump, the mirror opposite of Grandma Rhoda.

"Did you get a chance to see Dee and Jamie yet?" Grace asked.

"Uh-huh. They up in the house with Corinne, and child, they growin' like weeds," Aunt Cora exclaimed. "They said you was around somewhere with Mama. I told Evie the two of y'all would be out here in this drafty old room with Mama's junk she been accumulatin' for at least fifty years."

Aunt Cora, the third of Grandma Rhoda's children, had not been one to embrace her mother's love for sewing.

"So, what y'all doing in here, anyway?" Evie wanted to know.

Cora turned and, again, looked the room up and down, her nose wrinkling ever so slightly in a display of disgust. "Mama, I swear you need to throw most of this stuff out. No tellin' what you breathing in here with all this dust tracking about. Look at all them cobwebs up there."

"I don't want you messin' with any of it, either, you hear?" Grandma Rhoda railed right back. "And don't think I don't know where everything is in here. Now, what you want back here?"

"There you go gettin' all upset, Mama," Cora admonished. "Nobody gon' touch your stuff."

"Reba's looking for you, Grace," Evie said.

Grace groaned. "I haven't seen her or the baby yet."

"She still just as skinny after having that baby as she was before," Evie replied.

"What's going on with her and Corinne?" Cora asked, crossing her arms as she prepared for some special insight from Grace. "Daisy said she moved out from Corinne's and in with you, Mama."

Grace quickly intervened. "Mama's got so many of us over at her house that Reba's helping Grandma out during the funeral."

Cora's eyebrow raised to a dubious height. She nodded. "Oh, I see."

Grace knew her aunt didn't *see* at all, and she'd be on the prowl tonight to scratch out more information. Of course, that didn't mean Cora didn't keep her own family secrets locked up tighter than Fort Knox. Except for her youngest, 'Nard, her other children had left home and lived outside of Oxford with their families.

Grandma Rhoda walked past Cora and Evie, stopping for a moment to pat Grace's back. "You coming to the funeral home tomorrow morning?" she asked.

Grace nodded. "With Mama. I think we're supposed to finalize everything with the funeral director."

Grandma opened the door and led them out. The room's warmth dissolved into what had become a cool fall evening. Engulfed by the chill, Grace slipped her hand into the pocket that held the envelope.

"Mom—" The monosyllabic word had been stretched to a two-syllable shout by the time Jamie came jogging out of the hall and into the open breezeway. He pulled up when he saw Grace and the others at the end of the walk.

"Big Mama's here," he panted, out of breath. "She's looking for you. And Missy says we need to get our bags out of her car."

"Go on," she said. "And get the bags. I'm coming."

Grace turned to the women. "I've got to hand the kids off to Bobby's mama," she explained.

"She's pretty happy about it," Evie said. "She in there telling everybody that she's keeping Bobby's children."

Nodding, yet hoping her mother understood her dilemma, Grace started after Jamie.

"Bobby's sister says he's coming down to Byron's funeral," Cora said to Grace. "That's real nice of him to come such a distance, and he's bringing his new wife, too."

"Humph." Grandma Rhoda snorted her contempt. "It's a free country, and he can do what he wants to do, but why he want to come to the funeral? I didn't think Byron ever liked the boy that much."

"News to me, too," Evie agreed.

Meanwhile, Grace focused on setting one foot in front of the other, to make one step at a time as she silently damned Bobby Morrissey.

CHAPTER 18

Visitors to the house had doubled since Grace's arrival, making the air a trifle more stifling and the noise levels even louder. When Grace and Jamie located Dee, she was with Corinne. That, of course, was not the nightmare scenario Grace had imagined: finding Dee with Tamika and 'Nard while they planned a wild visit to Atlanta.

In fact, Dee and Corinne were sitting with Bobby's mother in a corner of the living room. Grace knew that, without a doubt, her mother would be cordial to a fault. She only hoped the same would come from Big Mama.

For decades, everyone in town had known Hazel Morrissey as Big Mama and, while the moniker could now be related to her size, from the very start, it had more to do with the tight authority she exerted over her family. As a child, though, Grace remembered a more mean-spirited name kids called her: Witch Hazel.

"Grace, I was telling your mama that I sho' do appreciate this chance to have Dee and Jamie stay with us." Her nut-brown face was shiny with sweat from the warm room.

Corinne pulled Dee's braids back so she could see her eyes. "You'll still be at my house during the day, sweetheart, and your other grandma at night. How lucky can you get?"

Beyond civil smiles and appropriate responses, Grace didn't react much to Bobby's mother. Big Mama hadn't taken well to Bobby's running after Grace first to college in Atlanta, and then to a job opportunity way up in Maryland, only to have Grace end up divorcing him, as she'd put it to everyone.

I didn't file for divorce, Bobby did, Grace wanted to scream to his family. With her self-esteem at rock bottom at the time, Grace would have continued to suffer his infidelities and contempt for the sake of the kids. Thank God he'd wanted out of the marriage; because in doing so it had ended her misery. And though Bobby had bouts with second thoughts over the years since their divorce, Grace never looked back.

She wondered if Big Mama ever asked herself why Bobby hadn't returned home to live after all the years since the divorce. And in that lay the answer. Grace had represented Bobby's chance at independence, too—from his mother; and for that, Big Mama would never forgive her.

On the other hand, his mother seemed to care as deeply as Corinne did for Dee and Jamie.

"I'm gon' speak with Ma Rhoda, Grace, and then we gonna go on back to the house," Big Mama said, pinching the neck of her dress away from her damp skin, and then fanning to create a breeze. "The family's gon' make sure to be at the wake and funeral," she added.

Grace nodded to the older woman before she reiterated their prearranged pick-up and drop-off of Dee and Jamie.

In the small town, Big Mama's house lay only a few miles and acres of deep woods away from where Grace's mother lived. That was a good thing, but Grace still tried to suppress the fears that attached themselves when her children were outside her care and control.

As Big Mama prepared to leave, Grace gave Jamie *the look*, meaning she was relying on him to look after Dee. He responded with a return gaze and nod that he understood the responsibility.

Grace hated putting this obligation on her son, and she hated even more that she kept it from her daughter. Of late, with Dee's access to a quagmire of dilemmas awaiting her in high school, Grace had demanded this duty of Jamie more and more.

After they left, Grace stood in the hallway with Corinne at her side.

"Honey, I can see the worry on your face, and as much as I want them to be runnin' 'round my house, I know they'll be fine over there."

"I won't worry much, Mama. Jamie will make sure his sister is okay."

"So, why you go and put all that responsibility on Jamie? He's just a boy himself."

The sting of guilt was sharp, and Grace was quick to retort, "You didn't seem to mind putting it on me when I was even younger." But as soon as she uttered the words, Grace regretted their barbed intent.

"I know, I know. I did my best, but I made a terrible mistake. You had to grow up so much sooner than your sisters—for me. But that don't mean you have to repeat my errors. You have to remember that, while Jamie's lookin' out for Dee, who's lookin' out for him?"

Grace swung her gaze to her mother, the words pricking at her conscience. *Don't repeat your mother's mistakes.*

"I am," Grace whispered angrily. "By all that's in me, Mama, I'm looking out for him." *Can you say you did the same?*

Corinne pressed her lips together, as though to trap any words not yet spoken, and the two women held each other's gaze while they broiled in the depths of what was unsaid.

A child's cry that droned in the distance had now come closer and won Corinne's attention. She tore her eyes from Grace and looked down the hall.

Gloria was marching right toward them with three-year-old Tavis perched on her arm.

"Mama, can you do something with him? I think he wants you," she claimed.

Gloria turned him so his little arms were outstretched in love—or was it desperation—at Corinne.

As her mother took Tavis from Gloria, cooing him in a low voice, Grace sighed and went in search of Reba.

She followed the sweet odor of cooked sugars and syrups and her younger sister's most probable haven—the kitchen. Reba had a knack for baking that could take her far if she allowed it.

Sure enough, there she was, standing in the kitchen and bouncing little Denzel in her arms.

"Grace—" Reba let out a little squeal and her face lit up at the sight of her sister.

"I knew I'd find you somewhere around the desserts."

"Grandma made tea cakes," she laughed. "And she let me make a fantastic red velvet cake."

"Mmm... It's so good to see you, girl."

The baby let out a wail of protest at being squeezed between the two women's hug, and they stepped apart.

"And little Denzel, too. Oh, let me hold him, Reba." She had last seen Reba in her final month of pregnancy, when Uncle Byron was undergoing surgery; and that had been almost five months ago. She took the baby from Reba and they sat at the table.

"He's beautiful, and with a head full of hair, already looking like you, you know." Indeed, he seemed to own their family's mouth and chin, but the dark eyes and strong nose... Grace wondered about his daddy, thinking any daddy would be proud of this bundle of joy.

She held the baby aloft and, upon clucking at him with an eager grin, he offered a toothless one back. Never mind about his daddy. She wasn't about to pressure Reba for those kinds of details.

"Thanks for your help when Denzel was born, Grace. And thanks for the other night, too."

She looked away from the baby for a moment. "So, I take it things are working out over here with Grandma?"

Reba nodded. "She doesn't ask questions, thank God,

and that's what I need right now." She clasped her hands in her lap. "No questions that I can't answer."

"Can you answer what's going on with you and Mama? She's taking it hard your coming over here and you—well, you're not saying much to her."

"I don't think that was ever our thing—talking, I mean."

"True, that's nothing new." She stopped bouncing the baby and looked at Reba. "But we didn't hurt Mama, either."

"I didn't do it intentionally, and I already saw her over here tonight." She crossed her arms defiantly and eyed Grace. "But, Mama don't understand when I try to get her to talk about things...about anything."

Grace nodded, sensing her sister's need for an accommodating audience.

"I know Gloria likes to boss me around, too, but if the truth be known, I had to leave from Mama's, just get away and leave, and figure things out."

"What kind of things?"

She hunched her shoulders childishly. "I been doing a whole lot of thinking lately, and I'm figuring I can't do anything with my life until I confront my past and my fears."

Grace smiled when Reba echoed Uncle Byron's almost exact words.

"I got a baby now—" she reached over and stroked the baby's chubby cheeks "—and I can't just be sittin' around waiting on Mama and everybody else to tell me and Denzel what we have to do anymore."

"You're sounding stronger than ever, Reba. And you're

right. You have to take control of your life. You talked to
Uncle Byron?"

Reba nodded quietly. "He liked listening to me, even
when I didn't know what I was saying or how to say it."

"That's the kind of person he was. So, are you taking
his advice, you know, about your fears?"

Reba drew a deep breath. "I don't know. I guess that
sort of depends on Mama."

"Oh?"

She raised her gaze to Grace and lowered her voice.
"Why don't Mama want to ever talk about our family
and the past?"

Grace frowned. "Meaning…?"

"Meaning our daddies. I wish I'd known mine. I don't
remember him and he died before I was barely in elemen-
tary school. Your real daddy died, too—and then nobody
ever mentioned them again. We don't even know any relatives on that side of the family."

It was true, and Grace had never given much thought
to a whole other set of relatives. She supposed she had
them, but they weren't any people she knew; and Mama
never brought them up. Neither had Uncle.

"So this is about you wanting to know your daddy?"

"Grace, have you ever wondered if your life might have
been different if your father had been around? I'm talking
'bout a daddy who'd read to you, tell you how pretty you
are when you dress up, and pick you up in his arms when
you walkin' too slow."

Of course she had, but Grace simply shrugged at her

sister. "To be honest, I don't think it matters since we had several of them available." She smiled. "We called them stepdaddies."

"I'm talking about someone who's your flesh and blood."

"Uncle Byron was always good enough for us." She peered at Reba and thought she understood. "But he wasn't your father, and no one will give you the answers you need."

"Don't you see? That's why I had to leave Mama's house. My sister wanted the bed I was in, the one man I'd just learned to talk to had died, and then my mama told me flat-out I didn't need to know about her husband and her life and why would I be so cruel as to bring it up now."

"She said 'her life'?"

Reba nodded. "Like I didn't matter. I got upset and left with Denzel, and here I am."

Grace now understood her mother's surprise that Gloria was involved in Reba's leaving. Corinne had actually been laboring under her own guilt at refusing what Reba wanted: information about the past. But why this sudden interest in family ties from Reba? Pangs from motherhood?

Denzel let out an unexpected groan that caused his little face to scrunch up before a loud wail followed.

Reba jumped from her seat. "O-oh, he just ate, so I think we might just be talking 'bout a serious diaper change."

It had been a long time, but Grace remembered the drill and smiled, holding him out to his proud mama. "It's late, too. He's probably tired from being handled by so many people."

Reba scooped him from Grace in a way that suggested, in only four months, she was mastering the intricacies of motherhood enough to be comfortable.

"We'll talk some more about this, won't we, Reba?"

Rocking the irritable baby as she backed from the kitchen, Reba smiled and said, "Sure. I promise."

Alone again, Grace let her head loll back against the chair. When her hand brushed her pocket, the rustle of paper reminded her of the envelope containing Uncle Byron's letter. Taking a deep breath charged with interest, curiosity, and more than a bit of trepidation, she slid her finger inside the flap opening and ripped the seal.

Inside were two sheets of plain white writing paper filled with her uncle's pitiable, slanted-to-the-left penmanship.

Recognizing it, Grace's fingers flew to her mouth. Oh, God, how she missed him and his uncanny ability to see into a soul. The first page was dated ten days before, and started out with a simple, *My Dear Grace*.

He opened by saying her reading his letter meant he had lost his battle to survive. He loved her and didn't want her to mourn at the expense of living once he was gone. The letter said he was tired, more than he'd ever been, and his strength, particularly in spirit, was drastically ebbing, due in part to his cancer's spread, and to prevent further anguish to Grandma Rhoda, he had decided to tell only Corinne.

Grace blinked her eyes quickly as she slipped the first page behind the second one and came upon her uncle's main reason for writing the letter.

He was concerned, he wrote, because over the last few

weeks, he had come to suspect that a terrible thing might have happened. And before he died, he had to make Grace aware of it, too. He asked her to seek out the truth behind his suspicions.

At the dire words, Grace's heart quickened even as her eyes hungrily ate up the frail script, skipping along the lines at breakneck speed during that first read, before sprinting ahead to the conclusion. And all the while, as the gravity of his words sank in, her heart burned—as though it were being squeezed in a vise.

The second time Grace read it did not make the pain any less; and her groan of disbelief at her uncle's words became a simple and painful whisper.

"No. No... Not Reba."

Before she could thwart their release, a puddle of tears flooded her vision as she brought the letter up to her eyes to scan the closing again, hopeful that she had misunderstood its ending. She had not.

Grace squeezed her eyes, clearing her view, and then dabbed them dry. Closing off her thoughts in compartmentalized little packets, she mechanically refolded the letter and placed it back into the envelope and stored it in her pocket.

Closing her eyes now, Grace's memories tilted and shape-shifted, becoming funny and delightful in one instance, to dark shadows best avoided in another.

No matter, her misty reminiscing was a calming balm against the cloying pall created by her uncle's death, the clustered family and her conflicted mood, now heightened by the disturbing contents of the letter in her pocket.

It was interesting how life could alter in a flash. Grace's previous complaint that she had little in common with her younger siblings wasn't true, and she should be happy that there was now common ground to share.

Only Grace was far from happy, and even less eager to embrace the possible commonality.

CHAPTER 19

Grace's sleep was being disturbed. She felt a hand pull at the bedcovers, and she rolled away from it.

Through a mist-shrouded consciousness, she angrily snapped, "No, I'm not going." She curled into a ball to escape the cool air that had alighted onto her warm skin. "Go away."

Lacking the motivation to move in her sleep state, the uncomfortable cool air soon draped her, and she reached out, blindly, to retract the covers, only her hand found contact with another.

"Stop it," she managed to mumble through stiff lips and a cotton mouth, and swung her arm wide.

The wild movement worked to rouse her further from the semiconscious dreamworld where she'd been languishing. And, in a matter of seconds, her eyes still closed, Grace knew exactly where she was: in Missy's bedroom sharing a four-poster double bed.

This time, a hand came from beside her and pushed, not so gently, at her shoulder.

"Wake up, Grace, for chrissake! You're having a nightmare again," Missy muttered. "This is the second one you had since you went to bed."

As the humiliation rose within Grace, she squinted through tight eyes and saw another pair staring down over her.

"Where's Dee and Jamie?" It was Tyra, Gloria's middle child, standing at her bedside.

"Hi, baby," Grace said, and yawned as she pulled the cover back up over her shoulders. "Why are you up so early?"

"Auntie, you talk in your sleep."

Grace paused a moment before asking, "I do?" She pushed herself up from the bed and then leaned back against the headboard, pulling her knees into her chest. "Dee and Jamie spent the night with their other grandma. They'll be over here this afternoon."

"Oh, okay." The child nodded in satisfaction as her two ponytails bobbed in unison.

"I told you they not here." Tamika's voice sailed into the room from somewhere near the vicinity of the door. "But no, you don't want to believe me."

" 'Cause you always telling stories," Tyra replied with a twist of her little head for emphasis.

Tamika left her spot at the doorway and came all the way into the room. "I do not," she challenged.

Grace smiled at the blossoming sibling rivalry. "Good morning, Tamika."

"All right, that's it. Get out, all of y'all, and close the

door behind you," Missy warned from beneath the covers next to Grace. "I'm trying to sleep."

Grace grinned. "Give it a rest, Missy. They were just looking for—"

Her attention wavered toward the doorway where Rambo's head had darted around the door and into the room.

"Good morning, ladies," he crooned as his eyes swept across the room, settling on Grace as she sat in the bed.

In a simultaneous thought, Grace recalled Missy's warnings about him and the fact that she'd slept in only a slip. Instinctively, she pulled the spread up to her bodice before she gave a boot to Missy's leg under the covers; but the warning kick had been unnecessary.

"Rambo, if you don't get your ass out of here—" Missy snarled as she turned over to face him.

"I didn't know y'all was still 'sleep," he explained. "I figured you'd be up by now. Okay, I'm going'," he interposed innocently, crooking his neck at his daughters before his eyes settled on the younger one.

"I been looking for you, Tyra," he said, his eyes flashing. "Girl, your mama waitin' for you to eat downstairs."

Grace watched stiffly as he shuffled Tamika and Tyra through the door.

"Come on out of here," he ordered, and the girls slipped out of sight around the door.

"And don't *you* come back no time soon," Missy admonished Rambo.

When he turned to close the door behind him, he gave Missy and Grace a wink-wink and a grin that stood out white from his beard.

"Pig," Missy spewed at the closing door.

"Did I imagine that or did he just pop in here on purpose?" Grace asked, surprised at what she'd witnessed.

"When no one's around to call him on it."

"He did say it was an innocent mistake."

"Yeah, believe that if you want, okay? He makes at least one innocent mistake a day." Missy sucked her teeth. "He's an arrogant prick and if Gloria doesn't know, she needs to be told."

"Maybe she already suspects he has a roving eye. God, how can she not know?"

"In that case," Missy reasoned, "imagine how she feels if she *is* pregnant again."

Grace shuddered, and wondered if her mother had also noticed this wanton nature in Rambo, hence the worry over her daughter and a possible fourth pregnancy. It all seemed to make sense why Gloria looked miserable. Her husband and her teenager were out of control, she had two very young children and she could be pregnant again.

Grace sighed. "That's why you can't be telling Gloria this kind of stuff. You can see she's got enough to deal with. Rambo will be gone in a few days, so just...stay out of his way."

"Oh, no way." Missy sat up in the bed and shook her hair loose. "This is my house, and I told you, if he puts his hands on me again, I'm ripping his balls out by the roots—and I mean it."

Missy's sincerity in her accusation and proclaiming her remedy was not to be denied. The idea of this kind of issue rising up was a disconcerting and tawdry thought that could only foment long-range repercussions in the family.

"Okay, you've got a point." Grace tried to lighten her tone again. "Nobody's asking you to compromise your principles. Let's just hope Gloria gets herself together."

"Rambo is her problem."

"We're not married to him, and they do have a family to consider. She's got three children and no outside job. She should work their problems out, go to counseling or something."

"Are you crazy, Grace? That's what you would do, stick it out for better or worse, like you did with Bobby. But I don't care if she's got ten kids and no job—if he's acting crazy, divorce his ass."

Stung by her sister's bull's-eye to her pride, Grace responded in a hurt voice. "Bobby and I did divorce when it didn't work out."

"Yeah, and he was the one who decided that."

Grace frowned. "There's a lot more involved when there are children to consider. You don't understand."

"I don't even want to hear that crap about I can't understand until I've walked the walk." She drew a deep breath before she turned to Grace, her voice softer.

"Aw, Grace, I'm sorry. I don't mean to be jumping on

you. I'm glad you're here, I'm glad you and Bobby divorced, and I'll just be glad when Gloria divorces Jackass."

"All I was trying to do is give him the benefit of a doubt through Gloria's eyes."

"Don't do that," Missy said, laughing. "She probably looking at him with the same fever Mama had."

Grace gave her a blank stare. "Huh?"

"You know what Mama used to joke about and say back in the day. 'The darker the berry, the sweeter the juice.'"

Grace rolled her eyes. "Are you serious?"

"Hello? All of our daddies are black as night, and, Mama, well she's about one shade short of a bowl of lemon pudding. Who can't figure that one out?"

Grace's grin turned into a whooping laugh. "Missy, stop it."

"You don't think our daddies just *happened* to be the blackest berries around, do you? Nope. That was the reason *why* Mama picked 'em."

Probably. "You are a trip, Missy."

Still chuckling, Grace rolled up from the bed and went over to her suitcase to choose her clothes for the day. Mama's choice in men—and there were a lot to consider—had been a constant; and she had certainly ascribed to the ditty Missy had recited, sort of reverse colorism in honor of the dark-skinned black man.

Grace's gaze slid over to Missy and their obvious array of surface distinctions. Corinne's marriage excursions had led to a motley crew of children who could create their own rainbow coalition—from light-skinned Reba to dark-skinned Missy. The rest of them were formed from a muted shade found somewhere in between.

From what Grace had gleaned from her mother's siblings, Corinne had been no shrinking violet, and had lived a full, exciting life in her younger days. Even now, Grace seldom heard regret from her mother—including the impact her choices left on her girls.

"Grace?"

She looked up from her wandering thoughts and closed the suitcase. "Yeah?"

"Are you getting married again?"

The totally unexpected question routed her thoughts to Theo Fontaine, and a blush warmed her face. She returned her attention to her suitcase.

"What kind of question is that?"

"You're seeing someone again. What's his name?"

"Theo...Theo Fontaine."

"So, it's possible you'd marry again?"

"Anything's possible. But right now, he's still just a friend."

"Which is code for you two haven't had sex."

"I... Uh, no," Grace stuttered, caught off guard by the question.

Missy grinned at her from across the room. "So, what are y'all waiting for? Didn't he make a move yet?"

"That's none of your business. Anyway, it's highly doubtful I'm gonna just hop into his bed right off—" Grace's voice dropped lower "—even if we want to."

"But you would marry again?"

"I have two kids to raise, remember, and I don't think I could ever subject them to a stepfather."

"Because you had one—twice?" Missy finished.

"Maybe…okay, yeah," Grace amended. "You can't be too careful."

"And that's why I'm not getting married," Missy declared as if to herself, and she stood from the bed. "Because you don't know what you're getting until it's too late. If I want kids, I'll just do like Reba."

Grace was reminded of her conversation with Reba last night. "Have you noticed Reba saying anything unusual lately?"

"No. She's barely made a sound since she moved in with Denzel."

"Last night when I talked with her, she has it in her head to learn more about her real father."

"Oh…what brought that on?"

"I don't know, but when I think about it, I don't know much about mine, either."

Missy came around the bed and leaned against the bedpost. "Our daddies died when we were kids. How are we supposed to know anything about them?"

"I think that was Reba's point. She asked Mama to share details and, well, Mama wasn't willing to go there."

"That makes no sense. Why wouldn't she?"

"I didn't ask Mama, but I'm sure she could have some issues with things, like all the men in her life keep dying and leaving her."

"Okay, that makes sense." She looked at Grace. "Does Reba understand?"

Grace shook her head and turned to Missy. "I'm thinking she doesn't care, she's waited long enough, and she wants answers now."

"Answers? Answers to what?"

"I don't know," Grace answered, frustrated.

"She dotes on the baby, for sure and she's sort of like you…won't let the little thing out of her sight." Missy's eyes widened. "You can tell Reba about her daddy."

"Me?"

"Why not? You're the only one of us old enough to have known all three of Mama's husbands."

"From a child's point of view only, Missy. But I can see both sides and I understand why it's hard for Mama going back there. Yet, I agree Reba has the right to know about her father."

Grace gathered the clothes she'd picked from the suitcase and returned to the bed. "I better get dressed," she said. "Mama and I are supposed to be going to the funeral home in a little while to check on the programs and see how Uncle looks in his suit. Daisy mentioned she might go, too. What about you?"

"Wouldn't miss it. Daisy talked about going to some new club last night that 'Nard heard about. I think they went out after we left Grandma's."

"In that case, who knows where she is this morning. What's Belinda and Glenn doing?"

Missy let out a painful moan. "Have you talked to her

lately, Grace? I mean, really talked with her? Oh, my God. Who knew she was that boring. You think Glenn did something to her? She's like a freakin' Stepford wife."

"It's more like she's enjoying her new house and suburban living, that's all, and she's playing dress-it-up. Lord knows we didn't have that opportunity growing up around here."

"Whatever…" Missy shot off the bed. "If she'd told me how she was gon' decorate one more room in her house, I swear I would've puked right there on Grandma Rhoda's plastic-covered sofa."

Grace chuckled. "It was that bad?"

"Worse. Gloria just up and left me there with her."

"I need to eat something." Grace slipped into her robe and grinned conspiratorially at Missy. "Didn't Rambo say Gloria cooked breakfast? You think she fixed enough for us?"

"Don't count on it."

"You can shower first while I call the kids to check on them."

Missy shrugged into her terry robe. "Christ, girl, give those kids a break for once."

As she sashayed past the bed, Grace picked up the pillow and threw it at her. Missy looked back with a wink-wink before she closed the door.

Alone in the room, Grace picked up the remaining pillow and hugged it to her chest. There were enough secrets in this family to fill a book and take a lifetime to explain.

Why did Uncle Byron think she was the one to extract this newest revelation?

She returned to her suitcase and searched around the bottom until she found the envelope with Uncle Byron's letter. Her heart thumped boldly as she looked inside to ensure all was intact. It was. All that was left was for her to do Uncle Byron's bidding from the grave and learn the truth. From Reba.

CHAPTER 20

Standing in the living room, Corinne could hear the muted laughter and activity that came from Missy's bedroom just above her. Much the same came from Gloria's family as they ate breakfast in the dining room.

She cocked her head and smiled, gauging what everyone was doing much as she did when they were children.

Children. You never stopped worrying about them. Corinne had done the best she could to raise all of hers; sometimes with, other times without, a husband. And like everything in life, you fare better with some things than others.

It was true, all her choices had not been for the best, and all her husbands had not been for the better.

Remorse. You live with it because you have no choice. Corinne knew she'd made mistakes and bad choices, with only Grace and Byron to help her through the lot of them. Byron, God rest his soul, had made sure she didn't live with regrets raining down. He had carried the burden with her.

Now that he was gone, Corinne had only to look into Grace's eyes to see her faults enumerated in all their glory.

When she told Grace she didn't know if she could go

on without Byron, she hadn't exaggerated. Her bond to her brother had developed over a long time, and a unity of thought became a part of what tied them together. It began—the seeds of their sibling intimacy—a long time ago, and then it nurtured naturally from there.

Their mama and daddy, Rhoda and Herbert Wilson, worked a small plot of land in South Georgia not too far from the Florida border. By the mid 1940s, when only four of the children had yet been born, Byron, the oldest, fell into the family well. Only little Corinne had seen him fall in and gone for help. Even at six, Byron had been resourceful enough to hold on to bucket lines long enough to get rescued. After that, he never complained when Corinne acted as his shadow. And that was only the beginning.

Corinne's brows peaked at the memory. She slowly limped, favoring her left knee, to the old armoire that housed the sleek, gray Sony television, pulled out the top drawer, and took out a white square of tissue paper.

Unfolding it, she revealed a piece of silk she had fashioned into a hemmed handkerchief that carried Byron's stitched initials. She planned to put it in the chest pocket of his burial suit.

Byron wouldn't have put up with a purchased silk handkerchief; but a gift she'd sewn by hand for him would be acceptable. He was the kind of man who bought only what he needed, not wanted. Kind and generous to a fault, he was never cheap, just careful with his money, hard-earned from his small school bus fleet.

Moderation, Byron always said, had been the key to his success at living life. He had learned that the hard way when it came to anger, a fact admitted only to and known by Corinne—especially anger that is produced by acts that fall beyond your control.

Byron made it a point of controlling his temper, and there was a simple reason for that: on the two occasions when he had lost control, there had been dire results with long-term consequences.

The first time Byron acted on anger without thought of its consequence, it had almost sealed his and Corinne's fates. They had come close, as children, to reaping a very different life, and possibly, even a short-lived one.

The incident, as they later referred to it, happened in the late 1940s.

Byron and Corinne had been eleven and ten years old, respectively, at the time, and the two oldest children of a black tobacco sharecropper. Their nemesis, Buddy, a white teenage boy who lived down the trail from their house in the rural district, hounded them with rocks, chases and threats laced with name-callings like *niggers, red niggers, colored trash,* and other variations of the same.

The terrors had grown progressively worse, and then one day, the inevitable occurred, when the threat was aimed at Corinne and took on a sexual tone. Byron knew he had to act before his sister was irreparably harmed.

On that occasion, Corinne and Byron methodically lit up the furnace in the drying shed with as many old wood-cuttings as they could find that wouldn't be missed. When the furnace became red-hot, they knew they had only to show their faces on the dirt path and Buddy would spit his hatred.

Their plan was to lead him to the tobacco shed, overtake him, and then throw him into the hot furnace. It was a simple plan made from an equal hatred. Later on, though, Corinne surmised that Buddy hadn't been as stupid as he'd appeared.

When Buddy chased Corinne into the hot, fetid shed, and the door slammed behind him, not a word was spoken. The dark quiet punctuated the change in power.

Even though more than five decades had passed since the incident, Corinne could still clearly see the dance of death they had posed as she and Byron, youngsters them-selves, moved toward their equally young tormentor.

Byron had thrown open the huge furnace door by its iron latch. The flames licked out in red and yellow fury just as Byron and Corinne leaped onto Buddy.

Amid the grunts the three created while they struggled on the packed earthen floor, none were more desperate than Buddy's as he fought his way out of their grasps and, in a tearful wail, fled from the flickering barn.

With the clear knowledge that Buddy had gotten away and would tell all the whites in town what they tried to do, Corinne and Byron started to cry. Had they forgotten that they'd be hung by the neck from old man Ransom's tree, never to see Mama and Daddy and Cora and their baby siblings? And what if they hung the whole family?

They quickly threw dirt into the furnace to quiet the blazing fire, and then set off to their house where they hid under the floor timbers to await their fate.

Of course, that expected fate never came to pass. Buddy never tormented them again, and they seldom saw him on their rushed hikes past his house. And on the rare occasions he was seen, nobody made eye contact because none of them wanted a reminder of what might have been.

With adversity came knowledge. Corinne and Byron learned they couldn't burn everybody who threatened them or called them *nigger*. Now, that would be some fire.

After years had passed and Buddy left the area, Corinne figured he had been as intimidated by his intended fate as they were by theirs.

But the incident was never spoken of and stayed between Corinne and Byron to this day. It had been too dark, too horrendous to fathom what a successful outcome of that simple plan, contemplated in anger, could have brought on. They had simply let its memory blend amid so many others garnered from those picaresque days spent together as children.

Growing up dirt-poor tobacco sharecroppers had taught Corinne's family to enjoy each other as wealth. To that end, the family finally moved en masse from South Georgia farther north, to Oxford.

And to this day, most of the family still lived in hiking distance of more family; and Byron and Corinne hadn't forgotten to practice the lessons learned.

But like always, things and people don't always go as planned, and Byron was no exception. The second time Byron lost control in anger, it had also been equally dark and horrendous, and the success of that outcome was yet to be realized.

Corinne sank to the chair sitting near the armoire. She just couldn't deal with those memories right now, not today. And with a shake of her head, she put them away. But she knew it would only be a temporary respite if Reba had her way.

Secrets. Corinne sighed with worry over Reba. But her daughter was a grown woman, as she so liked reminding her mama. She'd put that aside for now.

Corinne got back to her feet and refolded the handkerchief, carefully placing it back inside the tissue paper. She opened her handbag and pushed the tissue paper deep inside. Locking the purse's clasp, she set it back on the floor by the television, and then slowly made her way to the door. As always, her cane stood there, a silent sentinel. She reached for it, deciding she'd take it along to the funeral parlor.

She didn't feel very strong today. Not at all.

"Well, look at that," Daisy said. "They gave uncle a little smile, sort of like the *Mona Lisa*."

"She's right." Aunt Evie dabbed delicately at her eyes while she leaned over and peered into the casket. "He's got a little curve to his lips, like he's holding on to a secret or something."

"Let me see," Aunt Cora said, pushing forward. "Aw, he looks just like hisself, don't he, Mama?"

Aunt Cora sniffed loudly into the tissues she clutched before she and the others fanned out to make a space so Grandma Rhoda and Corinne could look at him now.

Grace and Missy lingered at the very back of the family group that had come to preview the funeral director's program as well as approve how Uncle Byron looked for his last public audience.

Mama, Grandma Rhoda, Daisy, Aunt Evie, Aunt Cora and her husband, Uncle Albert, were taking turns peering over Uncle Byron and giving their opinion on whether he looked happy, sad, fat, thin or, of all things, sick or healthy.

Grace, however, didn't care to hear the opinions. She felt drained and wanted to cry out her sorrow.

"C'mon over here," Missy said, nudging Grace. "Let's look and see who sent all these flower arrangements."

Seeing as the others weren't moving any time soon, Grace allowed her sister to veer her toward the flowers.

Earlier, upon first arrival at the Denison Funeral Home, Grace had experienced the familiar influx of emotional dissonance.

The square, unassuming building, with its massive, attached parking lot, opened its double French doors to reveal an almost palatial setting. Though it didn't seem like Uncle Byron's taste, this was the funeral home he had requested to handle his final rites.

Low ceilings with equally low lights closed in on their

small group while they had trooped in silence down a long, narrow corridor to an assigned room and the expected open casket that encased Uncle Byron's remains.

As their pace slowed along the ceramic floor in search of their assigned parlor number in the maze of hallways, one misstep into a wrong turn, and they found themselves in a sales venue—a room filled with the obligatory caskets for sale. Here, low-level Muzak had played as a ramrod straight salesmen whispered to a couple inspecting the products.

Backing out as quietly and as quickly as they could, they had retraced their steps to the main corridor and started the search all over for Uncle Byron.

So much had occurred from the time Grace had arrived that it all came to her in a flash of events now: obsequious chapel personnel, the smell of pine and something else faintly medicinal permeating the halls and tiny chapel, the opulent waiting room in muted pastel colors—complete with hanging chandeliers, vases and fishbowl planters filled with exotic flora. It was all sensory overload, and for the basic purpose of relieving a family's immediate grief.

Grace's head felt heavy and the pungent odor she couldn't quite identify was becoming oppressive; but she now found herself next to Missy as they took their turn to stand in front of Uncle Byron's casket.

With his eyes closed, he did wear a peaceful expression, like the others had said. In fact, Grace didn't know what she had expected, but he didn't look dead at all.

She batted her eyes quickly to keep her tears at bay

because he was dead. That's the reason they were here. That's why he wouldn't be around to help her and Reba or to solve all the other problems that popped up in the family. She'd have to be the one to save the family this time...alone.

"He does look, you know, happy," Missy said, obviously censoring her judgment for Grace's sake. She put her arm around Grace's shoulders.

"He does, doesn't he? Daisy was right, there is a bit of a smile on his face."

"He liked a good joke. I wouldn't put it past Uncle to tell them to make him smile just to keep us guessing."

"He did have a habit of surprising us when we least expected it."

Missy dropped her arm. "Maybe this isn't the best place, but it is as good a time as any to tell you since the subject of discussion involves Uncle."

Grace tensed wearily, not knowing what to expect anymore. "Tell me what?"

They stepped off from the casket and the others before Missy said, "You know he paid my tuition for school."

"Oh?"

"When he realized I wanted to go back and get my degree for real this time, he made a deal with me. If I stayed home and helped take care of Mama and just have a part-time job, he'd pay tuition."

That was Uncle Byron, all right, Grace thought, figuring out an answer that worked in everybody's favor.

"I didn't know for sure, but I can't say I'm surprised."

Grace smiled and nodded. "And I'm glad. He was always worried about Mama and thinking of the family."

"I know. Unfortunately, we didn't talk about it anymore before he died—it's just not what you bring up in a conversation to a dying man—" she exaggerated her voice "—ah, by the way, Uncle, after you're gone, will I still be able to go to school?"

"Is it too late for a student loan or something like that?" Grace asked.

Sighing, Missy said, "Tuition for the semester, even with extensions, is due next month before Thanksgiving break. I don't really know what I'm gonna do at this point, except drop this semester, get a full-time job, and start going again part-time next semester."

A cheerful voice, incongruent with the somber room, spoke out. "I'm sorry I missed your family out in the reception hall. I'm the directress at Denison's."

Grace turned from Missy and recognized the directress, as she titled herself, from the pictures out front.

"I'm Mildred Denison," she said, extending a red-tipped manicured hand toward Daisy, the family member nearest to her.

While Daisy introduced everyone, Grace thought the directress could easily have been going to a board meeting. She was impeccably dressed for the middle of a weekday. Death, of course, wouldn't care about the day, so it was best to be prepared in her business.

"I hope you found everything to your liking and as you requested," she said, directing her comments now to

Uncle Albert, presumably for no other reason than because he was the only man present in the sea of women.

Surely, Grace thought, since she was a black woman, she knew better than to embrace that presumption.

Uncle Albert cleared his throat and gave a clueless look toward Grandma Rhoda.

"We got the insurance policies my daughter, Corinne, mentioned to you on the phone last night."

"We have them right here. We brought them with us, like you said—" Corinne stepped forward with the help of her cane, opening her purse as she talked. "To use as collateral on the funeral until we find out exactly what my brother's policies will pay."

"Oh, that's right," Ms. Denison said, as if a bell had suddenly gone off. "You wanted to present your own policies as temporary collateral, but I didn't call you back this morning because I knew you'd be coming in," she added. "You'll be glad to know that it's already been taken care of."

Aunt Cora did a two-step, angling her way to the front of the group. "What you mean, taken care of?"

"Well, this morning, Mr. Wilson's, ah, excuse me, the late Mr. Wilson's attorney came by—"

"Attorney?" Mama asked, and then looked at Evie who could only shake her head of curls in bafflement.

"Yes. He showed me the proper credentials before he had us tally up the expenses. He then wrote a check for the entire amount." She smiled now. "And with a little extra thrown in for those last-minute details I told him might come up."

When Ms. Denison finished reciting her astounding news, a needle dropped into a haystack would not have made a louder sound.

CHAPTER 21

"Y'all know Aunt Cora wanted to call that attorney real bad," Daisy said, grinning as she held the front door open for her mother. "Did you see how her eyes rolled in the back of her head a little bit when that woman told us the bill was paid?"

"It sure was a surprise." Corinne stepped through the doorway with the help of her cane, and chuckled. "That Byron, I swear he was always full of surprises."

"More than you know," Grace said, not quite sure what to make of the announcement at the chapel. It had been a grueling day so far, and far more questions had formed than she had answers. She could only imagine what else the day held.

"Aw, look-a-there," Corinne cooed. "There's my little Denzel."

When Grace followed Daisy in and saw Reba in the living room, feeding the baby from a bottle, her heart was lifted.

"Hey, girl, how you and the baby doing?" Daisy asked.

"So, when did you get over here?" Grace wanted to know. Reba handed the baby off to her mother, who had already sat next to her on the sofa. "Not too long ago," she said, smiling.

Daisy dropped to the big lounger. "How'd you get over here?"

"Gloria."

"You not talkin' 'bout your sister Gloria, are you?" Daisy asked.

Reba grinned. "I called over here and she told me y'all were still at the funeral parlor, so she said she'd pick me up."

Grace looked up and saw a head appear, and then disappear from the interior doorway. She then heard someone on the stairs. It had been Gloria.

"You should just go' on and stay for dinner tonight," Corinne said with some hesitancy, "since you over here and all."

"Sure." Reba tugged the baby's leg. "We don't have any plans for a while, do we, sweetheart?" She looked up. "Didn't Missy drive y'all up? Where's she?"

"Oh, she went on and took Grandma Rhoda home," Grace said as she elicited grins from the baby by chucking his chin.

"Didn't Grandma say she wasn't ever riding with Missy again?"

They laughed, enjoying Reba's company as much as it brought a spate of relief from their earlier trip to the funeral home.

Grace rested a hand against Reba's shoulder. "Why don't y'all tell Reba about what just happened? I've gotta run upstairs a sec. I'll be right back."

"What happened?" Reba asked, looking around.

Grace left the room just as Daisy began her extended and probably infinitely more interesting version of their earlier trip. She and Reba needed to talk again, but for now, she went in search of her other sister, Gloria.

Grace climbed the stairs and started down the hall toward the bedroom Gloria shared with Rambo and her three-year-old.

When she neared the bedroom, she saw the door was closed, and just as she raised her hand to knock, she heard the unmistakable sound of sniffs. Gloria was crying.

"Gloria," she said, and rapped on the door twice. "It's Grace. Can I come in?"

She heard a flurry of activity and then knocked again. "Gloria?"

"Sure," a weak voice called back. "Come on in."

Grace pushed the door open. Her sister was lying on her stomach across one of Grandma's quilts that draped another of the four-posters Mama loved.

"Hey," Grace started, and sat next to Gloria's supine form on the side of the queen-size bed. She looked around and had almost forgotten that this was a bit larger and more airy than Missy's room. It had probably been a perfect temporary haven for Reba and Denzel.

"What you want up here?" Gloria asked suspiciously while she propped herself up by her elbows.

She had done a good job on her eyes. They weren't red, but she couldn't remove the stain of sadness from them or her mouth. Had something else happened? Where was Rambo?

"Reba's downstairs." Grace smiled and clasped her hands between her knees. "You know, that was a good first move you made, going over and picking her and Denzel up."

Gloria lifted her shoulders in a casual shrug. She crooked her head to look up, her eyes darting to Grace, but not sustaining contact. "My kids wanted to go over to Big Mama's with yours, so after I dropped them off, I stopped by and gave her a ride over here."

When Grace raised her brows skeptically, Gloria took a deep breath.

"Okay," she said. "So I can be a bitch sometimes."

Grace helped. "As well as mean and insulting to your sisters."

"Sure. That, too. But I sure didn't think her little ass would actually tell anybody."

"Best laid plans, you know. So, did you make it right?" Grace's voice held admonishment, but it was softly cloaked.

"If you mean apologize..." Gloria tossed her gaze to Grace before she turned away, as if in shame. "Yeah, I told her I was sorry."

"Good," Grace said, exhaling a breath.

Gloria rolled to her side on the bed. "You didn't come up here just to tell me what a good sister I am, so what's up?"

Actually she had, but Grace sighed at Gloria's still-hard shell. "We just got back from seeing Uncle Byron. Since you didn't come downstairs, I figured you might want to know how things went."

"All right," she snapped. "How'd it go?"

Grace frowned, and it must have shown deeply on her face.

"Jeez, I'm...I'm sorry." Gloria ran her hand through her tousled hair. "That came out all wrong. Sometimes I forget how close you were to him."

"Not just me. Mama. Grandma Rhoda. Surely you had to see how much he cared about all of us. His death is a big loss to this family."

"Was it hard seeing him there, at the funeral home?"

"Yes, it was hard, very hard." She smiled. "But you know Daisy. She made sure we didn't get too stressed."

"Did he look good?"

Grace nodded, and her throat became thick. "He looks like Uncle Byron, all right, and that means—" her voice wavered "—he really is gone." Her eyes misted quickly, something she hadn't meant to happen here and now.

But all it took for Gloria to let down her wall, it seemed, was to view someone else in pain.

"Oh, Grace." Gloria scooted up and then sat on the bed. "You were so close to him, and he loved you right back—but, it'll be all right."

Grace nodded in agreement. "It'll be hard knowing he's not there when I need him, that's all. And Mama, I worry about what she doesn't say, and what she's holding inside."

"Yeah, he was mama's support system, all right."

"That means now, more than ever, we've got to be around for each other."

For a moment the sisters gazed hard at one another, knowing they would say some things, but trying to gauge just how much to say.

"Gloria, what's wrong?" When she saw her sister shift on the bed, she caught her hand. "Something's bothering you, and I can tell you want to let it out." She squeezed her hand. "Go ahead, what is it?"

Just like when she was a little girl, her beautiful eyes squinted tight and her lips quivered before a sob would escape.

"I'm pregnant again, Grace, and...and—" She dissolved into sobs as she dropped her head to Grace's chest. "I don't want to be pregnant."

Even though the announcement was anticlimactic, it still created a thud in Grace's chest. She wrapped her arms around her sister's racking shoulders.

"Where is Rambo?"

Gloria's arms tightened. "He's not here. One of his friends picked him up after y'all left."

"Did you tell him?"

"No, but he already said he don't need no more children, and he's been pressuring me to get a job as it is." She let another pitiful sob escape.

"Surely, with you being pregnant, he'll change his feelings about another baby."

"No, he won't. We've been having other problems for

a while, and we're sitting on a string as it is. This is gonna break it, Grace, I know."

"Oh, Gloria, I'm so sorry about things. But you have to tell him. You know that."

"No." Her arms tightened around Grace again. "I'm telling you, and I know you won't say anything about this to anybody else until I decide what to do."

"What to do?" Grace could feel Gloria's chin tremble against her shoulder.

"Whether to get an abortion."

Grace didn't say anything. Her sister needed help, desperately so, and Grace didn't quite know what or how to help her in this moment—especially when this information Gloria carried tightly within had already been widely presumed by the family, maybe even Rambo. So, for now, Grace just rocked her.

It was later that same evening, and Grace sat in the La-Z-Boy, staring out the misty picture window. Her mood and inner turmoil were mirrored in the driving rain coming down outside.

The house was quiet as she waited for Missy's return. At Grace's insistence, her sister had driven over to the college to plead her predicament and get information on emergency loans. It was the least she could do in an attempt to protect herself since she wasn't prepared to share the news with Mama and the others, Grace argued.

So, for now, Grace sat and watched the gray day pass, her head swollen with furtive family secrets: Uncle Byron's suspicions, Reba's search into the past, Missy's tuition and now Gloria's pregnancy.

Earlier, Grace had rocked Gloria at her chest until they heard a car drive up. Rambo was back, and Gloria quickly scrambled from her sister's protection. Before she left the room, though, Grace had watched Gloria's amazing transformation—from a broken, confused woman to the beautiful disaster they all knew and would continue to love.

Soon after, Grace had watched Gloria and Rambo bound down the stairs together, smiling and waving as if from some surreal chewing gum commercial, before they left the house arm-in-arm.

"If you're gonna mourn, I guess this is the weather for it, huh?"

Grace's head swerved toward Reba's voice as she came into the living room through the kitchen. "Hey. I thought everybody was getting a nap in this rain. Where's Mama?"

"She's taking hers with Denzel. Mama know she loves herself some babies."

"They love her, too," Grace agreed. She swiveled the chair around from the window, and tucked her feet beneath her. Maybe Mama could adopt Gloria's baby. Grace shook her head. They had to think of something. Surely, Gloria had other options, even though they meant having the baby.

"What are you thinking about? I can always tell when you've left the room."

Grace slowly rose from her reverie, picking up the gist of what her sister was saying.

"It's called multitasking at my office. They expect you to do two, three things at a time."

"You don't miss your job back home when you come here?"

Grace's head shot up. "Actually, no," she said, and unfolded her legs.

Reba grinned. "Uncle Byron thought you'd make a great businesswoman because he says you're a born problem solver."

"Oh, he did, huh?" Grace asked, smiling. "Grandma said you and he talked a lot after he got sick."

She nodded, and now folded her waif-thin form onto the sofa. "I sat with him when Mama or Grandma Rhoda saw him. I didn't have much else to do, the baby had come, and I was still off from work. And then, I started visiting him by myself toward the end."

That's what Uncle Byron's letter had said. "What did you talk about?"

"Family, mostly. I brought up my daddy, the late, great Rufus Beneby." She let out a chuckle. "That Daisy always liked to pick at his name, our name."

"Well, you know Daisy. She manages to find humor and a dose of sarcasm in the least likely places."

"Anyway, Uncle told me what he knew about Daddy, and about him dying in that car accident in Atlanta."

"I remember him being reserved and introverted. Sort of like you."

"Uncle thought Mama should be the one to talk about him, but like I told you, she wouldn't say much."

"She's like that, Reba. You know it." Grace watched her sister answer her gaze. "Mama seldom talks about any of her husbands."

She looked away with a snort. "Just by talking, Uncle Byron ended up helping me figure out my life and how to get where I want to be."

"He talked about your fears and getting through them?"

She nodded. "And he was right. You have to work through a thing to come out healed on the other side."

"What about those fears?"

Reba looked down at her hands and nervously pulled at her fingers. "More than anything, Grace, I—I want to be a good mother for Denzel." She looked up. "I tried to explain that to Mama."

Grace frowned. "From what I know and see, you are a good mother, Reba. You love that little boy."

Reba smiled. "I know y'all think I've made some pretty dumb choices—"

"No," Grace said, shaking her head to disavow that opinion. "That's not true. Our worry comes from how you keep everything inside and won't talk to us about what's happening in your life."

"I tell *you* things," she said.

"Not about little Denzel." There, she'd said it, Grace thought.

"Denzel—" Reba hesitated, as though she weighed what she should say. "Is a part of me working through my fears."

"What?"

"It's like I explained to Mama and Uncle Byron. Denzel

introduced me to the things that, for so many years, I never thought I'd have—love and trust and pride in myself."

"You didn't think you had that? I'm not following you."

"It'd be easy to understand if you ever had your pride trampled and you didn't trust nobody, or your whole idea of love and relationships was just—" she shook her head "—screwed up." Reba rose from the sofa and went over to the window where the rain continued to flow in diagonal rivulets down the glass.

Grace watched her sister, trying to see through her words and hear what she seemed to purposely not say.

"Uncle Byron said I sounded like I was lost before I had my baby," Reba continued. "And I told him—" She turned from the window to Grace. "I told him Denzel restored my childhood, my faith, my innocence that was taken away."

"Taken away?"

Reba looked Grace in the eye, as though in a challenge. "Yes, it was all taken away."

Grace's brain assimilated what Reba had been saying, or maybe wasn't saying.

"Look, Missy's home," Reba said, staring through the window again. "She's running through the rain."

"Reba, wait." Grace stood, but her sister was already opening the front door for a soggy Missy.

As the two younger women commiserated over the weather, Grace sank onto the sofa, her brows furrowed in thought. She was unable to stop gnawing over Reba's uneasy words coupled with Uncle Byron's suspicions: restored childhood and innocence taken away.

It was after two in the morning when Grace sat straight up in Missy's bed.

Cold and clammy from the strong nightmare that had just released her, she was literally numbed by what had, in the quiet of the middle of the night, become crystal-clear.

Reba was telling her that her childhood innocence had been, literally, stolen. Uncle had suspected it. Grace's head pounded with the unsettling knowledge. *Reba had been molested*. Raped. Sexually abused. All of the above.

Grace threw back the covers and ran into the hallway, just making it to the bathroom in time to toss her stomach contents into the toilet. She gagged helplessly for another thirty seconds before she heard Missy come through the door.

"Girl, you all right?"

Grace held up her hand for her sister to go away, and with the other she turned on the water jets in the sink and splashed her face and mouth.

Grabbing a hand towel draped nearby, she pressed it to her face, and in a drunken walk, found her way back to the bedroom with Missy solicitously following.

"Will you say something, Grace? Are you okay?" Missy asked as she closed the door.

"Something I ate for dinner, that's all. I'm fine." She

grunted and managed to keep the bile down in her throat. Spying her robe, she quickly shrugged into it.

"Since you say you not having sex, let's hope that's all it is," Missy replied.

Grace had to get out of here, out of this room, assemble her thoughts, and scream, if necessary.

Missy's keys were lying on the dresser. Grace stuck her feet into a pair of house shoes, grabbed up the keys and, steadying the towel at her mouth, left the room.

"Where are you going with the keys?"

Grace hurried down the stairs and through the living room where Gloria's girls slept, sensing more than seeing Missy in her wake. She opened the front door.

It was still raining, but it had been reduced to a light shower. Holding her robe tight, Grace ran out into the filmy night to Missy's car, unlocked it and scrambled into the quiet, empty sanctuary.

The moment the door slammed shut, she dropped her face into her damp hands and the tears poured forth, helped out by her deep gasps from pain. She willed her body not to dry heave the truth that she'd found residing in her own dreams: shame, pain and the requisite silence about it all.

When Reba described it all for Uncle Byron, he had only suspected what Grace now knew.

In the letter he'd left her, Uncle Byron asked Grace to finish what he now couldn't—find out if she'd been molested, and then help her heal. *Help her*.

And who was Reba's abuser? Oh, God, that could be

easily deduced, she thought. Grace pressed the towel into her face, craving the earlier numbness.

The passenger door sprang open and Grace's head bounced up as she gasped. Missy had presented herself, dropping onto the passenger seat with a load in her arms, then slamming the door behind her.

Grace looked at her sister in the dark interior. "You scared me to death. What are you doing out here?"

"I brought you a blanket," she said, pushing it at Grace. "And one for me, too."

"What?"

"Well, if you're gonna sleep out here, you need a cover, and I figured you might want the company, too."

"You figured wrong." But then, sighing, Grace said, "Okay, but you have to get in the backseat and shut up. No questions if you want to stay. Deal?"

"Deal." Missy climbed over the seat and dropped in a heap into the back.

Grace's thoughts reeled. *Does Mama know Reba was abused, too? Is that why they argued before she left to stay with Grandma Rhoda?*

She spread the blanket over her chest and then leaned her head against the window and let the tears quietly drip down her cheek.

CHAPTER 22

Grace always thought the beauty of growing up in a large family was in the fact that there is always something or someone ready and willing to fill each moment of your time and space, lessening the opportunities to wallow in one's own misery. She'd decided that can just as easily become the downside.

That was how Grace saw it after the revelations from the night before. Right now, what she craved was the clarity of thought one finds in private reflection. That was not in her cards with a wake and a funeral on the horizon.

For the past twelve hours, she'd mulled over an irony she'd lived in spades: that by submitting to her sexual abuser, she had saved her younger sisters from a similar fate. Only she hadn't saved Reba. She blinked back the torment that accompanied the painful insight.

Grace picked up her iced tea glass and drank the last of its sweet, amber contents swirling amid the opaque ice cubes in one long swallow, extending this small piece of heaven for as long as possible before she set it back down on the dining room table.

"Hold still," Missy chided. "I'm almost finished." She expertly brushed Grace's hair into a tight, smooth chignon at the back of her head.

"Good," Grace said wearily. "I need a nap or something before we go to the wake tonight."

"You plan on sleeping in my car again if your nightmares give you a bellyache?"

She had not shared the real reason for her bolting from the house, so Missy's presumption, that the dream and upset stomach had required the temporary change in sleeping arrangements, was left uncorrected.

"No. It's definitely not my choice for a bed. I'll just avoid sweet potato pie after ten o'clock, that's all."

"I didn't know you still had those bad dreams."

"They come back ever so often," Grace agreed, shifting on the chair. "Probably because I'm away from home."

"Who else was that who had bad nightmares? Wasn't that Daisy?"

"No, she used to sleepwalk."

"She sure did—or at least that was the lie she told when she got caught outside." Missy laughed. "I totally forgot about that."

"Ouch." Grace flinched at a pulled strand of hair. "Don't make it too tight."

"I won't. Don't this remind you of the good old days when Mama lined all y'all up on the sofa to do hair for school?"

"They weren't good old days for us. We were all tender-headed and crying, knowing it was our turn next."

The front screen door banged shut, and soon after Gloria breezed into the room from outside.

"Missy, can you do Tamika and Tyra's hair when you finish with Grace?" she asked.

"Uh-uh. I'm not up for that," Missy retorted. "Why can't you do it?"

"You know I can't braid like you and Reba. She was gon' do it for me last night after dinner, but she never got around to it before she went back over to Grandma's." She plucked an apple from the bowl of fruit in the middle of the table and bit into it.

"You know, you are unbelievable," Missy said. "After what you did to Reba, you asked her for a favor? She wouldn't have had to go back to Grandma's last night if it wasn't for you."

"Well," Gloria said, flashing her eyes. "We can thank God Reba don't think like you and carry a grudge around forever."

Grace didn't want her empathy for Gloria diluted, so she closed her eyes and listened to them mix it up like saints and sinners. She wondered if Gloria's dilemma still had her insides tied and tumbled like yesterday. If so, Gloria wore her quandaries much better than Grace ever could.

"I swear to God, you take the cake," Missy sputtered. "And no, I'm not doing any hair for you. But you can take the girls over to Miss Betty's beauty parlor. She'll be glad to do their hair...for about twenty-five or thirty bucks."

Gloria let out a loud huff. "When you want to, you

can be such a witch," she said, and turned on her heels, leaving the room.

"And you're a lazy one," Missy yelled back. "Can you believe that? She got some nerve coming down on me."

Grace opened her eyes. "Cut her some slack, okay?"

Missy set the combs in her hand down. "Why? Why should I let her get away with being a selfish ass?"

"Because she's our sister and, well, she could have problems she's dealing with alone."

"Well, when you put it that way and make her problem so crystal-clear, I guess I can appreciate that," she said in her best sarcastic tone. "Humph. Puh-leeze," she grunted, then wiped her hands on the towel around Grace's neck.

"You're really not going to do the girls' hair?"

"If she don't take them to Miss Betty's, I'll do it, but only for my nieces' sakes, not Gloria's." She patted Grace's hair.

"You're finished already?"

"And you, girl, are beautiful again. Better looking than last night with your hair soaking wet and sticking out all over the place."

"Thanks." Grace touched her hair lightly before she looked at her sister. "It won't hurt to go easy on Gloria when she says, you know, stupid stuff."

"Listen, I've got my own problems and bad situations to deal with."

"You're talking about the school loan thing?" Grace asked.

Missy nodded. "Everybody I talked to listened with sad eyes, and they gave me lots of forms to fill out. But nobody was ready to write me a check or approve an installment plan."

"See, if my ship had come on in, I coulda wrote you that check you need so bad." Rambo came strolling into the dining room with a bottle of Coke.

"In your dreams, buster. What you want now?" Missy asked, gathering up the hair tools she'd used in the towel.

Rambo grinned and looked from Grace to Missy as he leaned against the wall. "Nothing. Y'all lookin' pretty nice for the middle of the afternoon just to be sittin' around."

"Don't be practicing your crappy lines on us," Missy said, rolling up the towel. "Your wife was looking for you. She needs you to take your girls to the hairdresser."

Rambo frowned. "All I'm doing is just chillin' for a minute, Missy, after throwing the football with Jamie outside." He crossed one leg over the other, and took a deep swallow of the Coke. "Don't be handin' out stuff for me to do."

"Dee's out there, too, isn't she?" Grace wanted to know.

"Yeah. I saw her with Tamika. They was hanging with some more kids from up the street."

"I'm going upstairs, Grace. I got to put some things together before the wake tonight."

"Sure, Missy."

From where she sat at the table, Grace watched her sister pick up the towel and then sidestep her way along the wall around the table in the small room.

When she reached Rambo along a narrow spot, she leaned away from him and he shifted against the wall, ostensibly to give her more space; but the shift allowed him to brush against—and then use his hand to steady—her. He put his hand on her butt. Missy skirted away from him with a backward look and left the room.

"That girl know she got one bad attitude," Rambo said, and turned up the Coke bottle again.

"I sometimes wonder if it runs in the family," Grace said, and leveled her eyes on him. "I'm talking about Gloria."

He laughed. "Oh, I know who you talking 'bout, all right. I live with her." He took another drink from the bottle.

"Why do you suppose she's all wound up like she is?"

"Hell if I know. She just runs hot and cold all the time." He moved away from the wall and sat at the table with Grace. "I don't even try to figure it out anymore. That is, unless you think you know and want to tell me about it."

Grace had only spent time with her brother-in-law in the company of the family, so they didn't know each other in a more bonded way as siblings or friends. She put up with his presence only because he was married to her sister. And, she presumed the same was true for him.

"Well, you are a big flirt."

"What?" He grinned, flashing big white teeth, but the humor didn't quite reach his eyes—beading right before hers, just as Missy described them.

"I think it was probably always a part of your charm, and what attracted Gloria to you at the start. But, after all these years of marriage, and three kids, I'd bet she doesn't think it's charming or sexy."

He straightened in the chair. "Why'd you say that? Oh...I get it. You think I'm trying to play on you?" The lazy grin came out.

"I doubt I'm your type or age range, but you're definitely playing on Missy, and no matter how innocent *you* make it out to be, Missy will call you on it if you keep pushing."

His smile crawled into a scowl as he jumped up from the table, leaving the bottle there. "Damn, if all y'all sisters ain't crazy." He stormed from the room.

When he left, Grace strummed her fingers and sighed. Uncle Byron would've warned him of the consequence of his actions and she'd only done the same.

She rose from the table, intent on going to find Dee and Jamie, only it was a complete surprise when she reached the doorway and met Bobby coming through the front door. Jamie followed on one side, with Dee on the other.

Grace stopped, and when he looked up, she asked, "What are you doing here?"

"We, ah, just got in a couple of hours ago, so I came by to see the kids." He looked from Jamie to Dee and grinned. "Me and Jamie threw a few balls outside for a while."

Grace knew the "we" referred to the young and tender Marilee. She'd love to be a fly on the wall in a room with Big Mama and the new wife.

"I'm talking about in Georgia, Bobby. What are you doing *here,* in Georgia?"

He shook his head. "I told you I was coming down to Uncle Byron's funeral. I even suggested we all drive down together."

She looked at the expectant faces on either side of him and knew something else was up. She honed her eyes onto Dee, who'd be straightforward.

"Mama, can we go to shopping at the mall in Atlanta with Daddy and Marilee?"

"Yeah. I can go to that new electronics store to get some more earphones," Jamie added.

Grace put her hands on her hips before she squinted at Bobby. "Jamie, Dee, let me have a minute with your daddy first, okay?"

"I need to change my shoes," Dee said, and raced off to the stairs. After a backward glance, Jamie lumbered after her.

"You look…great," Bobby said, smiling as he pushed his hands into his jeans' pockets. He stepped closer to Grace.

"You're going shopping?" Grace spoke in a low voice to him. "I had to scrounge cash together because you said you didn't have any money to help me get the kids down here, and the first thing you do when you get here is go shopping?"

"Y'all made it here, didn't you? And I told you I was gon' pay you back when we get home. Don't worry, I'm good for my share."

Don't worry? Grace took a deep breath.

"Aw, Grace, I know that pissed look of yours." He stepped closer. "Marilee wants to go find a dress for the funeral tomorrow, that's all, and we not gon' stay a long time, either. All they want to do is ride."

Crossing her arms, Grace sighed. "They're teenagers, Bobby, and there is no such thing as just a ride."

He exhaled a breath. "Well, excuse me for trying to spend some time with them. I thought that's what you wanted me to do."

"Bobby, I don't want to argue, and I'm not telling you what to do. The kids can ride, but you know they'll expect you to buy them something if you spend on somebody else, even your wife." She lowered her voice further. "And I don't have any extra spending cash."

Jamie sauntered back into the room. "Mom, can we go?" he asked. "I have some allowance money left over I can use for the earphones."

Grace was embarrassed that it appeared she was throwing finances into a benign car trip. Always the villain who walked around with her budget taped to her chest, she sighed.

"Sure, Jamie. Your dad will take care of whatever you need," she said, all the while holding Bobby's gaze.

He grinned at her and, looking past Grace, said to Jamie, "Go get your sister and tell her we got to go."

As Jamie stood at the foot of the stairs and yelled for Dee to come on, Grace crossed her arms.

"Make sure you get them back in time for the wake. It's at seven."

"We'll be back in plenty of time. You worry too much," he said, and playfully chucked her chin.

He was right. She did worry. In fact, she worried for the whole family because no one else seemed to see the need for concern on any level.

"Bobby Morrissey, is that you in there?" Corinne was coming in the room.

"Miss Corinne, how you doin'? You know you get prettier every time I come home and see you."

"Oh, I'm doin' fine," she said, beaming. "I saw your mama the other night, and she said you might be coming to the funeral."

"Yeah, I want to do all I can to support Grace and the kids through all this, you know."

"She appreciates you being here, too, don't you, Grace?"

Grace smiled as the kids walked into the room.

"Go on to the car," Bobby told them. "I'll be out in a minute."

"'Bye, Mama," Jamie said, and gave Grace a quick hug, following with one to his grandmama.

Dee did the same with a peck, and then they both went outside.

"Miss Corinne, it's good seeing you. Grace, I guess I'll talk with you later." He turned to leave.

"I almost forgot, Grace. I came out here to give you this." Corinne handed her a cordless phone from her pocket.

"The phone?" Grace asked.

"It's for you, honey. A Mr. Fontaine?"

From the corner of her eye, Grace saw Bobby pause in interest at the door.

"Thanks, Mama." She tried to keep the delight from her voice and the urgency out of her step as she turned to the staircase. "I'll take it upstairs."

CHAPTER 23

Grace ascended the stairs and looked for a private place to talk, but quickly deduced that Missy's bedroom would have to do.

She entered the bedroom where Missy stood at the mirror, inspecting her hair.

"Hey, what—" Missy started, but Grace pulled her into the hallway.

"I need some privacy for a minute, please."

Leaving Missy in the hall, she returned to the bedroom, closing the door behind her.

"Hello?" she said into the phone. She smoothed out the tremors in her voice and was surprised at the thumping from her heart. "This is Grace."

"Grace, it's Theo. Was that your mother who answered the phone?"

"Yes, it was." She took in another ragged breath. "Thank you for sending the flowers. They were beautiful. But how did you know where to send them?"

"There aren't that many funeral homes in Oxford," he answered with an inflection of humor. "So, things have gone well with you and the family?"

"We're coming along," Grace said. "The wake will start in a few hours, and then the funeral and burial is set for two o'clock tomorrow."

"It sounds like you're pretty busy," he began.

"I had planned to call you as soon as I arrived, but it's been a little crazy ever since I got here."

"I can understand," Theo said. "But as long as everything is all right…"

"Of course everything is fine," Grace lied. Actually, she wished she could unburden all that she'd discovered and taken on since she'd arrived, but, of course, that was out of the question.

"Except…except that I miss you," Grace added.

"You do?" Theo's heavy baritone voice cracked.

"Yes, very much," she said, and a smile formed unbidden across her face as she sank onto the bed. "More than I ever expected."

"I miss you, too, Grace. Maybe we should do something about it."

"When I return home next week, how about I invite you to my house for dinner," Grace offered.

"No, I was thinking of something a lot sooner," he said. "My meeting ended earlier than I'd planned, and suddenly I have a bit of time on my hands. I can still come down there if you—"

"Oh, Theo." Grace spoke up. "I can't possibly ask that of you." She nixed the idea in her head, though her heart reached out to the possibility. "I wouldn't feel right changing your plans. Anyway, the kids and I are dealing with down here much better than I'd expected."

"If you're sure you're okay."

"We'll get through things fine."

"In that case, I won't keep you," he started. "I'll call—"

"No," Grace stopped him, desperate to keep him on the phone. "Don't go yet."

"Okay...I don't have to," he said.

"Tell me about your trip to New York. How did it work out?"

It wasn't so much what Theo was saying but how he said it. Grace greedily listened to the tone and timbre of his voice, the familiar inflections that reminded her that their almost daily conversations for the past three months had possessed a renewal power all their own. She missed him more than she dared admit, and so what if it was a romantic notion?

"Grace?"

"I'm here," she assured him as she pulled from the reverie.

"I think that's the problem—you're there and I'm here."

"And unfortunately we can't do anything about it until I return next week," she whispered.

She closed her eyes and saw the smile he wore. She could see how he touched his graying temple, something he did when he was in deep thought.

He cleared his throat. "I'll be calling you again tomorrow," he assured her.

"And I'll be waiting," she replied. After she hung up,

Grace hugged her arms around her chest, not wanting to lose the warmth of the message that had radiated constantly through their conversation. He missed her.

Something warned Grace to look up. Missy was standing inside the closed door, smiling like a Cheshire cat.

"Don't even deny it," Missy said. "I think you got it bad, girl." Laughing, she then darted out the door.

With a resigned sigh, and feeling a bit of high school déjà vu, Grace left the edge of the bed, calling as she opened the door, "Missy, come back here, girl."

The Denison Funeral Home of Oxford had scheduled the first hour of viewing exclusively for the family. However, Grace had no expectations of anyone adhering to the times, and so expected family and friends during any of the four hours they were scheduled to use the chapel.

She made sure, however, that at least she and her sisters would remain present and available for the entire time to greet, introduce and thank visitors who thought enough of Uncle Byron to honor him by paying last respects.

Only a mild protest had emanated from Jamie earlier at having to wear pants made of something other than denim, fleece or nylon. It was to the contrary with Dee. She was excited about a chance to dress up and that was another warning bell to Grace.

With Tamika's help, no doubt, Dee appeared downstairs at the last minute in a bias-cut black skirt with a ruffled hem that ran from mid-thigh on one side and ended at the knee on the other side. And she had on lipstick that wasn't anywhere near the color of her lips, something that had never been an issue at home before for a fifteen-year-old.

Marilee, it turns out, had helped her choose the skirt during their impromptu Atlanta shopping trip, and Tamika had shared her favorite lip color, Sunburn. Had it not been for Missy's and Daisy's insistence that she looked fine, and Mama's pulling at the skirt to gain another inch of covered thigh, Grace would still be home getting Dee dressed again. As it were, that minefield had been maneuvered, albeit not totally to Grace's satisfaction.

However, as it is with family, when they alighted from the sedate black limousine that had transported them from the house to the chapel, Dee sought out her hand as everyone paired off along the paved walk that led to the entry, all bad feelings and ill will put aside. Grace squeezed her hand, content with the moment.

"Are you scared, honey?" she asked.

"A little," Dee answered.

It was no wonder. Dee and Jamie never had to deal with death head-on and at an age where they could understand the consequences of mortality. It probably made her feel small and vulnerable.

At that moment Jamie came up from the other side, and though his hands were jammed into the pockets of his slacks, he gave Grace a reassuring smile, which she returned.

"Are we going to have to stay the whole time?" Dee asked.

Grace didn't answer. So much for the wonder in the moment.

Exhaling a deep breath, she led them through the doors.

Uncle Byron's wake was being held in one of Denison's chapel rooms specifically designed to accommodate big groups. The room had a wide aisle down the middle and a succession of pews lined up, one behind the other, on either side.

A large, eighteen by twenty-four photo of Uncle Byron had been set on an easel and stood at a forty five degree angle to the burnished oak casket. The upper end of the fancy coffin, as Uncle Byron would have referred to it, was opened to reveal his enigmatic countenance, replete in his best suit and Corinne's silk handkerchief that bore his initials.

The perfume from the flood of flowers conquered the slightly metallic and medicinal pine odors that permeated the halls. A huge and colorful spray of flowers—from the family—covered the lower end. Spread in a curve about the floor, and some peering from makeshift easels, were rows of plants, flowers, bouquets and baskets, sent in sympathy and respect to the family.

Grandma Rhoda, surrounded by Reba, Aunt Cora, Uncle Albert and Aunt Evie were already inside the chapel, having just been delivered by another funeral limo a few minutes earlier. Belinda and Glenn were driving their own car and had not arrived; nor had Gloria and Rambo who were also driving in order to transport their children.

When Reba began to cry as she took her very first look at a passive Uncle Byron, it was as though a trumpet had sounded and everyone's grief crawled from that place of safekeeping and showed itself.

And with that initial wail, the chapel was soon filled with both the regular relatives and then the kinfolk seen only at times like these. Mama's other sisters, Lettie Bea, Margaret, Fontella and their husbands, all from other parts of Georgia; the sisters' children—cousins whose names Grace remembered, but that was about all; and their husbands and children, whose names were never known. All came with mournful faces.

Some grieved silently, like Grace and Corinne because by now the tears had been spent. Others wept noisily and uncontrollably, as though the tears and grief had been saved up for this moment and had no choice but to come out as a deluge.

But no matter the manner and no matter the amount of grief, Uncle Byron was gone and everyone was keenly aware of that fact.

CHAPTER 24

After her first ninety minutes at the wake, Grace moved to a pew toward the back of the chapel. She was exhausted, and so were the kids. Jamie and Dee had slouched down on either side of Grace, held under her arms that were stretched around their shoulders.

She was beginning to think like Dee; Grace wanted to go back to the house and prepare for the long tomorrow. After the funeral, the hardest part would be over, and she held on to that thought.

"Hey, Grace." Bobby slid onto the pew with them.

He wore a white shirt and slacks, and Grace appreciated his bow to dignity tonight.

"Hi," she said, and as she straightened, so did the kids.

"Hey, Daddy," Dee said, stretching and yawning at the same time.

"Hi, Pops." Jamie half stood to greet his dad with a complicated slap-handshake-squeeze.

"Y'all look pretty busted," he said, grinning at their tired faces. "Mama said when we leave, y'all can just ride back to the house with us. That way, Grace, you don't have to drop 'em off."

For once, she found no fault with this plan. "Thank you," she said. "Where's Big Mama, anyway? I should thank her for coming."

"Last time I saw her, she and Marilee was over there somewhere with your sisters."

Grace could see them now. They were near Uncle Byron's coffin in earnest conversation. She could only imagine Daisy's take on it later.

"Is your friend, Theo, coming all the way down here to the funeral?"

Grace frowned as she digested his words.

"Theo's coming, Mama?" Dee asked while Jamie looked on in curiosity.

The phone call this afternoon, Grace figured, had clued him in, but she never told him Theo's name. That would have come from the kids. She suspected Bobby was shrewd enough to ask enough questions to get a name.

"No," she said evenly to Dee. "He's not coming here." She then drew a bead on her ex-husband.

"I've said this before, Bobby. I'm not discussing who I see with you."

With a snort, Bobby looked around before he turned back to Jamie and Dee. "When I get ready to go, I'll be waiting by the front door, so keep your eyes peeled, okay?"

When he left them, Grace leaned back on the pew. "Theo did call this afternoon—and it's Mr. Fontaine to you, Dee—and he asked how you two were faring with the funeral and all. And, well, I told him we were all good."

"Aw, so that means he's not coming, after all?" Dee asked. "I wanted him to come."

"You only met him once," Jamie said.

"So? He's pretty cool to be old. Bernard's cool, too. Look, he just came in," she said, peering across the room. "I'm going to find Missy." She hopped up from the pew.

"Mom." Jamie turned to her. "Bernard said he'd teach me how to drive if I come visit Grandma next summer."

"He said what?" Grace asked, following their gaze.

Jamie stood, too, and followed his sister. "I'm going to buy a soda."

Grace's stare finally landed on her young cousin of criminal intent, 'Nard. It was funny hearing Dee and Jamie call him by his given name. Of course, they hadn't been around long enough to adopt their cousin's short-ened version.

Bernard Duncan, aka 'Nard, had strolled into the chapel with four other young men; at first glance, all seemed of similar intent: a study in laid-back insolence.

She looked closer. 'Nard had recently started his dreads, with locks that extended no more than three inches. They seemed to strike out on their own, and at every angle imaginable, like a halo of curly thorns.

The harsh dreads did nothing to toughen his pretty-boy face one iota, and Grace suspected that might have been his original intent. He wore a waist-length black leather jacket over black jeans and black leather boots. His platinum chain necklace matched the chunky platinum bracelet that peeked out from the wrist of his unsnapped sleeve.

Grace thought it surprising that her young cousin seldom wore rings, had no visible tattoos and, beyond the single hoop earring in his ear, had no visible piercings. She didn't know if that could be said of the other boys behind him who slouched into the chapel, as though not sure they would be welcome. They, too, wore jackets and over-sized jeans. But unlike 'Nard's dressier shirt, they wore something more akin to a T-shirt under their jackets.

'Nard, stopped, kissed, hugged and chuckled as he and his friends made their way through family and friends to Uncle Byron's casket. Once there, they stood quietly a moment before abruptly turning away. He said some-thing to one of his friends before he walked toward the pew where Grace was sitting.

"Grace." He eased next to her onto the seat. "You don't ever come home anymore."

"They don't need me babysitting you anymore."

"Nope, guess not." He blushed.

"Anyway, home is somewhere else now. Can't stay here forever, you know. It'll happen to you one day."

"Yeah, it will. But with Uncle Byron gone, I might just take off sooner than I'd planned, do something different for a change."

"Like what?"

He shrugged his shoulders. "Uncle Byron told me you might know someplace I might be able to show my artwork up in the D.C. area."

It was well known in the family that 'Nard loved to paint and draw, but Grace, like everyone else, had presumed he'd packed up his acrylics and drawing pencils for a gun and holster.

"Oh, really? I didn't know you were still interested in art."

"Oh, man, that's in my blood." He slapped his fist to his heart. "I won't ever give that up completely. I just walked away for a while."

"What happened?" Grace asked.

"Well, just between me and you, cuz, Uncle Byron caught me and my boys in what you might call an embarrassing situation a while back."

"Oh?" She furrowed her brow. "Like what?"

"Let's call it attempted robbery of the vehicular kind." 'Nard paused. "So he made me a proposition. If I added something else to my life, he'd let it slide that time. And since we'd been talking about my drawings, well, I sort of liked what he was sayin'."

Grace mulled over his words. "Now that he's gone, you know he doesn't have anything over your head. You can do whatever you want."

"That's right, but I feel funny, like I'm lettin' him down if I don't finish what we started. It's not like a job over at Mickey D's, you know. Uncle Byron said people pay big money for nice art." He nodded. "I think I could do that."

"With some training and discipline, maybe even art school, I'm sure you can, 'Nard."

He leaned back into the pew. "You know your kids are a trip. They 'bout the only people who called me Bernard since I left high school—what?—seven years ago."

His friend signaled him at the door. "Listen, I gotta jet. But, ah, we need to talk again before you go back home, you think?"

"Sure. I'll make sure we do before I leave. Maybe you can come up and visit one weekend. I'd like that. We'll make some rounds to the artsy spots."

"Sounds like a plan." He bent and gave her a hug. "Later, cuz."

Grace shook her head. She had actually invited 'Nard to her house; but he hadn't seemed so criminally inclined as he talked about his dreams. Obviously, Uncle Byron had seen something in him worth saving. She smiled. Wait till Daisy heard about her partyin' buddy going straight.

Grace stood and saw Gloria sitting by herself. She went over and slid into the space next to her.

"Hey," she said. "We haven't had a chance to talk since the other day. How're you feeling?"

She looked at Grace and then turned away. "I'm still pregnant, so what do you think?"

"For one, I can tell your mood hasn't improved." She leaned over and whispered, "You still haven't told Rambo?"

Gloria crossed her legs in the short skirt, and then uncrossed them, preferring instead to cross her arms tightly against her chest.

"I don't know what to say to him."

Grace lowered her voice. "And the abortion?"

"I haven't decided."

"You haven't decided because of Rambo or because it's not what you want?"

"It's my body and my decision," she snapped.

Grace could tell she was parroting rhetoric. "And that's the reason why you don't dare get an abortion simply because Rambo doesn't want a baby."

"What am I going to do with another baby, Grace?"

"Love it the way you love your others. We're your family and we'll stick by you even if Rambo decides not to—and you still don't know that he won't."

She pressed Gloria's hand and rose from the pew. "I gotta go. Aunt Evie is signaling for me."

Grace walked the short distance to Aunt Evie. "You wanted me?" she asked.

"Who is that tall, white man over there?" Evie asked, and motioned near the casket. "He just got here and signed the guest book." She looked at the book on the easel stand and interpreted the wide scrawl. "His name is John Sheffield." She looked up. "I thought maybe he worked at Byron's office, but I never saw him before. Do you know him?"

The name, if not the face, was familiar, and then it struck Grace. "Yes, he's the John Sheffield that paid the funeral bills—Uncle Byron's lawyer."

"Oh, that's right."

"We called his office in Atlanta and they said he'd get back with us. I guess he decided to just come to the wake instead."

At that moment Mrs. Denison, the directress, came in, shook hands with Mr. Sheffield, and then walked him to the front pew where Grandma Rhoda and Corinne sat, along with the other sisters and various relatives.

"I guess she's planning on introducing him to us,"

Grace said, watching from a distance as Mr. Sheffield shook hands with everyone.

"Why don't we just go on over there and meet him, too?" Evie suggested.

"Sure," Grace said, but now she saw that the whole row of relatives had turned as a unit and was looking at her and Evie at the door.

"Why they looking at us?" Evie wondered.

"I don't know," Grace said, equally puzzled. "But they want us to come over there and meet him."

They didn't have to traverse the entire room because Mr. Sheffield had already started toward her. He held out his hand before she had a chance to say anything.

"My name is John Sheffield, and you must be Grace Morrissey, Byron Wilson's niece?"

"I am," Grace said.

"I've heard so much about you from your uncle."

"You have me at a disadvantage there, Mr. Sheffield. I don't think Uncle mentioned you even once to me in all the times we've talked."

"Nonetheless, he left me with an important duty to relay no later than tonight."

Grace remembered how she'd felt when Grandma had mentioned a letter, and then later on, after she'd read its contents. This moment was feeling eerily similar. She cocked her brow to indicate she was ready.

"I have the duty of informing you that you are named in your uncle's will as the individual to carry out the provisions of that will."

Grace took a step backward and her hand came up to her chest. "I—I was named what?" she asked.

"Oh, my Lord," Evie said.

Mr. Sheffield took a deep breath and smiled at them. "Ms. Morrissey, you are the appointed executrix of Mr. Wilson's estate. You've been asked to carry out the orders your uncle requested and designated in his last will and testament."

CHAPTER 25

"I promise you," Grace said, shaking her hands, "I didn't know anything about this. I don't have any idea what this whole executrix duty involves, and I sure didn't ask for it."

She had been repeating the refrain to the family ever since she got the word from the soft-spoken attorney who had appeared at the wake. The news he delivered had spread quickly among the family present in the chapel, relegating Uncle Byron to an almost secondary subject at his own wake.

With the exception of Corinne and Grandma Rhoda, most of those present hadn't wanted to believe Grace was just as surprised as everyone else by the news.

Mama had understood the confusion on Grace's face. And when Grandma Rhoda had taken her aside, all she'd asked was, "Is that what Byron told you about in that letter?"

And Grace had answered truthfully to her grandma Rhoda. "No, that letter said he wanted me to take care of Reba. He was worried, and wanted me to continue what he started—get help for her."

Grandma had nodded her understanding, said she

wasn't surprised that Uncle Byron had picked her to handle his affairs, and that was that.

Now, back at the house, Grace could only pace across the living room in the company of her family and wonder what was in store.

"Does anybody really know anything about what Uncle Byron did?" Gloria asked.

"We know uncle had a business," Daisy said. "Before that, though, didn't he drive school buses for the county?"

"Until he bought them," Grace said, knowing some of the story from the attorney. "And then leased them and the service back to the county." She stopped her pacing and sat. "He's always liked being a businessman. I think he was a good one, too."

"Damn, I didn't know he owned those school buses," Rambo said. "That was pretty smart, but he sure didn't live large. Wasn't he staying with your grandma?"

"Livin' large don't always mean you got money, honey," Daisy chided. "In fact, most times it means you owe money."

"Why are we discussing money? You don't have to have a lot of money to have a will or an estate," Grace argued.

"She's right," Glenn said from the doorway. "And chances are, you won't really know any details about what's going on until you have the reading of the will."

"Unless Uncle told Grace something she's not telling us," Gloria added.

"I told you, I don't know any more than you do," she said.

"You know when they gonna read the will?" Gloria asked.

"Do you?" Missy asked, too. She was curled up on the sofa next to Belinda, and hadn't said much.

"Mr. Sheffield said that, as executor, I could arrange the date, so I told him to set it up in the next few days since I have to go back home next week. The only issue is contacting everyone who needs to be there."

"Oh?" Daisy asked, her interest peaking.

"Yeah. Mr. Sheffield's office will be contacting everyone Uncle Byron named in the will, so they can be present, too."

Missy whirled her feet from the sofa and sat up. "You mean, it's possible he may have left something for us in his will?"

"You got my cell number, right, Grace?" Daisy asked, grinning.

"And, since a lot of the family is here for the funeral," she said, ignoring Daisy, "it makes perfect sense to have the reading as soon as possible."

When her comments instigated a barrage of questions and observations, Grace realized her mother was missing. She had apparently snuck out while everyone talked about Uncle Byron and the possibilities left in Grace's care.

As Grace left the room, she heard someone comment, "I heard an executor gets paid, too, because this is, like, a job." She sighed.

When she entered the kitchen, and didn't see Mama, the only other place she might have headed would be her bedroom. Grace climbed the stairs and went in search of her at the end of the hall.

The door was ajar, and she could see her mother sitting on the edge of the bed with only a single bulb on at the nightstand. She was still dressed in the dark suit she'd worn to the wake.

Grace rapped against the door, then pushed it wider.

"Mama, are you all right?"

Corinne slowly turned her head toward Grace and the door. "Come here, Grace, and sit down with me."

Closing the door behind her, Grace moved across the room, not sure what to expect in her mother's appeal.

"We were all downstairs, and suddenly you were gone," she said

"I know. I've been thinking, and that don't even include the news you got tonight."

Grace nodded. "Go ahead. What's on your mind?"

"Your grandma said something to me tonight. It was about that letter Byron left you."

Grace's breath caught in her throat. "She did?"

Nodding, Corinne asked bluntly, "What did it say?"

Grace hesitated before she took a deep breath. Secrets. She hated them. "It said he thought Reba had been… molested when she was younger." Her voice had petered down to a whisper.

Corinne straightened, then turned more fully on the bed to Grace and revealed the overwhelming sadness that crowned her eyes.

"Like you?" Corinne said.

Grace simply nodded.

"And was she?" her mother pressed.

For a moment Grace halted, then nodded again. "I think so, Mama. She hasn't come out and said it directly, and not to Uncle, either, but—" Grace clasped her hands to her chest. "Uncle was sure enough to be worried, and from what Reba's been saying, I believe she was."

Corinne's eyes fell shut, and then she covered them with her hands. Grace knew it was to block out all the guilt and comprehension and shame.

"Oh, Lord, Lord. How much of this rain you think we can take?" Corinne mourned.

Tears streamed down Grace's cheek. "Mama, did you know about any of it?"

"A few weeks ago she told me how she remembered she'd been fondled and violated when she was little, and...and I told her maybe she wasn't remembering right, and was she sure. But she didn't change her story. She had dreams, she said, when what happened wouldn't leave her, and it would show up crystal-clear. She said in order to move on with her life, she had to let it out, and let it be known."

A sniff came from Corinne. "Grace, I was too shocked at first to even believe her."

"What else did Reba say?"

Corinne dropped her hands and looked up. "Reba said it was killing her, keeping it all inside, and Byron told her she had to let it out. Now, I'm scared Reba is bound on letting it out to everybody."

Grace took her mother's hand. "Mama, we can't let her keep on thinking it's in her head. Uncle Byron was right. She already says we don't think much of her. We have to support her telling it, and hear her out." Grace bowed her head. "We owe her that for all these years she suffered in silence."

"You didn't tell everybody, Grace, and you all right."

"I told Uncle Byron, Mama, and then he told you. And I'm not all right, not by a long shot." She closed her eyes. "I have those dreams too."

"Oh, Jesus, what have I done? I let you down, and now Reba." She looked at Grace, her eyes floating in tears of remorse. "I didn't know, I didn't see it until it was all too late."

She rubbed her mother's hand. "Mama, you did the best you could."

"I'm so sorry."

"We have to do something for Reba. Uncle Byron has made her strong, but it's up to us to let her know we understand, and most of all, support her." Grace's mind raced for a solution to a dilemma that would now most likely have to be crossed.

"We can still talk with her without involving the other girls, can't we?" Corinne asked.

"I don't know, Mama." Grace's chest tightened. "We've kept this secret going on over twenty years," she said. "We were lucky it's been ours for this long. Don't you think Uncle also realized that the silence had to end when he suspected Reba had been abused? It's better we tell it than for it to be discovered."

Corinne nodded, resigned to the inevitable. "You know, Grace, when you were born, I loved you so much. People use to say to me, 'You love that baby more than God hisself, and you gon' get punished for that.' So every time I'd get pregnant after that, I was paralyzed with fear that I wouldn't love them as much as I loved you."

"Oh, Mama, don't be saying things like that." She grabbed up her mother's limp hands again. "All parents feel that way. I felt that way with Jamie. But then, when I saw my baby girl's fat, scrunched-up face, I knew I could love her as much as I did Jamie." Grace smiled. "It's different, but the same kind of love."

"But mine persisted." Corinne paused. "It still does."

Grace raised her eyes to her mother's while vigorously shaking her head, the tears careening in different directions.

"You love us all, Mama—it's just different, like I said."

"Maybe," her mother replied. "And maybe this is the punishment."

Grace turned and just sat there, defeated. She didn't know what to say. Her mother was determined to bear this great guilt internally, as they had all been taught to bear life's cruelties.

"Byron and I tried so hard to make this go away," Corinne whispered. "When you left here and got married, and had a baby, we thought it was over and behind you." She turned her stare on Grace. "You don't know what your uncle and I did to make this nightmare end." She looked away as a quiet sob escaped. "And now, it's all come right back to haunt us."

"Oh, Mama." It was then that Grace's tears flowed in earnest. "And look at what I did. I let that bastard take advantage of me because I thought I was protecting my baby sisters from him." She sniffed and wiped her nose with the back of her hand.

"I don't want my other girls to know," Corinne said woodenly.

Her mother's pain was palpable and Grace hoped she'd never have to face such a dilemma among her loved ones.

"Mama," she began gently, "we won't be able to avoid it. Missy and Belinda will figure out it was their daddy who raped me and Reba."

Grace was huddled in the bed and drifting through a troubled sleep when she heard Missy come into the room.

She sat up and rubbed her eyes and watched as Missy prepared for bed.

"Hey, did I wake you?" Missy asked.

"No. I was tossing and turning, not really sleep," Grace replied. "Everybody's gone?"

"Yeah. You, my dear, are the talk of the town."

"Please, spare me the details."

"I came up looking for you, but you were in the room with Mama." She looked at Grace as she stepped from her slacks. "The door was closed. So, something going on?"

Grace sighed. "No, just talking. Tomorrow's going to be a big day."

"Yeah, I guess. Is your boy coming?"

Grace gave her a quizzical look.

"Theo, girl, your *friend*. Who else?"

"Oh," Grace said, easing into a gentle smile. "No, he's back in Maryland. I wouldn't ask a friend to come this far to a funeral for someone he doesn't even know."

"He'd be coming for you, silly rabbit, not Uncle Byron." She shrugged into her pajama top. "'Course, Bobby came for you, too. And with his wife. Now that was a novel idea. By the way, do you know I'm actually older than her?"

"Bobby's not a friend like Theo."

"Well, at least you're starting out as friends with Theo, and that's more than I can say for you and Bobby. Considering his wife, he's still being ruled by the head downstairs."

"Bobby and I started out for all the wrong reasons. We both wanted to escape, and instead made our own prison."

Missy sat on the edge of the bed and lotioned her legs. "When you talk like that, I think of poor Gloria. She's in a prison, too, with all the time in the world to consider mistakes."

"I won't ever discount Bobby or our mistakes because we created two wonderful children in the process. Gloria may not say it, but she thinks the same way."

Missy tilted her head and stared at Grace. "Who named you?"

"Huh?"

"Your name. Grace. Did Mama ever say how she chose it? I swear, there's just something about when you start talking that shows how...special you are, and how differently you think."

For the first time that evening, Grace relaxed with a grin. "No, she never explained why she chose it, but she used to tell me that you grow into your name."

"Oh, hell. So, does that mean I'm going to be a *miss* all my life?"

"Only if you don't get over this last boyfriend and find another one."

"You, too. Get over Bobby and his bride and move on. I'm thinking this Theo could be a good start. When can I meet him?"

Grace's grin widened. "What makes you think I'd introduce him to you pack of wolves?"

"See... You were looking miserable earlier, and I got you to smile."

She leaned over and hugged Grace.

"What was that for?"

"For my big sister hearing how I needed to see her, and then coming to stay at the house during the funeral." Her smile beamed. "Thank you. You always look out for me, and I love you for it."

"Promise me something, Missy."

"Sure," she said, adjusting the covers.

"You know I love you. I don't want you to ever doubt it, not for anything, and no matter what. Promise?"

Missy held the cover still as she looked at Grace.

"Is this about Uncle's will? You make it sound so serious—"

"Just promise me, okay?"

"Okay, okay. I promise I'll never doubt your love for me." She snuggled under the cover, and gave Grace a cautious look over her shoulder. "Christ, we sound like two lesbos making declarations in bed in the middle of the night."

"If you don't hurry up and get a boyfriend, there could be talk."

"They already started about you. Thank God, Theo's now in the picture."

Grinning, Grace tossed the pillow at her head.

CHAPTER 26

Early the next morning, on the day of Uncle Byron's funeral, Grace borrowed Missy's car and drove to Grandma Rhoda's house. When she arrived, Reba answered the door.

"Hey, Grace. Why are you over here so early?" She squinted through sleep-swollen eyes, and had obviously just awakened. "The funeral's not till two o'clock."

"Is Grandma still sleep?"

She nodded, but then looked alarmed. "Is everything all right?"

Grace came inside and followed Reba back to her bedroom. "Yes. A lot happened last night."

"I know. That was some surprise when you found out what Uncle Byron wanted you to do."

"It was. That's not why I'm over here. Later on last night, I talked with Mama."

"About what?" She opened the door to her room. The baby was asleep on one side of the double bed, and the covers were thrown back on her side.

Grace followed her in and, closing the door, walked to the edge of the bed and stroked the baby's cheek.

"He's so perfect, Reba. It's easy to see how you say he's restored your faith in yourself." She sat on the bed.

Reba sat, too, cross-legged in the middle of the bed. "What did you and Mama talk about?" she asked again.

"You, Reba, and what you told her happened when you were a little girl."

She sat straighter, now wide awake. "Are you here to tell me I don't know what I'm talking about, like she did? Because if you are, you can just go." Her lithe form slipped off the bed and she went for the door, but Grace moved just as fast and met her there.

"No, Reba, I didn't come to tell you that." She looked at her sister's strong face, the full lips and brows, and thick hair. They had different fathers, but they were the same. "I came to tell you I believe you because I was abused, too."

Reba backed up a few steps as her sister's words sank in. "Grace, you?"

When Grace acknowledged her question with a nod of her head, Reba began to cry. Grace swaddled her in her arms, and they sat on the bed.

"Do you want to talk about it?" Grace asked.

"Was it Daddy Fletcher who...who touched you?" Reba used the name the youngest children had called him.

Grace closed her eyes tight. She had no real memory of her biological daddy, Richard Brooks, and her first step-father, Rufus Beneby, had been nothing but quiet and kind, though distant—the opposite of Fletcher Johnson, their second stepfather. Mr. Johnson, as Grace called him, was a cruel alcoholic who had brought his own brand of horror to her childhood.

"Yes," Grace answered, nodding. "Mr. Johnson sexually abused me over four years—almost the whole time he was married to Mama."

"I remember the first time it happened. I was in second grade. It was the first week of school and I wore that pink skirt Mama made. After that, I didn't want to come home from school with him."

"How long did it continue, Reba?"

"Until he died, when he broke his neck." She looked at Grace. "Why didn't you tell anybody?"

"For the same reasons you probably didn't. He told me how everybody liked him, even Uncle Byron, and no one would believe me—that I'd mess things up because my sisters had a daddy again. I also didn't want Mama in jail or my sisters dead." As Grace remembered, warm tears soaked her eyes.

Reba pulled back from Grace. "I've been having these awful dreams. They're like nightmares. Everybody in my dreams keep turning into Daddy Fletcher, and then...and then he starts touching me, putting things inside me, and I scream to tell everybody, and then I wake up."

Nodding gently, Grace said, "I have them, too. They started when I got married. After I divorced, they actually went away. But lately, they've come back again, and really strong. The same kind you're having."

"I talked with Uncle Byron, and I couldn't bring myself to tell him what happened to me, what with him being so sick and having his own problems to deal with. But I told him how I was feeling, all lost and everything. He listened, and told me to let out whatever it was that was bothering me. Sometimes I think he knew what I was going through."

Grace smiled. "I think he did, too."

"Does Mama know about you? When I told her what happened, that I needed to tell her everything, she didn't want to believe it at first. Then she told me no purpose would be served by bringing it out now. She wanted to let bygones be bygones."

Grace put her hands on Reba's shoulders. "I finally told Uncle Byron what Mr. Johnson was doing to me. I was just around Dee's age, and I was a wreck, trying to be everything to everybody, and it was killing me."

"You told Uncle?"

She nodded. "And then Uncle told Mama. But soon after that, Mr. Johnson fell down the stairs while he was liquored up." Grace sighed. "You have to understand our mama. She's sick with guilt that it happened to us and she didn't know, but she also thinks, now that we're free of the abuser, we can just go on with life. I don't think she understands how deeply it's shaped our lives."

"Lord knows it changed mine," Reba said.

"Mine, too. I'm divorced and still don't understand what happened in the marriage. I don't want to make the same mistake twice, so I close myself off."

"That's what I did with Denzel's daddy."

"What happened?"

"I met him last year, I thought I was in love, and then

the nightmares and stuff started. It scared him, I pushed him away, and we broke up just as he was transferred from the city to Denver. And then I learned I was pregnant."

"Does he know about the baby?"

She shrugged. "He tried contacting me, and Uncle Byron told me I should respond and tell him about his child. So, I did. I told him everything, Grace, and he still wants to send for us, but I told him I have to get healed from this first."

"Oh, Reba, I'm proud of you. I think you did exactly right. But you must talk with Mama. She's just as torn as we are, and she has another worry, as well."

"I know," Reba said. "I love all y'all, and I would never blame Belinda or Missy or love them any less for the horrible things their daddy did."

"I just think our sisters are going to have a hard time with this if they ever find out. And that's why Mama's afraid."

"The funeral car is gon' be here in fifteen minutes," someone shouted from downstairs.

Upstairs, Grace was dressed, but she was now sewing Daisy into her dress, Missy was still in the closet selecting yet another outfit, and with Mama's help, Gloria was downstairs trying to finish dressing Tavis and Tyra.

"Breathe in a little more," Grace urged Daisy. Her sister was half bent onto the dresser, and Grace hovered over her with needle and thread as though she were working a fine piece of tatting.

The side of the dress managed to split just after Daisy zipped it up, and there had been no time to find a replacement. Thankfully, there was a jacket that would cover the exterior signs of repair made by Grace's lightning-fast stitching.

"Thank God, Grandma Rhoda taught y'all something after all that time you spent over there in her sewing room," Daisy panted, still holding her breath.

The sewing room. Grace thought it had become a metaphor for her life thus far. It was in that room where she had been torn into pieces, literally and emotionally; yet sewing had preserved her sanity. She had learned how to pick up pieces and put them back together again, sometimes stronger and better than before. Was it too late to teach that to Reba?

"Grace..." Missy's voice was panicky. "I don't have any stockings. Please, do you have extra ones?"

"Sure. Look in my bag."

This was how she'd imagined it had been when her other sisters, so close in age, grew up together; pandemonium on occasions such as this: what belonged to one of them might as well have belonged to all. She had imagined they shared everything, and even without much money, it must have been a wonderful life, filled with love and free from...abuse.

But it hadn't been as she'd imagined. The dream she'd dreamed for her sisters was supposed to have been different from the reality she experienced.

A tear clouded her eye and she blinked.

"Ow, Grace," Daisy bellowed.

"Sorry," she said. "Missed a stitch."

The lineup of cars had been changed that morning with the funeral home, courtesy of Grace. She wanted all of her sisters to ride together, and that included Reba. It was important to her in light of what the days to come could bring.

Jamie and Dee wanted to ride in the car with their older cousins, which included Bernard. She agreed.

The line of limousines looked elegantly somber against the quiet backdrop of Grandma Rhoda's empty street. The October day was clear with the sun shining. It was as good a day as any for a funeral.

As Grace and her sisters quietly stood outside the fourth funeral car in a line of six, on a signal, one of the funeral directors took hold of Gloria's hand and helped her step into the car from one side. Another gentleman opened the other door and began helping them load from that side, as well.

Gloria's skirt was absurdly tight, and when she stepped up, it seemed on the verge of splitting on the spot. Grace could only hope it held up for the rest of the day, or at least until they'd returned to the safety of the house since she hadn't thought to bring more needle and thread.

Once they had settled into the funeral limo, the solemnity of the occasion seemed to close in on Grace as well as her sisters, but for all of one minute, though.

There was a silent pall at first as everyone gained their bearings in the limo's small universe and came to terms with the reason for all this. The driver, partitioned off, could have been a world away.

Then, as if cued, Missy started with the observations, with Daisy acting as her backup.

"Did y'all see all that makeup Mr. Denison's son was wearing?" She shook her head. "Man, he got more on him than poor Uncle Byron."

Daisy didn't need an opening, and spoke up.

"I don't guess you know, huh? Both of his sons wear that stuff, and that ain't all. But I tell you, for where they be going when the sun goes down, hell, that ain't nothing."

"What are you talking about?" Belinda asked.

Daisy slapped her knee. "I didn't tell y'all? 'Nard took me to this crazy club the other night, and we saw one of the brothers there."

"No, y'all didn't," Reba said.

Gloria stomped her foot. "Now, I'd heard about one of them, you know, dressin' up, but I thought it was just gossip."

It was hard to keep a stoic face with Daisy in the car.

Reba, sitting next to Grace, gave up and began to laugh. "Are y'all for real?"

"I heard the whole stinkin' story the other night," Daisy said.

"Say it ain't so," Missy said, shaking her head. "And that youngest one, he is so damn pretty, too."

"That could be a rumor, you know, and none of y'all

know what you're talking about." Belinda delicately sniffed into her handkerchief. "So, what did you hear?"

Grace tried to head off the gossip. "Daisy, don't you start that stuff. For heaven's sake, we're in a funeral procession."

"But, I swear to God, Grace, this is for real." Daisy was now giggling herself.

"At the club," she continued, "They was sayin' Daddy Denison got wind of what his son was doing after hours, and went down there himself, and ended up catching the oldest boy decked out to the nines, in women's clothes. I mean, he's a flamin' transvestite—"

Belinda squealed. "No, girl."

"Yes, he is. And when the daddy called the oldest one on it, he told his daddy that his brother was doing the same thing, at the other table."

Gales of laughter rocked the funeral car.

"Y'all are awful" was all Grace could exclaim amid her own laughter.

"I tell you," Daisy said, wiping her eyes. "These funeral boys can be strange. They got money, but they strange as hell."

"No stranger than these motorcycle cops out here doing wheelies to get attention," Missy said. "Watch this."

When one of the cop escorts came close to the window, his sleeves rolled back to expose his upper arm muscles, Missy got his attention.

"Hey, honey," she mouthed, and, crooking her finger at him, blew a kiss. When he grinned back, then sped ahead on his back wheel, the sisters laughed.

Within fifteen minutes, they had arrived at the church and the doors to the limo were thrown open.

With heads bowed, the sisters dutifully wiped tears from their eyes as they emerged from their car. The invited mourners who looked on presumed these were tears from spilled grief. They didn't know they were celebratory tears of a shared union of sisterhood, the results of thigh-slapping, head-thrown-back laughter Daisy and Missy had managed to elicit in the backseat of the funeral limousine.

What must the driver have thought they were doing back there, laughing so hard? No matter, God bless her sisters. They might have to atone for a few things one day, but no one could elicit a smile the way they could, and in the worst of circumstances.

As they lined up with the family and then walked in the processional to the third pew amid Uncle Byron's hand-clapping church congregation, Grace felt a tinge of guilt from the fact that she was bringing a little of the carnival to this occasion herself. Stark images of the upright, urbane Denison brothers—who stood like sentries at either end of Uncle Byron's casket—became interchanged with those of Amazon women, dressed to the nines in loud, party dresses and glittering high heels. Grace blinked away the image.

In the moment when one of the brothers came precariously close to them, Missy pinched Grace's thigh, and all Grace could do was press her handkerchief to her mouth to suppress a smile, try not to study his face for traces of makeup, and remind herself that Uncle Byron would think it okay for her to smile, even laugh, today.

When the ceremony was over, the congregation stood in unison for the recessional, and Grace faced the audience of mourners for the first time.

And that was when she saw him. Theo Fontaine. Her heart literally surged as she looked again. It was him. He stood at an aisle seat near the back, and he watched her, too.

"Grace, where you going?" Daisy asked. "We're getting ready to go to the graveside."

"Don't leave me," she said over her shoulder. "I'll be right back."

"Where she going?" she heard Missy ask, but Grace's attention was on the stone steps ahead and how they'd take her back into the church, and hopefully Theo would still be there. What was he doing in Georgia? In Oxford? Hadn't she asked the same thing of Bobby? And Missy had answered, "For you, Grace."

She climbed the seven stone steps and as she turned the corner, collided into Theo.

Without a word, he caught her to him, and they hugged a warm hello, capped by a peck to her cheek.

"Oh, my God, Theo." Grace's heart thumped loudly. "You came, after all, all the way from home?"

"I didn't think I'd get a chance to see you before you returned to your grandmother's house."

They separated, and for a moment, before her questions were answered, she simply saw the man, a handsome one in a black suit and crisp white shirt. It highlighted those beautiful gray wings he sported at his temple. And his arms still held her waist.

"What are you doing here?" She reached up and smoothed the faint outline of lipstick she'd left on his cheek. "The last time we talked—"

He smiled. "No, the last time we talked, I was in Atlanta. You didn't ask me, and I didn't say. I wanted you to tell me you needed me, and I'd planned on driving down for the funeral."

"So, how did you know where to come?"

"I called you again this morning, on my way out of town, in fact, and I spoke with your sister, Missy."

"Oh, you did?" Grace wasn't sure if she wanted to hear this. "Go on."

"Well, she said you were getting dressed, but since I was in town, I might as well attend the funeral and reception afterward at your grandmother's." He smiled. "So, technically, she invited me, and gave me the address to the church and house."

"Grace, come on."

She looked down over the railing, and there was Missy, looking up and smiling, and beckoning with her arms.

"The limo is ready to leave, and that better be Theo."

Theo waved as Grace nodded to her sister. She turned back to him. "This is definitely a surprise."

"I know, and you hate surprises," he said.

Grace smiled. "I'm working through my fears. You have my grandmother's address, right?"

"Yes."

"Meet me on the porch there and I'll talk with you when we return from the graveside, okay?"

His smile grew wider. "I'll be there." They squeezed hands before Grace quickly maneuvered down the steps and headed for the limo.

That wasn't as bad as she thought it could be. *Work through your fears.* Things were happening fast with Theo, and she didn't have time to think. But, don't things happen for a reason?

The reason for Theo's appearance hadn't manifested itself yet, but she guessed she could hold on until it finally did.

CHAPTER 27

When the family alighted from the funeral limousines at grandma Rhoda's house, cars had already pulled onto the grass surrounding the sprawling address as well as taken up the length of both sides of the street.

Grace searched the crowd for Theo's face. He would already be here.

And then she saw him. He stood apart on the porch as he talked with Dee, Jamie...and Bobby?

Grace took a deep breath and darted a mean-spirited look to Missy who walked alongside her.

"You see what your meddling has done, don't you?" she asked.

"What?" Missy asked innocently, but then corrected herself almost immediately when she followed Grace's gaze. "Oh."

"Is that all you have to say? You didn't even tell me he'd called."

"Aw, go on and admit it, you're glad I encouraged Mr. Lookinggood to come."

Grace drew in a sigh. "I'm glad to see him, but I didn't want him to meet all the family—at one time—just yet."

"I know what you mean…some of the branches do take some time gettin' used to. I suspect Theo and Bobby won't pull guns and knives with the kids hanging around, but go on." She pushed Grace ahead. "Rescue that poor man from your ex."

Grace looked back and gave Missy a censuring glare, but quickly made her way to the small group on the porch.

She was about to speak before Dee burst out with, "Mama, you said Mr. Fontaine wasn't coming to the funeral."

Grace flashed a smile of acknowledgment as she moved to stand near Theo. "At the time I didn't realize your aunt Missy had invited him."

"He was hanging out by himself, so we came over. Dad followed us," Jamie said, offering the details.

Bobby's muscle worked in his cheek. "I wanted a chance to meet the man who's gonna be 'round my kids. Know what I mean?"

"Indeed I do," Theo said, nodding to Bobby. "It's been my pleasure."

Rocking back on his heels, Bobby asked, "Fontaine, huh? That's with an 'e'?" At Theo's nod, he pressed on. "So, you work in the D.C. area?"

"Yes, I—"

"Theo," Grace interrupted. "I should take you to meet my mother and grandmother. They're probably inside by now." She looked at her children. "It's late and you should be hungry, so why don't you go on inside and get your-selves a plate of food? They should already be made up on the back patio."

After the kids said their goodbyes to Theo and walked away, Bobby said, "Now, you were saying something about where you work."

"Bobby, I appreciate you coming to the funeral to support the kids," Grace said. "But it ends there, okay?"

She took Theo's hand and they walked away.

After a few steps Theo laughed. "You think he's going to pull up a police report or a credit history or something like that?"

Grace smiled. "Please, don't laugh. There's no telling what he'd try."

"In that case, I should warn you I lead a pretty boring life on paper."

"I still don't know how you came to be in Atlanta," she said.

"I have a meeting there on Monday. After I got back from the New York trip, and knowing you were just south of Atlanta, I came in early on the off chance that I might get to see you." He squeezed her hand.

"And, of course, you got lucky with that phone call Missy intercepted."

"Do I get to meet her?"

"Be careful what you wish for. I've got five of them curious to meet you, too," Grace said.

They had made their way to the back parlor where long tables had been set out and were now being weighed down by covered trays and pots of food. Her mother and grandmother were seated not too far away.

"Mama, Grandma Rhoda, I want you to meet a friend of mine from Maryland," Grace began, and introduced Theo.

"You've come a long way, so you must be a real good friend," Corinne said, smiling.

"You're right, Mama, he is," Grace amended, and smiled at Theo.

"It's nice of you coming all the way down here," Corinne added.

"Grace, I don't believe you ever mentioned his name, but I'm sure I heard it from Byron," Grandma Rhoda commented with a cryptic smile. "You like my l'il Gracie?" Grandma Rhoda asked, her eyes sharpening.

Taken aback by her grandmother's comment, Grace looked at Theo.

"Yes, ma'am," he answered quickly. "I sure do."

"Good. Then you take care of her, or you might have to deal with me."

"And the rest of the family, too." Missy came from behind them and thrust out her hand with a beaming smile. "I'm Melissa Johnson."

"You wouldn't by any chance be Missy?" Theo asked.

"Yes," Grace said, and suddenly her sisters surrounded her. "And this is Reba, Belinda, Gloria and Daisy."

One by one, Theo managed to survive each sister's inspection in relative calm and quiet assurance, charming them as he had with the children. Grace, on the other hand, held her breath as if she were the one under scrutiny.

But as they talked and smiled, and the minutes counted up to five, ten and then twenty, with no calamity occurring, Grace became assured, unguarded and less defensive about Theo's interest in her. In his favor, he had been brave enough to walk a gauntlet of relatives, and in their territory, for her. That had to mean something.

Now they were saying goodbye again on the front porch.

"The worst is over, you know," he said. "I've met your family. And I like them."

"I haven't met yours," she said, smiling bravely.

His bright smile was heady in the afternoon shade. "We'll make it the first order of business when you return home."

They walked to the edge of the porch.

"I won't stay," Theo said. "You've got people to greet, family to care for, and I'm keeping you from them."

He leaned into Grace and, grasping her upper arms, placed a light kiss on her lips. She imagined that he had lingered for a moment longer.

"Grace, the funeral may be the reason for the shadow I see in your eyes. But if it's not, and there's anything I can do, promise you'll call me?"

She nodded. "I'm glad you came."

He stepped off the porch. "You have my hotel number," he said matter-of-factly before he turned and walked across the grass to his car.

Grace hadn't trusted herself to say much as Theo prepared to leave. His offer of a wide shoulder and an extra arm to lighten her burdens was tempting.

All she'd needed was a little impetus in his direction,

and she might have taken off with him in his car. Now that he'd left, she felt inexplicably empty.

She moved to the very edge of the porch and watched him leave, one hand pushed into his pants' pocket, the other swinging casually in counterpoint to his long stride.

"I don't know why you want to keep something like him hid up there," Daisy said. "I always knew you still had it in you, I just didn't know if you knew how to use the damn thing," she teased.

"This is exactly why I kept him away—so y'all don't jump to conclusions," Grace argued. She had returned to the house after Theo left and was now resting her feet.

"No conclusions to jump to anymore," Daisy insisted.

"Well, next time you see him, you'll have to come to my house."

"Hey, that's slick, too," Daisy said, and saw Gloria headed their way. "Oh, hell. Here comes trouble, you think?"

"Did y'all know Aunt Evie's brothers are here?" Gloria asked when she joined them.

"I haven't seen 'em," Daisy said.

"If I do, I'm making them leave. Mama and Grandma Rhoda don't need to know they're even here," Grace said. "You remember how they treated Uncle Byron when he and Aunt Evie divorced."

Daisy scanned the room. "Where is Evie, anyway?"

"She knows they're trouble. She's probably trying to get them to leave," Gloria said. "By the way," she said, giving Grace her attention. "Your name is poppin' up in everybody's mouth. They're trying to figure out why *you* are handling Uncle's *estate*." She stretched the words out.

"You know, I am so tired of this. Anybody wants to know, tell them to ask me," Grace said.

"Go'on, sister." Daisy grinned. "You bad."

"Ya'll ate?" Gloria asked.

"Nope," Daisy said.

"Me, neither."

"Then let's get something," Gloria suggested. "I know where the Mother Board at church hid the good stuff."

Leaving the comfy sofa, they moved into the hallway, passing a few people. They entered the kitchen with Gloria leading the group, but as soon as Gloria cleared the door she abruptly stopped in her tracks, and Grace and Daisy crashed into her back.

They were all trapped by the frozen tableau playing out in front of them. The sisters' eyes squinted, and their mouths gaped at Missy's hand in midflight as it headed for Rambo's left cheek. Within another second, her knee lifted to find an endpoint at his crotch.

Grace wasn't sure if they realized they had company.

"I warned you to keep your nasty hands off my ass, you sick bastard," Missy screamed.

"Owww—" Rambo let out an excruciating groan when her knee found its target.

"Damn, woman, what's wrong with you?" Rambo managed to groan out while doubled over. "Shit, that hurt."

"What's going on?" Gloria managed to say, and moved toward them. "What's happening?"

"Your husband is a no-good bastard, that's what. Keep him the hell away from me," she said, pointing at him as she strode to the door. "Because the next time he puts his hands on me, he's gon' need a hospital bed."

While Gloria rushed over to Rambo, Grace and Daisy moved out of the door. Missy's mouth was stuck out and her brows were angled in unbridled anger as she marched from the room.

"Did you hear that?" Gloria ranted at the still-bent-over Rambo. "You tell me what happened right now."

When Daisy paused, as though she would go back into the kitchen with Gloria, Grace stopped her.

"Let her handle it, Daisy. We need to find Missy."

"No, you go get Missy. I'm staying right outside this door because I want him to act like he gon' get upset with Gloria. I will kick his ass myself."

Grace took in a deep breath. She knew this might happen, and she had even warned Rambo. And what would Gloria do? Pregnant and already feeling unwanted, she had to pick sides between her sister and her husband, and then suffer the ignominy of Rambo's public outing. Grace left to find Missy.

Missy was pacing in Reba's bedroom when Grace got there.

"Are you okay?" Grace asked.

"Grace, that pig put his hand up my dress." She stood

with hands akimbo. "Did you hear me? I'm fixing a plate and getting stuff out of the oven, and he comes up behind me and puts his whole damn arm up my dress."

"He won't forget what he did any time soon. You gave him a hard kick in the you-know-whats."

Missy's face finally unclenched. "Yeah, I did, didn't I? But, Grace, he's does this bump-and-touch stuff every time they visit, and I was just getting tired of it."

"I know. I saw him yesterday when he brushed against you."

She seemed relieved that there was a witness. "You did?"

She nodded. "After you left, I told him not to try it again or you were going to react. He didn't take my advice, and it serves him right. I just hate you had to be the one to teach him the lesson."

"I bet he's in there telling Gloria some crap that she's believing. Suppose he tells her I came on to him?"

Grace smiled. "Don't worry about what he's telling Gloria. She's not stupid. She saw what we saw, and you were no willing participant. But, he is her husband, and we have to respect whatever she decides to do. We don't have to like it—"

"And we don't have to live with it, either. I'm not going back to Mama's house if he goes. I swear."

"I'll make sure Gloria knows she and the kids are welcome, but he can't return. And then I'll let her explain things to Mama."

"Thanks, Grace." She hugged her sister.

"You sure you're all right?"

She nodded against Grace's shoulder.

Suddenly there was a crash, followed by heightened voices. When Grace and Missy opened the door, Reba had just arrived.

"Somebody just crashed into Grandma Rhoda's table on the porch," she announced.

CHAPTER 28

"Oh, God," Grace said as she quickly walked toward the disturbance with her sisters. "You don't think it's Rambo making trouble, do you?"

"Or Daisy, for that matter," Missy added.

But when she, Missy and Reba went out onto the porch, there was new trouble, but a different sort.

Nathan Parker, Aunt Evie's brother, had crashed into one of the small tables set up with food. Grace figured if he wasn't drunk, he was probably damn close to it. Aunt Evie was trying to coax him from the patio area with little success while a couple of cousins had begun cleaning up the mess of broken dishes and spilled food.

Mercifully, this was all happening on the back porch with only a spattering of guests, and not inside with Grandma Rhoda, Corinne and the older family members and guests.

"Oh, hell," Missy said, turning in the opposite direction. "Let me go find Uncle Albert and Daisy. They can haul his ass off the property."

Nathan and his brother, Royce, were two men Uncle Byron had not liked. He never spoke his reasons to Grace, but it was widely known that while he was married to Evie, they were banned from their house. The men's long-standing hatred worsened when he divorced Evie.

And while Grace was not privy to why they divorced, surprisingly, it was an amicable split. To her credit, Evie continued to involve herself with the Wilson family, hence everyone still called her "Aunt Evie."

So, there was no reason for the two men to have shown up, except to cause trouble.

Grace's aversion to them was far more specific. Nathan and Royce Parker had been good friends with her stepfather, Fletcher Johnson, her molester. For all Grace knew, they could all have been birds of a feather.

When Grace approached Aunt Evie, she was talking to Nathan as he picked himself up from the concrete floor and then propped up against the brick wall. He was a burly man in his fifties, the younger of the two brothers, with a bald orb for a head.

"Grace, would you look at this fool falling all over the place? I told him he had to go. He knows Byron wouldn't want him here, and makin' a fool of himself at that."

"She's right, Mr. Parker. You should leave before Grandma Rhoda comes out here and sees you. All you'll do is upset her."

"I ain't got no problem with Grandma Rhoda. She's a nice lady. We just came by to support Evie." Nathan Parker flashed a greasy grin at Grace, baring a gold-covered incisor. "We heard how you been put in charge of everything for Byron, so we just tryin' to see 'bout Evie, you know."

"Nathan, you don't bit more know what you talkin' about than do Royce," Evie said.

"Mr. Parker, you have to leave right now," Grace said, shaking her head.

Another man, though not quite as tall, appeared through the door and stepped out onto the back porch. It was Royce, the older version of his brother, Nathan, with a beer belly that rode atop his low-slung leather belt.

"Nathan's got it right. Everybody know Evie was the one married to Byron, so how you think we feel when we heard it's gon' be you handlin' things?" He let out a cackling laugh, as though he held a secret. "Now, I wonder why is that?"

His words were more slurred than his brother's, and he took a swig from the beer bottle he held in his hand.

"Royce, y'all need to go on." Evie was turning one brother toward the path through the grass and pulling the other along with her hand. "Both of y'all drunk and you know whatever Byron did ain't none of your business."

Grace was as upset as Evie. But it was yet another comment on the draw of Uncle Byron's money or the lack thereof since nobody knew anything of his finances.

"I'll drive them home, Grace, and then come back."

"Leave me alone," Royce demanded, and swung the bottle he held, though all he caught was air.

"I ain't goin' nowhere right now." Nathan shrugged off Evie's hand.

Already anxious from this long day that seemed to

have lost poor Uncle Byron in the shuffle, this was the pro-verbial straw. Grace was angry, stretched thin, and primed to lash out from the pressure.

"Who the hell do you think you are?" she demanded of the men. "Coming into somebody else's house, and after a funeral, for God's sake, talking your trash? Hell, yes, you're leaving right now. Get out." She pointed to the grassy path in the back.

"Come on," Evie said to her brothers, pulling their arms. "Please, y'all, c'mon."

Nathan laughed and pushed away Evie's arm. "I told you we don't have to go. Byron not around no more."

"That's right," Royce agreed.

Nathan chuckled and leered at Grace. "I bet you miss him, huh?"

"You have no respect for the dead, do you? You would come here and tramp on Uncle Byron's memory just because you didn't like him?"

"What memory?" Nathan laughed and leaned in close to Grace's face. "Hell, he wasn't nothing but some pervert who couldn't even get it on with his wife."

Grace was a study in stone. "What did you say?"

Royce had sidled up to them. "That's why he put you in charge of everything," Royce agreed.

"Yeah, you was his favorite go-to," Nathan said. "'Cause he liked his girls…little."

"Nathan." Evie's shock was worn on her face. "You done gone too far now." She pulled his arms. "Get on out of here."

Grace's anger contorted her features as the world around her turned red. "Uncle Byron never touched me. Why would you say that? He was like a father—no, he was a father to my sisters and me. How can you say something like that?"

"Because it's true," Nathan slurred. "He was messin' with you for years, he was a certified pervert. Ha, ha," he chuckled. "We know."

"Hey, what's goin' on out here, Grace?" It was 'Nard's voice coming from behind.

Grace wound her fist and swung at Nathan. "You're a liar. He was the only thing good around here." But she missed.

She swung again and this time made contact, but he must have swung back because almost immediately she felt a blunt shock to her ear. Even so, she balled her fists and went at him again, and again, her anger so white she saw nothing in front of her eyes, only a red rage backdrop behind her grief and shame.

"Byron was a low-down fucker. You let him get away with it, and you know it."

"No, he wasn't," she cried as she swung her arms. "He wasn't the one."

"Yeah he was. Fletcher told us all about it."

"Fletcher? He duped both of you. It wasn't Uncle Byron, you crazy bastard. It was your friend, Fletcher Johnson. Fletcher molested schoolgirls, Fletcher was the monster, and I'm glad he's dead."

Someone had Grace by the waist and was pulling her

away as she screamed at the men, and that's when the words began to echo in her head, as though they were on some kind of a surreal tape loop. *It was your friend Fletcher Johnson. Fletcher molested schoolgirls, Fletcher was the monster.*

She'd said it out loud.

"What?"

It was Missy's shocked exclamation reaching Grace's ears.

"Grace, what are you saying?"

From some part of her brain, Grace could detect that a commotion had broken out. Scuffling, bodies in motion, cursing. Grace saw it all, as though she were now disembodied and viewing a movie. More and more people piled onto the porch.

"Grace?" Missy was pleading. "What are you saying about Daddy?"

"Mama, what's wrong with you? Dee, go and get Daddy right now."

Grace backed up. She had to get away from all this confusion, if only for a moment, and she turned to the door, fighting against the strain of people who were pouring from the house to come outside.

"Answer me, Grace. You can't just go," Missy screamed at her.

When she got inside the house, all Grace wanted was some guaranteed privacy away from everyone. And she knew where to go. She walked to the other side of the house and through the breezeway to the sewing room.

Grace opened the door and went inside. When she flicked on the lights, the quiet peace was like a blanket of warmth, and she started to cry—

Without warning, the door flew open and Grace's head jerked around. It was Missy and Daisy.

CHAPTER 29

Missy raced into the little room ahead of Daisy.

"Grace, didn't you hear me out there?" Missy cried. "You can't say something like that and just leave."

Daisy was shaking her head. "Grace, honey, what's going on? You just blew up out there."

"I didn't mean to let it out that way, I'm sorry." She wiped her hand across her face, only now aware that her ear ached.

Reba rushed through the door next, followed quickly by Belinda and Gloria.

"Somebody tell me what's going on?" Belinda asked. "I have never been so embarrassed. Gloria said Aunt Evie's brothers accused Daddy of being some kind of a child molester."

"Not Aunt Evie's brother's," Missy said, and she hugged her arms around her middle. "It was Grace." She turned to their oldest sister. "Is it true what you said? Please, say something."

"Oh, God, this is not the way you were supposed to find out."

"Grace..." Gloria slowly moved toward her. "You have to explain what you meant out there."

"I didn't mean for it to come out that way—" Grace started, shaking her head.

"But, is it true?" Belinda whispered.

"Yes, yes, it's true," Grace shouted. "Every bit of it." She took a deep breath. "Mr. Johnson raped and abused me for four years. See, I've said it."

Amid her sisters' stunned silence, Grace's voice lowered as she turned to look at Reba, who still stood just inside the door.

"I said it, Reba."

Reba bent her head, but her words came out loud and clear.

"He raped me, too."

With the initial shock wearing off, the sisters sat quietly in the sewing room, some on the floor, some on stacks of material, and talked. But first, they made sure no one else in their rank carried the same secret that had weighed on Grace and Reba.

When they were satisfied Fletcher Johnson had injured no one else, they released their hurt. Their voices were heavy with pain and much still remained unsaid, because there were no words to express comfort for someone abused, and repeatedly, by another family member.

"If I had known how understanding everybody would be, I don't think I would have waited so long to say something," Reba said from her spot on a stack of cloth.

"Lord, I wish I'd known," Daisy said. "It must have been hell keeping this inside, y'all."

"After I was grown, I never thought I'd have to tell because I didn't want Missy and Belinda to suffer for one moment for Fletcher's sins," Grace said.

Belinda let out a little moan as she rocked back and forth. "Oh, God, this is so horrible."

"Now I know why you said you'd always love me," Missy said. "I remember that."

"Yeah," Grace said. "Mama didn't want all this brought up because she thought it would hurt us as a family."

"But don't it hurt just as bad if you can't tell anybody what happened?" Gloria asked. "You can't keep something like that inside forever."

"True," Grace said. "It eats away at you. That's what secrets do."

The door opened again. This time it was Aunt Evie.

"Grace, you in here? Your children are worried and looking for you. Can I talk with you a minute?"

The sisters got up to leave, exchanging embraces as they did.

"Grace, we'll talk some more," Missy asked.

She nodded. "I'll get Aunt Evie to bring me home later. I've got to see the kids."

When they were alone, Aunt Evie looked Grace in the eye.

"Grace, I'm so sorry for what my brothers did."

"Jamie and Dee, I need to let them know I'm all right."

"They're okay. They're with their daddy. You're the one I'm concerned about, though. Do you know what you were saying out there? And more important, is it true?"

Grace looked at her hands and nodded. "I never wanted my horrible secret to come out in so public a way. I've guarded it because I knew a lot of people could be harmed, and now, look at what I did."

"You did it defending your uncle Byron."

"I know." She felt the tears begin to flow. "How could they say those things about him, Aunt Evie?"

Evie patted her hand and sat by her. "I'm going to tell you some things that aren't for public consumption, all right? First of all, you were right to defend your uncle. He's none of those things my sorry-ass, no-good brothers said."

"I know that."

"Byron was gay, though." At Grace's raised brows, she went on. "He tried to change and go straight right about the time Fletcher Johnson broke his neck. That's how we met when I used to tend bars.

"Anyway," she continued, "we hit it off well, and there were no secrets between us. I knew about his past, and well, he knew mine, too. Neither of us were angels, and we realized after about three years, that it wasn't gon' work for us. So we divorced, and promised we'd stay friends, and we did. He even gave me his house in our divorce just out of love."

"Did your brothers know this about Uncle?"

"No, but, now that I hear Fletcher was that kind of man, I'm thinking Fletcher probably told my brothers that lie about Byron just to pass blame if something ever got out about him being a pedophile. When we never had kids, and then divorced, I believe my brothers figured it was because of what Fletcher had told them."

The sewing room door was thrown open again.

"Here you are," Bobby said from the door. "Jamie saw your sisters coming from this way."

"Mom—" Dee and Jamie both raced over to her and they hugged.

"Mama, you looked scary out there," Dee said.

"I know. Those men were saying some ugly things about your uncle Byron and before I knew it, I was setting them straight. I didn't mean to do it that way and scare everybody. I'm sorry."

Evie stood. "I need to see if I can fix anything out there."

Bobby stuck his hands in his pockets and came farther into the room, and that was when Grace saw that Marilee had come in, too.

"You oughta know the police are on the way," he said. "Your brothers started fightin' everybody," he said to Evie. "And 'Nard, he pulled a gun when he saw your brother hit Grace."

"What? He had a gun out there?" Grace asked.

"Yeah, but get this. The damn fool's got a permit to carry one around." Bobby shook his head. "It's a mess, but at least it's all outside."

"Where's Mama?" Grace asked.

"I told Daisy I'd get you home, and she's gon' make sure your mama and Missy get home, too. Cora's taking care of your grandma."

Evie hurried to the door. "Let me go."

When she left, Grace looked at the kids and saw the questions in their eyes.

"We'll talk tomorrow," she said. "I know you have a lot of questions, and I promise I'll answer every one."

"But, Mama, is it true what you said?" Dee's voice was tiny and petered out at the end.

Grace nodded tiredly. "Yes, and it was a long time ago. That's probably why I'm so protective of you, you know?" She and her daughter hugged. "I'd like to sit down and talk with you about it later."

"Jamie and Dee, y'all go on to the car with Marilee. I want to speak to your mama for a minute, and then we'll be out of here."

Grace perked her brow at Bobby, her curiosity aroused.

"Marilee, I want y'all to stay in the car until I come out." He handed her the keys.

"Come on, kids." Marilee seemed out of her element, but she smiled tentatively at Grace. "I'm sorry about all this for you."

Grace nodded as they left, and then turned her gaze to Bobby. He was visibly affected, but she wasn't sure whether it was from all the commotion and confusion or the shocker Grace had let out.

"So, what do you want?"

"Want? What do you think, Grace? Some answers."

She sighed. "It's been a long day, and I don't need any more riddles."

"Grace, I'm your husband, and I never even had an idea

about—" he couldn't say it and blustered on. "And you...you never let on what happened to you."

"Did you ever really want to know?" She pressed her hands into her pockets and walked around the room. "It's not the kind of thing you go around telling and then explaining at the drop of a hat."

"That's not the point. I was your husband and I should have known. I should have been told about something in your life as serious as that."

She gave him a look of incredulity. "That is the point. When were you ever consistently my understanding partner? And when would have been the right time?"

At his silence, she looked at him. "Should I have told you on our wedding day? How about after one of our arguments during that next ten years—the ones about *your* sexual needs? Or maybe I should have explained my dreams and flashbacks to you after you'd shame and blame me for daring to refuse you sex?"

Grace let out a hollow chuckle. "You don't remember the names you called me back then, Bobby." She turned to him. "I do. Every last ugly one."

He seemed appropriately chastised as he rubbed his chin. "Okay, I'm sorry. I guess I was young and...and maybe stupid about some things."

"You won't get an argument from me on that one."

He stood from the wall and raised his hands helplessly. "I can't change our past and you won't forget it. So, I just wanted to say I'm sorry about all that's happened. And maybe it's my fault that I made your life worse."

"Bobby, listen. What I am is not your fault. It's nobody's fault but the man who abused me. When I married you, I think I wanted to marry a man with father qualities. The sad thing is, I didn't know my father, but I knew my abuser."

Grace stepped away from him. "I was messed up from the start and I pulled you into my hell, and it didn't work."

"What are you going to do now?"

"I'm going to heal, Bobby. That's how I'm going to save myself."

He walked to her. "Come on, I'll take you home."

"No, I think I'll stay here a minute. I can always get Evie to drop me off."

"You sure?"

She nodded. "Tell the kids I'll talk with them tomorrow and that I'm fine."

Grace turned her back to the door in a silent dismissal and waited as he quietly exited the room.

When she knew she was alone, she heaved a deep, unsettling sigh that shook her tired shoulders, and looked around the room. The ghosts that had swirled before and made her sick didn't appear this time and she felt strangely liberated.

At a stressful time like this, she sometimes wished she had some vice she could turn to, lose herself within, and reappear when she was mentally ready to deal.

How that must feel, to revel in a wanton, selfish indulgence. She had lived her own life safely…too much so because her own childhood had been lost to someone else's recklessness.

Maybe it wasn't too late to lose herself tonight. She thought of Theo's offer of help—she could go with him to his hotel and separate herself from tonight's pain, if only for a short while.

She felt in her pocket for the paper with his number jotted down, and stared at it for almost a minute before she made a decision.

CHAPTER 30

A car drove up to the house, and Corinne, along with Reba, rushed to the door.

When she saw that Bobby was the lone form to leave the dark SUV, Corinne's heart dropped. Where was Grace?

She didn't wait for him to get to the porch.

"Where's Grace, Bobby?" she hollered across the lawn. "Daisy said she was coming home with you."

He shook his head as he walked up to the porch to meet them.

"I talked with Grace for a minute, and then she changed her mind about coming right now. She said she'd get Evie to bring her later."

Corinne turned to Reba. "Tell somebody to call Evie over at Mama's."

Reba stuck her head back in the door and screamed the request into the house.

"I wish you hadn't left her over there, Bobby."

"Did you say something to her to make her change her mind about coming home?" Reba demanded.

"Now, don't be gettin' on me." Bobby fussed. "She's

all right. In fact, she says she feels better it's all out in the open." He looked back at Corinne. "She just didn't want it to come out like it did. She feels real bad about that."

"So, she's just sitting around over there?" Reba asked.

"I left her back there in Grandma Rhoda's sewing room. That's where she wanted to stay for a while."

Corinne wondered on that. Grace's love affair with that room had always been hot and cold, and Corinne never knew why until Grace told her and Byron how Fletcher first found her in there and stole her childhood. *Raped her.*

The stab to Corinne's heart was strong and she wanted to take all that hurt away from her children and let it reside in her, where it ought to be. She let unspeakable horrors get to her children. She was to blame.

That Grace would stay in the room meant what? Some breakthrough? Grace had told her last night that despite what everybody thought, she wasn't *all right*. Maybe she had found a kind of peace since the secret was now out. Corinne could only hope for that.

Bobby climbed the porch steps and came to her. Corinne could swear she saw a bit of sadness there. He spread his arms out and hugged her.

She couldn't help herself, but she still thought Bobby was like a confused child, and that he'd lost much more than he ever imagined when he divorced Grace. Maybe he was just realizing that.

"Miss Corinne." Bobby fumbled for words as he released her. "I don't know what to say."

"Don't worry about it, son. All of us will be fine, including Grace. You just go on and take the kids back to your mama's house. Grace will see them tomorrow." She nodded again. "It'll all be okay."

He drew a deep breath as he, in turn, nodded to Reba. Turning on his heel, he loped down the porch and back to his car.

As Corinne and Reba started back into the house, another car swerved into the yard and parked behind Missy.

"That's Aunt Evie," Reba said.

She was driving Byron's Lincoln, the one he had delivered into her custody when he'd become too ill to drive.

Bobby tooted his horn at them before he pulled off with the children just as Evie slid out of the Lincoln.

Reba peered into the dusk. "I don't see Grace."

Evie skipped across the grass in the heels she'd worn to the funeral, an event, in light of the recent happening, that seemed distant.

"Grace not with you, either?" Corinne called.

"Well, I would've brought her, but she said she didn't want to come home just yet."

"Come on in," Corinne said, and trudged back into the house, leaning heavily on her cane. She settled onto the big lounger at the picture window.

After climbing the few steps to the porch, Evie followed Reba inside.

"Did everything ever settle down over at Grandma Rhoda's?" Reba asked.

"Oh, yeah. The sheriff hauled off Royce and Nathan for disorderly conduct and trespassing."

"What about 'Nard and that gun?" Reba asked.

"He was the one trying to keep order, and he had a valid permit for that gun, so they didn't try to take him in."

"Has anybody seen Belinda?" Missy had come down the stairs and into the living room.

"I haven't seen her or Glenn," Reba said.

"They left Mama's right after all the trouble started," Corinne explained. "She just didn't want to be there, and I said I understood."

"Why is everybody disappearing?" Missy asked, her face childlike as it tightened in anger. "Is this how it'll be from now on, all of us going separate ways, scared we might step on each other's toes or secrets? I want my family back, Mama. I don't care what's happened today. I want us all together again."

Corinne looked helplessly at Missy and didn't know what to say. She wanted her family back, too.

Reba threw her arm around Missy's shoulders and walked with her to the sofa where they sat.

"I've got something for you, Missy," Evie said.

She fumbled in her purse as she walked to the sofa and, extracting a slip of neatly folded paper, extended it to Missy.

"It's from Grace. She wanted me to give it to you."

Missy took the paper, and then slipped her finger between the folded edges to break the taped seal. Her head was bowed as she read the message.

Corinne's patience ebbed away. "Missy, what does it say? And don't give me that 'it's between us' talk. I've had about enough of that. Now, what did Grace say?"

"She said she loves me, Mama, and that she'll be back tomorrow, but she wants some time to think." Her voice was raspy from the hardscrabble tears she'd cried earlier. "She called Theo Fontaine to pick her up from Grandma Rhoda's house."

"All right, then. I think I'm going upstairs." Corinne pushed herself to the edge of the lounger, and after gingerly finding her grip on the cane, eased her body from the chair.

Corinne was bone-tired. The funeral had culminated in the same way as most of their family gatherings—Grace likened them to carnivals. And her children were every which way to the wind.

Missy and Daisy were strangely quiet and distant, Belinda didn't want to be found, as did Grace, Gloria had locked herself in upstairs, and Reba—well, Reba was back home, but she had her own baby to tend.

Byron was dead and buried, her children no longer needed her. She felt alone and, suddenly, very tired. With a push from the cane, she climbed the stairs to her bedroom.

Grace had closed her eyes and remained silent for the entire trip to Theo's hotel back in Atlanta. Thankfully, he had not pressed her for answers to questions that surely swirled in his head, and Grace did not freely offer any. She simply wanted time away to think.

When they arrived at the Airport Westin Hotel, he valet-parked the car for her convenience, and they simply exited the car, entered the hotel and went straight upstairs to his room.

To his room.

Grace hadn't thought through the whole plan of calling Theo. He seemed a raft in her river of despair, and she simply wanted to hold on for at least a while. For at least tonight. And he was willing to let her.

As they rode the elevator to the fourteenth floor where he had a suite, Grace looked at Theo. A tall, impressive-looking man with clean, serene features. He wasn't a pretty boy. He was a man's man. Handsome and rugged. He had changed from his earlier black suit to slacks, and his shirt was tucked neatly inside his belt. There was no beer belly here.

Her thoughts flicked like a butane lighter to Nathan Parker, his accusations, her revelation, and the confrontation. Grace sagged against the elevator wall.

As she stood there, she felt Theo's arms slip behind her. He caught her to him, and she rested her head against his chest. And he still said nothing nor asked anything of her.

Ding. The chime caused Grace to open her eyes just as the elevator doors opened, and with his hand curled at her waist to guide her, they moved the short distance together to his door.

When they entered his suite, to Grace's surprise, Theo took it upon himself to care for her. With only minimal words spoken between them, he set her on the bed, slipped off her shoes, ordered up a pot of tea, and then he asked her to tell him what was wrong.

How could she refuse his request?

"Remember when I told you I didn't want to come home?"

Theo nodded.

"I'll tell you why." And she did. Grace told him the whole story of what had happened over the last few days, up to and including all the dreadful events at the house that followed the funeral. She told him about her nightmares and her fears, and she didn't leave any part out, no matter how unsavory.

On the contrary, she felt relief at unburdening herself with the details of so much misery she had kept cataloged in yellowing mental files for so long.

Theo was more than a stranger, but not yet so close an intimate wherein shame and expectations would block certain disclosures. They talked for hours as Grace sat upright against the headboard and Theo sat in a chair pulled up at her side.

When she had cleared her dark storehouses of information, they sat silent in the dim, unlit room, neither desiring to move.

Finally, Grace broke the silence.

"I'm much more than you bargained for, Theo Fontaine," she said, smiling. "I give you permission to throw me back in the water."

He grinned before he left his chair and turned on some of the lamps. The warm illumination took away the edge from the elegant room and the subject matter, as well.

"We all have a past," he said. "And there's toxic material in all of them. But you're one up on most of us."

"How so?" she asked.

"You at least *know* the monster you have to fight." He sat back down, then leaned toward her, taking her hands between his. "I don't want to throw you back, Grace Morrissey."

Grace's eyes shimmered. "I don't think I could've said this a week ago, Theo, but I do want a relationship with you."

"You do, huh?" He smiled.

"I know I've got to work hard at it, and overcome some—"

Crouching forward, Theo dropped his hands on either side of her on the bed and kissed her—slowly at first, and then firmly, deeper, as her hands came up around his shoulders, rising to his neck to hold him there.

When they broke apart, Theo raised his head and smiled. "Don't say things like that unless you mean it."

Grace sighed. "I do. But I don't think it's going to be a cakewalk for us. When I divorced Bobby, I built this small world for me and my kids. Everything was about them or done with the idea to protect them. In a way I used them to protect myself, too."

"That's understandable. You didn't want the same bad things from your childhood to harm your children."

He leaned back in his chair and studied Grace a moment.

"What?" she said.

"I know it's not a popular concept, but maybe you should allow someone to take care of you for a while. I think you're tired of taking care of everybody else. But, you were taught not to complain, so you keep on, always moving to the next problem or fire to be put out."

She thought about what he said, and it held some truths.

"You even felt responsible for your sisters' and mother's safety, and it kept you from telling on your abuser."

"That's more complicated. My mother had all of this hurt going on in her life," Grace said. "So, how could I tell her about my hurt and add to her problems? It was less complicated to keep the secret for as long as I could hold on."

"And you never broke that silence. Neither did your sister?"

She shook her head. "Because there was nothing unusual about keeping secrets in my family. You learn to function around them. I think a lot of families are like that. There are levels of sharing, and you learn not to scratch too far below the surface."

"So, how does Bobby feel now that he knows your past affected your marriage?"

"He sees where he didn't help things. But, on some level, I knew I'd never make a successful marriage because a part of me was always walled off."

"Is he still in love with you, Grace?"

"He's married. But the real answer to your unasked question is, I'm not in love with him. The saddest part of all is, I probably never was."

Theo stood from the chair and sat on the bed so he could face Grace. He closed his hand around hers once more.

"It's late. We should work out the sleeping arrangements before you keel over from exhaustion."

Grace stiffened, and albeit imperceptible, it was detected by Theo.

"You tell me what you want to do. If you'd like me to take you back to your mother's house tonight, I will. If you want to stay with me tonight, I welcome you, whether it's beside me or not."

Grace placed his hand to her lips and kissed it. "I want to stay with you tonight, Theo, but I'm scared." She squeezed his hand. "I want this kind of intimacy again, but I'm afraid I need baby steps—"

"I know, and we can make it work. You tell me what you want."

Grace nodded. "Tonight, I want to sleep with you holding me. I don't want nightmares tonight, just a dreamless sleep and you next to me, making me feel safe. I want to feel that happen."

Theo reached to tuck a strand of hair behind her ear and smiled.

"Done," he said.

"Wake up, Sleeping Beauty."

Grace frowned, and cracked her eyes, and saw Theo's dark brown ones twinkle back at her. Self-conscious, she swallowed, and with her lips pressed primly together, grunted a greeting from somewhere deep in her throat that she edged with a smile.

"Did you sleep well?" he asked.

Pushing herself into a sitting position, Grace looked at the other side of the bed where she last remembered he lay as his hand held her to him. She looked for the pillow he had squeezed between them. It was tossed aside.

"I thought you slept in bed with me—"

"Sadly—" he grinned "—I find I am not completely made of stone, so I slept the last few hours over there." He motioned with his head. "In the chair."

She grinned back. "I'm glad."

"Huh?"

"That you're not completely made of stone."

He smiled. "I went down and got some breakfast for us, and a few toiletries for you—croissants, juice, a toothbrush, an assortment of lotions."

"Oh, you're a prince," Grace said.

"Only the best for Sleeping Beauty."

Grace slid her feet onto the floor. Self-conscious once again of Theo's shirt she'd worn to bed, which only reached to her mid-thigh, she quickly stepped into the bathroom.

"I'll take a quick shower and freshen up," she said over her shoulder.

He stood and crossed his arms, grinning at her modesty. "You do that."

She'd forgotten the toothbrush. Smiling, Grace tiptoed over to the table and grabbed up the toiletries, before she scooted back to the bathroom.

After Grace brushed her teeth and located a shower cap, she took a long shower. It was heavenly and she felt as though the weight of the world were being washed from her shoulders.

As she dried off under the warm rays of an overhead heat lamp, a hard rap sounded against the bathroom door.

"Grace."

Theo's voice was muffled from the other side.

"It's your sister on the phone. She says it's important."

Quickly wrapping the towel securely, she opened the door for Theo. He handed her the phone before he walked away, giving her privacy.

"Hello?"

"Grace, thank God I found you. It's Missy."

"Missy?" Grace sagged against the bath counter to counteract what could only be bad news. "What is it?"

"We're at the hospital. And it's Gloria. She's been in an accident."

Grace's world swirled.

"I— I'll be right there."

CHAPTER 31

The brightly lit tiled corridors that led to the emergency room crackled with activity, despite the fact that it was a quiet Sunday morning outside the hospital building.

"Maybe I shouldn't have gone off and left the family like that," Grace muttered. "Everyone was so fragile after the blow-up."

"You didn't do this, Grace," Theo said, and hugged her to him as they rushed down the wide corridor. "Stop beating yourself up."

"What was I thinking?" she said in sharp reproach.

When they turned the corner, they almost ran into Daisy.

"Where is she?" Grace asked.

"Through here. We told Mama to stay home with the kids because they're real scared."

"And where's Rambo?"

Daisy looked back at Grace over her shoulder. "Walking around and looking like a sad chump. I saw his ass crying a few minutes ago."

Grace was surprised at that depth of feeling from him. She didn't think he cared at all, what with the way he treated his wife.

They entered the ER and followed Daisy through a partially filled waiting room, the people looking more bored than sick.

While they walked, Daisy explained, "The doctor hasn't come in yet. He's checking on the tests and lab results they've been running."

"Tell me what happened."

"She left the house, we think to go talk with Rambo wherever he was staying last night, and when she didn't come back home, we didn't worry. But then we got a call from Rambo before daylight that the paramedics found her and the car crashed into a telephone pole out on the highway."

"Broken legs, arms?"

"We don't know anything right now." They reached the room. "The doctor should be here any minute. Go on in and I'll get the others."

Grace took a deep breath and looked over at Theo before she went in. "Thank God she's not—"

"I know," he said, and took her arm. "Come on in and see her, and then you can ask the doctor all your questions."

Grace went into the room and saw her sister in the bed, helpless and small among all the twenty-first-century apparatus set up around her. Her eyes were closed and her hair was sticking out from all angles on the white pillow.

Sitting in the corner of the observation room, and out of her initial line of sight was Rambo. He had on a jogging suit and sneakers, and his hands were pushed deep into the pockets. He didn't say anything, but she didn't think it was from anger. His eyes were closed, too, almost as if in prayer. She cleared her throat, and Rambo opened his eyes.

"Hi, Grace." He straightened in his chair.

She nodded and introduced Theo. "How is Gloria?"

"She takes short naps, but other than that, there's no broken bones or anything, thank God."

Grace leaned over her sister. "Oh, Gloria," she whispered, and moved to squeeze her hand until she saw the IV line. Grace smoothed her sister's brow instead, and watched as Gloria opened her eyes.

"Gloria, it's Grace."

"Hey," Gloria said, blinking her eyes to focus. "Are you all right?"

She smiled. "I'm fine. You're the one we're worried about. I leave the house one evening and look at what happens."

Gloria smiled, too, and looked past Grace. "Is that Theo behind you?"

He stepped up. "Hey, there. We were pretty worried about you."

"I told the paramedics I was fine, but when I couldn't tell them my phone numbers, they strapped me up and brought me here."

"That's exactly what they should've done." Grace sank to the chair near the bed as the door opened and her sisters filed in. Daisy, Belinda, Reba and Missy, followed by the doctor, formed a curve around the bed.

"Grace," Theo said, whispering at her ear. "I'll wait outside the door for you."

She nodded as he squeezed her waist, and then she watched him leave, greeting her sisters one by one on his exit through the door.

"Good morning, and such a lovely morning filled with lovely ladies."

Dr. Harcourt's amiable greeting was returned by them in unison, and worked to break the ice.

He proceeded to flip the metal chart open and explain Gloria's condition.

Grace had instinctively reached out for the sister's hand next to her. It was Missy. Exchanging a quick smile, Grace grabbed it and squeezed as Dr. Harcourt spoke of normal heart monitor readings. When she looked down the line of sisters, she noticed that all of them had done the same as she, holding a sisterly hand for Gloria's recovery.

"Let's see, we've done a head CT just to make sure there's no bleeding on the brain." He looked at Gloria. "You know you were confused at the scene."

"What's that?" Missy whispered to Grace.

"A CAT scan," she replied.

"Oh."

"But she can't go home just yet," the doctor continued, "because we'd like her monitored for a full twenty-four hours to rule out any brain trauma and ensure that her mental status remains stable."

Rambo had stood from his corner spot and moved so he was just on the other side of the doctor.

"So, there's no damage we need to worry about?" he asked.

The doctor turned slightly. "Oh, Mr. Gatlin, I didn't see

you back there. Ah, let's see, we don't think there's an issue at this point, that's why we want to make sure her brain is fine so she can go home." He looked down at Gloria.

"You know, there must be a reason why a healthy woman plows into a telephone pole?" He referred to his chart again. "I understand there was a funeral yester-day." At the nods, he said, "That could very well have been the trigger for stress."

"I had so much on my mind, I guess, and I just wasn't paying attention and lost control of the car." She started to cry. "I'm just glad I didn't hit anybody."

Rambo moved to the head of the bed and took her free hand. "You'll be fine. Just wait. Before you know it, you'll be back home with me and the kids."

"One more thing," the doctor said as he flipped the chart closed. "We do the standard tests for these kinds of accidents. We checked your urine for drugs and your blood for alcohol, and they were both negative." He turned and smiled at Gloria and Rambo. "And of course your pregnancy test is positive."

Rambo didn't know. The slight lift of his brow was telling. Missy had a self-satisfied grin, while the other sisters simply smiled.

When the doctor left the room, the first one to burst out with excitement was little Reba.

"Oh, my God, you're pregnant, Gloria."

"Oh, I knew it," Missy bragged.

Daisy slapped Rambo hard on the back. "I guess you gon' be a daddy *again*."

But Grace looked at Gloria. Her eyes were shut, as though she didn't want to look at Rambo.

"Why don't we give them a few minutes, now that we know she's going to get through this, huh?" Grace suggested.

As everyone filed out, Gloria said, "Wait, Grace." She then looked at Rambo who had stayed at her side. "I need to talk with Grace for a minute, and then we can talk, okay?"

"Sure," he said and, avoiding Grace's gaze, he stepped out of the room.

Grace turned back to her sister. "Gloria, he didn't know, did he?"

Her head rocked on the pillow as tears rolled down the sides of her eyes. "No, and last night when I left Mama's house to go see him at his friend's, I told him I wanted a divorce."

"Oh, Gloria. What did he say?"

"He didn't want one, but I told him he'd embarrassed me around my family once too often." She looked at Grace through her tear-stained face. "After what he did to Missy, I can't stay with him."

"And if you leave him, what about the baby? Will you keep it?"

"I know my window of opportunity to do anything is closing fast. I still don't know what to do."

Grace leaned down and hugged her.

"I understand, and whatever you decide, I know the family will support your decision, even Missy, because she loves you, too."

"All we have is each other," Gloria said between sniffs. "I know that. That's what Mama always says."

"And she's right." Grace decided to ask her sister the question she knew was in the backs of their heads.

"Gloria, it was an accident, wasn't it? You just weren't paying attention to the road?"

More tears flowed. "I couldn't hurt myself and leave my children. I love them," she said.

"Okay, okay. I believe you. I'm going to let Rambo come in. Don't let him upset you, and don't talk about any decisions in the hospital. Wait until tomorrow when you're home." She gave her a kiss to the forehead before she left.

When she left the observation room, Rambo was standing just outside the doorway, alone.

"Grace," he said. "Did she say anything else about what happened?"

She turned to him. "She was upset from when she talked with you earlier."

"She told you, huh?"

Grace took a deep breath. "She did."

His mouth turned into a sneer. "And I bet you told her to drop me like a hot potato."

"You'd lose the bet." She turned squarely on him. "I

told her that whatever decision she makes, all of her family will stand behind her, even Missy."

"I know y'all don't like me."

"Tell me, Rambo, what is there to like?"

He let out a hollow chuckle and then punched his fist into his palm. "Yeah, you got a point there. I don't know why I do crazy things, sometime." He looked at Grace. "I can see you don't believe me, but I love Gloria and the kids. Hell, I got another one on the way, and she wants to divorce me."

"I don't doubt you love your kids, but what about your wife? If you love her, prove it. Better yet, prove it to her."

"Huh?"

"Go in there and support her. Don't go in there accusing her, or bringing up the divorce. Just be in there. And another thing, if you can't figure out why you do the things you do, and you really love your wife and kids and your baby on the way, you should both see a marriage counselor."

He sighed. "Yeah, well, thanks for talking to me. I know what I did yesterday was stupid and reckless, and I swear, I'm gonna apologize to Missy."

"Ah, I wouldn't go near Missy any time soon. Free advice."

He nodded, and a little smile appeared. "Yeah, I guess I should have taken it before."

Rambo pushed the swinging room door and went in to his wife.

Grace wondered why she hadn't sought a marriage counselor. That was pretty simple. It takes two to save the marriage and Bobby would never consider someone else's advice about his life.

She looked around and saw Theo at the end of the hall near a coffee machine. She went to meet him.

"So, how did it go?" he asked, and handed her a blistered cup of orange juice.

"My beautiful sister is still a beautiful disaster. However, I think maybe we had a breakthrough with her husband."

"Sounds promising, but remember what we said last night?"

"Mmm... We said so much, didn't we?" She smiled as she pulled back the tab on the juice. "But I know, I can't fix everything, so stop trying."

He grinned. "But you're a work in progress, so it'll take time."

"Grace, are you going back home with us?" Reba called from down the hall. In fact, all the other sisters had congregated there.

She looked at Theo. "I think I will go with them, Theo." She looked down at her clothes. "Besides needing to change my funeral outfit, our family crises require all heads present."

"I understand. I'm glad you thought about me last night when you needed someone."

"One of the better decisions I've made lately. Maybe you can come back to our house for Sunday dinner this afternoon? Jamie and Dee will be there."

"Thanks. I wouldn't miss it." He leaned in and gave Grace a lingering kiss on the mouth. "I'll see you later, then."

She stood and watched him disappear around the corner before she turned to join her sisters, a pleased smile on her face.

CHAPTER 32

"Go right in, Miss Morrissey, please."

Grace thanked the receptionist and entered the huge office with carpet deep enough to sink her heels.

Across the room behind a dark and massive desk, John Sheffield, Uncle Byron's attorney, stood and was now coming around the desk to greet her.

"Good afternoon. And, please, Ms. Morrissey—"

"You can call me Grace," she said. "It's just simpler."

He smiled. "Then, Grace it is. Please, have a seat."

She sat in a big winged chair in front of his desk in the plush office.

"You know, that's just the way Byron was," he said. "He was never big on impressing people, and to look at him, with his conservative and simple dress, and quiet life-style, he was quite an unlikely millionaire."

Grace swallowed hard, and then shifted in her chair. "M-millionaire?"

"At least," the attorney said gently, smiling.

"Uncle was worth a million dollars? How?"

"He was very, very careful with his money, but that was after he made a windfall with the fleet of buses he owned."

"His little school bus company?"

John Sheffield grinned. "That little school bus company owns fleets all across South Georgia and rural townships where they don't have regular services. He started it back in the seventies and it's just snowballed from there because he kept putting his profits into more investments and expansions."

"Oh, my goodness," Grace said, still shocked. "I don't think anyone in the family knew this."

He smiled. "And he wanted it that way. He had a true belief in education and entrepreneurship, and I think he did extend a helping hand to the family in that regard."

Grace thought about it and realized that it had always been Uncle Byron who came to the family's rescue when a necessity was involved.

"Your uncle believed in you very much. I'm guessing that's why he made you executrix of his will, which, I might add, you'll be happy to know provides well for individual family members as well as his extended family."

Grace could only nod at this sensory overload she was receiving.

"You'll find he has provided the funding for an education trust which will help any family member who wishes to continue their education beyond high school."

Grace fanned herself as a nervous giggle escaped. "Oh, my goodness, Mr. Sheffield."

"Just call me John. Byron did." His face became serious.

"Of course, these things as well as other provisions will

be explained to the entire audience present for the reading of the will after our meeting. However, there is one matter that must be dealt with before we get to that actual reading, and it's this."

He opened a folder lying on top of the desk and removed two oversized envelopes. He passed one of them to Grace.

"What is this?" she asked, and was overcome with a sense of déjà vu, like when she received the letter from Grandma Rhoda that had been from Uncle Byron.

"Byron left very specific instructions for me, as his attorney, to give this letter to you. You must read it in my office, and before you leave, you must decide whether to leave the office with it as your possession, or burn it."

"What?"

"I also have a sealed copy of the same letter—" he held up the one on his desk "—which will stay with me, never to be opened unless certain circumstances occur."

"And they are?"

"I can't divulge them."

Grace sat back in her chair. "Boy, Uncle sure never believed in making things easy."

"Anything worth having is worth the work." He picked up the envelope on his desk and prepared to leave. "I will give you a sufficient amount of time to review the contents of Byron's letter, and when I return, you can give me your decision."

With a nod of his head, and a smile of encouragement, she supposed, John Sheffield left Grace in the huge office.

Grace tapped the letter against her hand and could feel the tension throbbing in her temple.

Taking a deep breath, she opened the sealed envelope.

"Grace, was that enough time?"

She raised her head and looked toward the door. The attorney was standing in the middle of the double doors waiting for her okay to enter.

Grace nodded and then bent her head as she pinched the bridge of her nose. Almost thirty minutes had passed, and she'd barely noticed it.

When she raised her head, she saw that a box of tissue had appear mysteriously at the desk's edge. She pulled a tissue out.

"And your decision, Grace?" he asked, standing patiently behind the desk.

She took another deep breath. "Burn it."

Later that evening, Grace strolled leisurely through her mother's house. She looked at it with new interest, and explored it in ways she hadn't before. Then, she went to find Corinne.

"Mama, can we talk a minute?"

"Why are you looking so sober?" Corinne had her knitting out and was busy working on some project for little Denzel. "After the reading of Byron's will this afternoon, I'd think you'd be in a better mood. The girls are." She bent her head and looked at Grace. "Why didn't you want to go out and eat with them?"

"Because I wanted some time alone to talk with you."

"Oh?" She dropped her hands to her lap. "What about?"

"I know the whole story, Mama." She sat next to her on the sofa. "I know how Fletcher Johnson died."

The knitting needles dropped from her mother's stiff fingers, yet she didn't move her hands. She just stared at Grace.

"So much is now beginning to make sense to me, Mama, and for years I was never sure. But now, I am."

Corinne looked away as her whole body slumped against the chair, and her hands fell to her lap to join the needles.

"How...how did you find out?"

"Uncle Byron told me."

Her gaze leaped to Grace.

"He couldn't depart this earth and leave you vulnerable, even after so much time had passed. That's how much he loved and trusted you."

"And you."

"And me," Grace agreed. "You know, I swore I was finished with secrets and in the blink of an eye, I inherited another."

"Byron and I had no choice, Grace. We had to do what we did, otherwise, there would've been no justice."

"I know, Mama."

"When you told Byron that Fletcher was touching you and making you do things, not one time, but for years, Byron wanted to get a shotgun and shoot him like a dog in the street." She rubbed her tearing eyes.

"Grace, you don't know how hard I had to work to keep him from doing it. The next day after you told him, Byron came over and confronted Fletcher about it. He denied it, of course, the drunk fool.

"They were all over the house, just fussin', and then at the top of the stairs, just fightin'."

"And then, Fletcher was sort of perched on that top stair, and whether Byron pushed him or he fell, it didn't matter. The end result was that he hit those wood stairs head-first and hard." She shook her head in memory. "I can still hear that thump in my head, and then he rolled down the stairs like a big cannonball." She took a deep, strangled breath. "And he landed on me, cracking my already bad leg. Messed it up for life."

"You'd just come home from the hospital." Grace helped with the story.

She nodded. "I was on crutches with my leg, and I couldn't even get up the stairs, so the police didn't have a problem believing my story that he fell down the stairs by accident." Corinne looked over at Grace. "I didn't tell them that Byron had been here when it happened."

"Uncle Byron left while you called an ambulance?"

"He checked for Fletcher's pulse, and there was none, and I was in so much pain from my leg. He didn't want to leave me, but I told him to put the phone nearby and to get out of there. I'd tell the police a simple story. And it worked."

"Except that I saw Uncle's truck over here that day. And later on, when I heard he told the police he hadn't been here, it puzzled me, though I never contradicted his story."

"Lord, Grace, we didn't know you saw his truck." Corinne looked away. "For years after Fletcher died, we kept thinking the police would reopen the case for some reason and find out we lied. We never slept easy for causing a man's death, or felt good about it. But it was justice for what he'd done."

"It changed your life," Grace said.

"I swore I'd never marry again after Fletcher died, and I didn't. No dates, no boyfriends, no nothing. His death was the best thing that happened to this family, and I wasn't gon' ever let my girls be put in jeopardy again. I think I spoiled Missy and Belinda because of it."

"I understand why Uncle Byron felt so strongly about being the father figure to us. He felt responsible for Fletcher's death."

Her mother sighed. "He never had children, and y'all never had a father. It was a perfect arrangement, the way he saw it. He never regretted anything he did for y'all."

"I regret I had a part in turning his funeral into a free-for-all."

"Byron would've been proud of you defending him. He always worried about Evie's brothers and their filthy mouths, but Evie can handle them. She loved Byron too much to let them hurt anything or anyone he loved."

"You and Uncle Byron have been through some times," Grace said. "When I think of all the decisions you've had to make…"

Corinne tilted her head. "The thing is, you have to just go on ahead and make them, because you never know how they'll come back to haunt you."

Grace grabbed up her mother's hands and, raising them up to her mouth, kissed each one.

"You know, Mama, I used to think the scariest thing in the world was to become my mother." She grinned. "Now, I'm thinking it's the only thing I'd want to become."

Dropping their hands, the two women, so different, yet so similar, embraced.

In looking back over the past week, and considering the number of surprises—not to mention revelations—that had been borne by them all, Grace finally understood the gravity of her mother's favorite saying, *God makes the back to bear the burden.*

Indeed, Grace decided her mother must have some kind of back, and could only hope that when she was tested, she would do her mother—and Uncle Byron—proud.

"You know, Grace, Byron's spirit is still around. I can feel it."

"I do, too, Mama. But you know something else, his goodness will be felt for a long time in the family if I have anything to do with it."

Grace sat up and smiled at her mother as she remembered the provisions set up in the will. Actually, she did have everything to do with it. And Uncle Byron himself had made sure of that.

Descendants of Rhoda Gibson Wilson

Rhoda Gibson = Herbert
Wilson
-Deceased

Children of Rhoda Gibson and Herbert Wilson:

Richard = Corinne — Rufus — Fletcher — Byron = Evie — Cora = Albert — George — Lettie Bea — Margaret — Fontella
Brooks   Wilson   Beneby   Johnson   Wilson   Parker   Wilson   Duncan   Wilson   Wilson   Wilson   Wilson
-Deceased   -Deceased -Deceased   -Deceased   -Deceased

Under Richard Brooks and Corinne Wilson:

Grace = Robert   Gloria = C. Rambo
Brooks Morrissey   Brooks   Gatlin

Jamie   Tavis
Morrissey   Gatlin

Denise   Tamika
Morrissey   Gatlin

                      Tyra
                      Gatlin

Under Rufus Beneby:

Daisy = Lester   Rebecca
Beneby Cooper   Beneby

                      Denzel
                      Beneby

Under Fletcher Johnson:

Belinda
Johnson
=
Glenn
Townsend

Melissa
Johnson